Manaen: Prophet to the King is a must read. It will make you laugh, cry and think deeply. It shows you the life of Christ through the eyes of a man who was there through his birth, life, death, and resurrection. It is a love story of an orphan boy who finds a father, a woman who finds true love and a rich and powerful man who finds a savior. It brings fresh insight to your spirit and joy to all who read it.

—Rev. Donna T. Moore, Pastor
City of Refuge Worship Center, NC

MANAEN
PROPHET TO THE KING

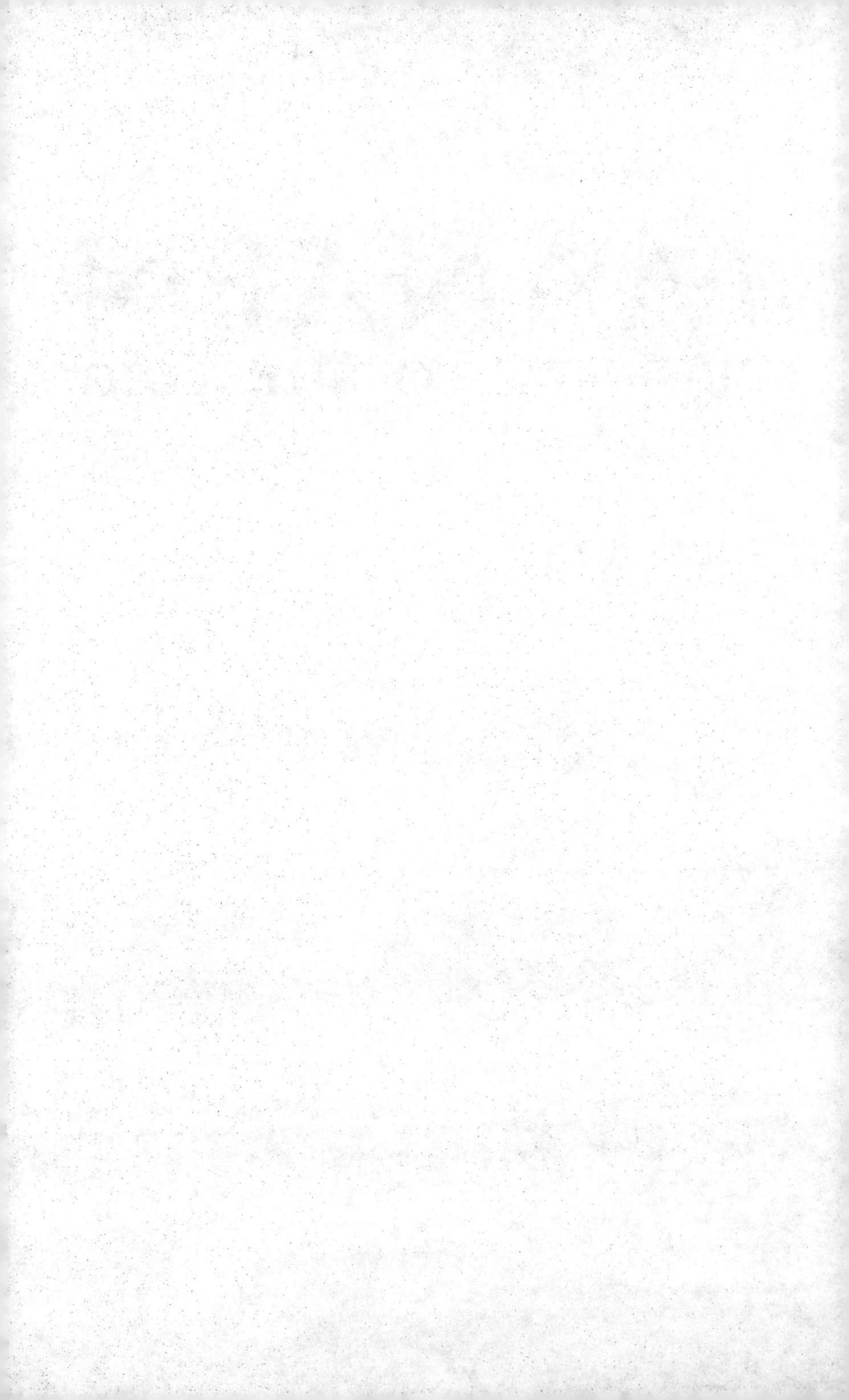

MANAEN
PROPHET TO THE KING

Robbie Munn Bayler

Tate Publishing & Enterprises

DEDICATION

This book is dedicated to the following:

My Lord and Savior, Jesus Christ, for a new life and the gift.

My husband, Ken, who has made my writing possible and put up with me while I did it.

Rev. Nina Henry, who has believed in and encouraged me for almost forty years. Thanks, dear friend and sister in Christ. We've traveled down many roads together through laughter and tears.

Rev. Donna Moore, my pastor, employer, and friend. Thank you for keeping me motivated and laughing. Your joy, wisdom, and biblical knowledge have helped me beyond measure.

Without all of you I couldn't have written this book.

ACKNOWLEDGMENTS

My undying thanks to:

Betty Owens, for all of your assistance. Your input was so valuable.

Wayne Boger, for the amazing garden he created and cares for at our church. It has been such an inspiration as I have written this book. Thanks again Wayne.

Jane and Melvin Reece, for the inspiration I receive each time I visit your mountain cabin. Christ seems so close there.

David Holcomb, for buying me my first computer. Thanks, "cuz."

Rev. Ron Durham, my professor at Christ to the World Bible College, who was the first one to tell me I could and should write. Thank you for believing in me.

FOREWORD

It has been my pleasure to know the author of this book for almost forty years and to watch her life as it impacts those around her. She lives the Christ-life and imparts that life into everyone she meets. Only eternity will reveal the number of those whose lives have been changed and positively affected for the Master because of Robbie Munn Bayler.

Manaen was born out of Robbie's heart's desire to not only impart the wonderful message of salvation, but to do it in an interesting and entertaining way. In this book, she has done just that. We can see the distinct possibility of this being a true story (rather than fiction) of a man who was born into the degenerate, but wealthy and powerful, Roman hierarchy. The influence of those he has been taught to despise opens his mind and heart in a direction he never expects.

Robbie has portrayed Jesus Christ as the man or joy he

surely was. She has also captured the life and dedication of first-century Christians and accurately portrays their influence on their neighbors, society, and world. The reader will find himself or herself viewing his or her own life from a different perspective. He or she will be reminded in this book that what we do and how we live far overshadows what we say. The reader will also be challenged to live the life God has given with courage.

—Rev. Nina M. Henry
Missionary to Asia Pacific

"Antipas, what's happened? Have the Romans invaded?" he asked him. The second remark was their standard joke from when they were boys and had been sent to Imperial Rome to be educated. It was thrown in now as an attempt to calm the panic in his friend's eyes, but Antipas was neither calmed nor amused.

"Manaen, my father's dead! Do you realize what this means?" Antipas shrieked. His voice was shrill with terror. "My life really is in danger now! Help me hide!" His eyes rolled wildly in his head as he searched for a hiding place. "They'll surely kill me now. Help me, Manaen. Please help me."

Manaen had never heard the arrogant, self-indulgent Antipas use the word "please" before, so he knew he was desperate. He grabbed his friend's arms and shook him in an attempt to calm his frenzy.

"Stop it! Calm down, and think, Antipas. It was your father who killed your family members. You're actually safer now if he really is dead. Are you sure of his death?" He pulled Antipas down the hall to his own rooms where the boy waited.

"Where is Agrippa? Philip doesn't worry me, but Archelaus is as much of a tyrant as Herod was. Do you know where they are, Antipas?" He was trying to get more information about the situation as well as calm the man's fear.

As Manaen looked into the worried face of his friend, he saw the glaze of fear in his eyes and spit on his lips. He realized that Antipas was incapable of coherent thought. He spoke quietly.

"Never mind, my friend. Come with me to my room and I'll post a guard. I know the guards that we can trust. You'll be safe. You will also be king of part of your father's territory."

Chapter 1

The sails of a black, high-decked Phoenician galley that was headed for the Pillars of Hercules billowed in the breeze as two boys in their early teens ran across the beach. Leaping and spinning, they spread arms as if they were sails trying to catch the wind and glide away. Joy surged through them as they ran and shouted at the birds that they had disturbed in their rambunctious dance across the sand.

To them, this unexpected early release from the confines of their classroom was a gift that meant an afternoon of freedom. They were intent on enjoying every remaining minute of their day. Too soon they were being sent to Rome to continue their education, but for now they were free here in Caesarea. Free to enjoy the Mare Nostrum. Free to be boys.

"Antipas," Manaen shouted, "I'm the captain of that great ship. No, I'm the owner, and I own all of the galley slaves pulling on those long oars. I'm the richest man in the world, and I sail my ships all over the world, even to Cyprus and Athens and Rome. If you want, I'll let you be my captain." Quietly, he added, "Wouldn't that be something, a king for a captain!"

Excited, he went on.

"We'll sail the seas, conquer the world together, and discover places where no one has ever been. Would you like that, my royal friend? Would that ease your boredom, or does it have to be dancing girls?" They collapsed on the sand, laughing.

"Oh, yes, Manaen, I'll sail with you. We'll collect spices, silk, and all of the riches of the world. We'll explore far islands and drink all of the wine we find hidden there, and we'll conquer the natives. We will make them be our slaves, and they will have to do everything we tell them. They can't hide their riches from us; we are the conquerors!"

Pretending to thrust a sword, Antipas threw back his head and laughed a wild, reckless laugh.

"Let's put all the men and ugly women in chains to sell as slaves. The beautiful women will have to dance for us whenever we want. And cities! Yes, let's build great cities, even greater than my father has built. We'll have rowdy orgies, eat roasted hummingbirds, and race chariots. I'll beat you every time. Let's go to the Orient, to see the people with almond-shaped eyes and yellow skin, and force them to give us all of their silk. That's all that our women will wear, and we'll make them dance for us wearing that cloth and nothing else. Won't they be beautiful?"

"Yes, very beautiful, but if we drink all of the wine, we won't be able to enjoy the dancing girls. How many layers of the cloth will they wear?"

"Only one layer, my friend, only one!" Antipas whooped with laughter as he rolled in the sand. Then he grew very still and quiet.

"Manaen, what did you mean about a king for a captain?"

"You will be king when Herod dies." Manaen's eyes seemed to focus far away, as he too became still and quiet. "And you'll build a great city, and a beautiful young girl will dance for you and…"

"No, Manaen. No more!" Antipas' voice sounded shrill and brittle with fear as he tried to whisper through chattering teeth. "One of my older brothers will be king when my father dies. Mariamnie is my father's favorite wife. One of her sons will be chosen. Aristobulus or Alexander will be the next king. I'm too young and insignificant and my mother's not a favorite. I would never be chosen. Never!"

"No, you're wrong. Mariamnie may be the beautiful, favored wife, but she'll be killed—and so will her sons. Your father will see to that. He's quite mad with his thirst for power, you know. You'll become king of Galilee and be known as Herod the Tetrarch.

"How can you say that? How do you know what's going to happen?" he snapped.

"It's just something I seem to know—a premonition, something I know about future events. Some people call me a seer and some a soothsayer. I hate it when they do that!"

"You're crazy! That's what you are! And don't ever say that about me again. If anyone heard you, they would have me killed." The boy's eyes were dilated with fear, and he seemed to be trying not to scream as he swung his head around to see if anyone was close enough to hear what was being said.

"What if our bodyguards were to hear you? They would surely report such treason, and we could both be killed!"

He was panting now with fear.

"I understand that, but it's true. And whether I say it again or not, you will still become a king when Herod dies. But, don't worry; I won't tell anyone. They'll find out soon enough. Antipas, it's in the hands of the gods. There's nothing we can do to change it."

"Maybe not, but you can stop saying it!"

Neither boy spoke as they stood up and watched the ship sail away into the Great Sea. They could still hear the creaking of the oars in the oar locks and the snapping of the whips on the backs of the slaves pulling the gigantic oars inside the holds of the slave-driven ship.

Antipas, with eyes that looked like the eyes of a frightened animal, spun away with a wild laugh and ran up the dune, calling out to the only friend he had ever known.

"You're the one who is mad. Catch me if you can, my crazy friend."

CHAPTER 2

Rome, *the city of seven hills, the seat of all learning, the center of the world. What a dirty, filthy, stinking cesspool. What a mess.* Manaen's thoughts raced as he looked down on the city from one of the seven hills. He was panting from the exertion of running up the hill, trying to escape from the things that were troubling him. From this vantage point he could look down into the city and see the Forum that Julius Caesar had built and the new one that Augustus was building. *Is nothing ever good enough for these people? They replace new buildings with even newer buildings just for their own self-aggrandizement. These Roman emperors are as bad as Herod!* There were the viaducts that fed water into the city and there sat the Ara Pacis. *Ara Pacis, Altar of Peace indeed! There is no peace in this place!* He was filled with disgust as he pondered the things that took place here: barbaric things, debauched things, things that until lately he had participated in willingly. Men sold their souls in a thirst for power. Both women and men sold their souls and bodies in the quest for love and survival.

Antipas is in his element here. He has become totally Roman in his thinking and morals. Morals. That's a joke. Maybe I should say in his lack of morals. Manaen sat on a stone wall and started tossing rocks down the hill harder and harder as he thought about his cousin and friend. *I wish Herod had never sent us here. Antipas has become more and more immoral, and the more immoral he becomes, the more angry and self-indulgent he becomes. We never have a civil conversation anymore because he is either drunk or hung over from being drunk. All he seems to care about is getting a woman in his bed and wine in his belly! I know that he fears for his life, but his lifestyle isn't helping him any. He has always been fearful and self-indulgent, but he seems to be out of control here. I couldn't believe what I was seeing when he had his servant almost whipped to death for not serving his wine at the right temperature! And to hear him shout at me to back off when I tried to stop it and tell me that I could be next was too much!*

He realized that he was throwing the rocks at a tree with a vengeance. *I wish I could hit him in the head with a rock and knock some sense back into it! I am really tired of his attitude and hearing him talking on and on about Pax Romana!* He slammed his fist into the tree and then yelled in agony. "Now that was a really stupid move!" He stood rubbing his sore, bleeding knuckles. "To Hades with him anyway! To Hades with them all," he shouted at the tree, instantly feeling foolish.

He began to pace back and forth. Like an animal in a cage he walked a few paces and turned, walked a few more paces and turned as his thoughts raced out of control. *Pax Romana! Roman Peace! What a farce! Peace at any price. Peace that was actually purchased by barbarism of the worst kind. Their supposed knowledge is king. The Senate is too powerful and corrupt to be anything but a joke—a very bad joke.* He thought about men who stood around in their togas posturing as they spouted ridiculous drivel that passed as wisdom.

Well, everyone knows that if you say a thing loud enough and long enough, people will begin to believe it. He spun around and posed in a mockery of their rituals, then strutted across the mountain top like one of the effeminate senators he knew. "Blah, they make me sick!" Rage burned in his belly like a hot coal and he could feel the bile of his anger in his throat. He tried to push it down, make it go away, but it was no use.

God, how I hate this place! Why was I ever so excited about coming here to be educated? Oh, yes, I'm educated now. I understand the stupidity around me all too well! Why don't I just do as the Romans do while I am here in Rome? Well, I guess I have been doing just that, but lately I can't bear it. I've bedded my share of the women, fought my share of the fights, and downed my share of the wine! The only thing I ever gained was very short lived pleasure. Well, there were the headaches, sore muscles, and nausea! I'll admit that! Maybe it's Nebo's influence over me. He has always tried to teach me things I wasn't interested in learning; things about his God and how to grow up to be a decent man. Maybe I was listening after all.

As a boy I was so anxious to drink the wine, watch the beautiful women dance, sail the seas, be a man. Now all I want to do is return to the desert and a simpler way of life. His thoughts would not be still. They were as restless as he was as he paced back and forth on the hilltop. *Oh, how I would enjoy quietly sitting in the temple in Jerusalem, listening to the rabbis teach the Law and talk about their God. How foolish they seemed to me as a boy; but now, even though I don't understand this Yahweh they serve, there seems to be more wisdom in that foolishness than in the paganism I have found here. At least the Jews offer sacrifices of bulls, sheep, and goats, not sacrifices of men, women, and children. And they don't have prostitutes for sale in their temples. Yes, I think maybe Nebo was right! Maybe there is a better way to live.*

God, how disgusting all of this is to me and I don't even know why. I only know that it seems to be the stupidest form of insanity, and the basest of ways to live.

Manaen turned to go to the villa that he shared with Antipas, but he was stopped in his tracks by what he saw. The sky was so red from the sunset that Rome seemed to be on fire; even the buildings reflected the light. He began to shake as he realized that he was being given a premonition of what was in store for Rome. *I don't know how I know, but I do know that Rome will burn and untold numbers will be lost in the inferno. God, I've got to get out of this place before I lose my mind. God? What am I thinking? Is there really only one God as the Jews proclaim—one God, almighty, all-powerful, all-knowing, creator of all things?*

He started down the hill then turned and ran back to the top, still fascinated by the illusion of Rome burning in the setting sun. He thought about Herod pretending to be a Jew in order to rule over the Jewish people. *I wonder what he really believes. One thing I know for sure, the gods of the Romans are nothing but wood, stone, gold, whatever. If they do have any power at all, it's only used for evil! Why do I want to return to*

Jerusalem? Herod has gone mad in his quest for power. He's killing his own family members and anyone else that he distrusts. And who is to say who can be trusted? I'm a family member, but what if he gets it in his mind that he can't trust me? Will he kill me too? I would die before I betrayed his trust in me, but does Herod understand that? Or does Antipas, for that matter? Where will it all end? Will it ever end?

Manaen was a young man in the prime of his life, handsome and sought-out, the desire of many women, and the life of every party. Yet he was lonely, lost, and dejected. He stood gazing sadly at the city stretched out before him. Like most of the people who populated this place, he was forlorn, heartbroken, and world-weary. *I have to get away from this stinking hellhole. But are Judea, Galilee, or Samaria any better? Idumea certainly isn't.*

He jerked his head up as a sneer curled his lips in aggravation. His eyes began to look like hard black marbles. *Why speculate? We can't return until Antipas' father—the mighty, mad king Herod—summons us home. Antipas thinks Herod has forgotten he's alive. Considering what's happened to some of the other members of his family, maybe it is best if he has. Antipas would live longer that way. Jupiter's priest, is there no rest?*

Shaking his head and picking up his scrolls, he jogged down to the bottom of hill. *Why do I dread this banquet tonight? No, it won't be a banquet; it will be an orgy, a drunken brawl! There will be half-naked dancing girls and not all of them will be slaves. Some will volunteer! King Solomon called them foolish women, and they are just that! The people will gorge on the lavish fare until they vomit. Then they will go back and gorge some more. Wine will flow like water until people don't even know their own names. The worst part will be the men and women behaving like prostitutes, only they'll be selling their souls rather than their bodies. Every one of them will think they are smarter than anyone else in the hall. What absurdity!*

Surrounded by a swarming sea of humanity, he made his way back to the villa. The mass of people around him seemed like debris from the storms of life that had washed up on the barren shores of the Roman aristocracy. They appeared broken, and they cluttered the landscape wherever they came to a stop. Hopelessness was their constant companion; despair a way of life. Beggars held out empty vessels hoping they would be filled, with disappointment as their only reward.

Sly-eyed women watched him as he strode pass and thieves studied him to see if there was anything of value to take. From his bearing and clothing they regarded him as one of the nobility, but not an over-indulged, easy mark like most of the noble class. Considering his size and the confident way he strode through the crowds, they decided against making any foolish moves. Besides, they reasoned, he probably had guards nearby.

Manaen's thoughts would not be still. *How can I be so totally alone in this mass of people? I feel like a duck with a broken wing floating on the Great Sea. The sharks are closing in for the kill and there's no protection, no help for me. I'm part of the household of Herod the Great. I'm an educated man, even by Roman standards; friend, companion, and cousin to Herod's son, Antipas; yet I don't really belong anywhere. I feel like more of a misfit than these wretched people in this plaza and just as hopeless.* Clutching his scrolls and shaking his head to clear his thoughts, Manaen trudged back to the villa.

CHAPTER 3

Antipas was furious. That was obvious from the sparks of fire that seemed to explode from his eyes.

"He's calling us home, Manaen. Back to that stinking backwater called Judea," he snarled through clenched teeth, "and for me to marry some desert dung heap. I don't care if she is the daughter of Aretas, King of Arabia. I don't want to marry her."

"Calm down, Antipas. It can't be that bad. What else did he say?"

"He says that we have had the best education money can buy from the rabbis in Judea, and the rabble here, and it is time for me to think of my future." His breathing was ragged, and his body was tense as anger raged in his eyes. "What does he mean the 'rabble here'? We have had excellent teachers here. At least we have learned something other than the *Pentateuch.* I won't go, I tell you. I am staying right here, and there is nothing he can do about it! Is there?"

His shoulders slumped as panic replaced the anger in his eyes.

"He can't make me marry this dung heap, can he? Jupiter's priest, they live in the rocks like snakes." Antipas had gone quickly from anger to whining.

"Antipas, my friend, you know as well as I do that if Herod is calling us home, we have no choice except to go. If he has decided you are to marry, what else can you do? How do you think you can bypass his will? Are you the great Herod, who rules his part of the world and tells everyone else what to do and when to do it?"

Antipas didn't respond. He sat sulking.

Manaen's eyes were kind as he regarded his friend.

"No, you're his son; he simply misses you and wants you home. He thinks that he knows what's best for you. We've been gone six years. And how can you know that this Nabataean princess is a dung heap?"

"Because all of them are dung heaps, camel dung at that!"

Manaen couldn't help laughing out loud as he spoke.

"Perhaps she's the fabled desert rose. Aren't you tired of the flesh pots here? Surely you have had enough of these skinny, anemic Roman women and look forward to our beautiful dancing girls at home. There'll be lots of them at your wedding. Remember the silk fabric we were going to bring back from the Orient? You could insist on that at the wedding. No! I have a better idea! Maybe it is time for you to start your own stable of beauties. A string of horses would be nice too." Manaen laughed again.

"No, Manaen. You can't make me laugh this time, but you're right. We'll have to return."

"So it seems."

"Has it really been six years? What else have we learned besides intrigue and debauchery?" His anger was cooling now, but in its place was a bitterness that Manaen had come to see more and more of lately. Bitterness, anger, and a cool craftiness dominated the expression in Antipas' eyes these days. Being in Rome had done nothing to enhance his temperament. He was more self-indulgent and arrogant than ever. It seemed that his childhood friend had been replaced by an angry tyrant.

"Oh, I hate to leave it all," Antipas continued, "but you don't mind at all, do you? What is wrong with you?" His voice was heavy with contempt. "Don't you realize that we'll be back under his thumb? Who knows how long we can stay alive in that precarious position? I'd feel safer under the hooves of a runaway horse."

"Is it Rome you hate to leave, or is it the lovely Aletia? Or, perhaps, it's your favorite cousin, Agrippa? Now that's one who really does bear watching." Manaen's eyes and thoughts seemed far away now. "Don't ever leave your back unguarded with Agrippa, Antipas. He is dangerous. He'll take your kingdom if you let him. Archelaus would also kill anyone for power. And when you marry, be very careful how you treat that princess."

Antipas hated it when Manaen got like this. He seemed to be in another world, a world where Antipas couldn't follow him.

"What do you mean 'my kingdom'? Don't start that nonsense with me again. After all these years I thought you had come to your senses." Antipas' lips were so stiff with fear that he sounded like he was hissing. "I still think you want to get me killed!"

His head swung from side-to-side as he looked around for listening ears. "Stop this nonsense now! I won't listen to it anymore!" Antipas wanted to run from the room and find a hiding place, but he was afraid to leave Manaen alone and risk someone else hearing his ramblings.

"You are mad!" he snapped.

"No, Antipas, I'm not mad. You will rule. Hear me well. You will rule." Manaen seemed to rejoin Antipas as he smiled at his friend. "Well, we had better get ready for our trip. When and how are we leaving? Have the servants been instructed to pack our things? Do we have passage? Don't just stand there staring at me with your mouth hanging open. That's dangerous here in Rome, considering the fly population. Why are you looking at me like that, Antipas?"

"Do you realize what you are saying when you get like that?"

"Like what? Oh, you mean when I … yes; I tell you facts as I know and understand them. They will happen—I just don't know when. You'll see in time. Meanwhile, don't worry about it or talk about it. Just expect it."

"Don't worry about it, he says! What you're saying could cost me my life, and you tell me not to worry! I'd leave you here in Rome, but I am afraid of the damage you could do with your strange gift, if it is a gift. Sometimes I think it is a curse! There are enlightened people who would say that you are quite mad or demon possessed. Do you know that?"

"Yes, I know many 'enlightened people' who think that anything unfamiliar or uncontrollable is madness." Manaen's voice was thick with scorn.

CHAPTER 4

"Hasn't it been fantastic weather for our trip, Antipas? No storms, not even a small gale. You are looking tanned and healthy. In fact, I have never seen you looking better. Being out in the open has been good for you; that is, once you stopped retching and got out of your cabin," Manaen chuckled.

"That's really amusing, Manaen. I hate the outdoors. I hate the fresh air. I hate having nothing to do, and most of all, I hate this foul, stinking ship. The food has been atrocious, the service even worse, and there are no women."

"Well, well, you are in a good mood, aren't you? Antipas, look around you. The Mare Nostrum is calm and beautiful with colors ranging from azure to indigo. The sky is blue without a cloud in sight. Look at the wood this ship is made from and the colorful sails. Do you ever see the beauty around you?"

"Oh, stop trying to change the subject! If the great Herod was so anxious to have us back at home, why didn't he send one of his ships and the proper servants, including a cook, to accompany us home? And speaking of the sky being so clear blue, clouds would probably mean wind and a little more wind would certainly get us home faster! Did you consider that in your grand dissertation regarding the Mare Nostrum and the sky?"

Antipas' arrogant face grew red with anger as Manaen started laughing.

"Don't you dare laugh at me! You are…you are…!" Antipas began to sputter as he tried not to laugh. "Oh, for the love of Neptune and all of his host!" he swore. I hate it when you make me forget what I'm angry about." Manaen made a face at him, and Antipas roared with laughter, but it didn't last long. After a few moments he spoke.

"Sometimes I really am a royal pain. Why do you put up with me, my friend? And why are you my friend? The only friend I have ever had, as a matter of fact. What keeps you coming back for more of my abuse? Why have you always been so loyal to me?"

"Why have you been loyal to me? You're my only friend too, you know. The only friend I've ever had, so I guess we have that in common. You're also the only family I've ever really known. We put up with each other because we both know that we are all that we have. We are a habit to each other. I hope it's a good habit, Antipas. I hope that I'll be as loyal and faithful to you as Jonathan was to David."

"Back to the old teachings? It seems to me that you are turning there more often of late. Why is that? We've traveled and seen the Acropolis at Athens and the temple at

Pergamon with the altar of Zeus. We've seen the temples of Trajan, Athena Polias, and Athena Nike. We've visited the Parthenon and Erechtheum." Antipas smirked. "And we've seen some lovely statues there!"

"Yes, and we've studied Pericles' laws, Plato's *Republic,* Socrates' philosophies, and Homer's *The Illiad* and *The Odyssey.* But why are we reciting our studies?" Manaen turned to study his cousin's face.

"Because we've learned Greek and Latin, mathematics, literature, and all the sciences, but you keep going back to the plagued Hebrews and their *Pentateuch.* Why are you never satisfied? What drives you? Have you not learned enough? Are you still questing for knowledge?"

"No. I'm yearning for peace. And I don't mean 'Pax Romana!' This peace of Rome is more brutal than anything I have studied. It is worse than a scourge—destroying everything in its path, killing, raping, and plundering all in the name of peace."

Manaen tried to explain his thoughts to his old friend.

"In our chronology of our studies, we didn't include Anaxagoras. He taught that the universe is governed by a supreme mind that brought form out of the chaos of nature. He believed that people, by thinking for themselves, could likewise bring order into human affairs. I keep going back to that and comparing it with this Hebrew God. Perhaps the two lines of thought are not so far apart."

"You're thinking like an old woman!"

Manaen could see the contempt in Antipas' eyes, but he continued.

"Perhaps Anaxagoras and the Hebrews came closer to

the truth than we realize. Perhaps there is a supreme mind, or Supreme Being, even above the Caesars and Herods of this world. Have you ever thought about that, Antipas? Or have you ever dared think such treasonous thoughts?"

"Yes, I have heard those things, and I didn't forget Anaxagoras." He rolled his eyes in boredom. "I just don't think his teachings are worth considering. My father, who is an Idumean, took up the Hebrew faith and now worships as a Jew just so that he can rule the Jewish people," Antipas replied sarcastically.

"I know that." Manaen was getting angry and struggled to keep it under control.

"Well then, if there is this Yahweh the Jews are so fond of, why has he allowed Rome to take over his land and his people? And, why has he allowed my father to prosper in his hypocrisy?" He tossed his hair and looked down his long hawk-like nose to study his finger nails, adding scornfully, "No, cousin, it's just another myth, just like the Greek's philosophies and all the rest."

"But you attended the temples in Rome." He fought to stay calm. *A display of temper could cost me my head!*

"Oh, yes. I'll worship at the Greek and Roman temples. Whichever is more profitable or pleasurable at the time. And—you must admit, cousin—the temple prostitutes are most pleasurable."

Manaen could sense that his relationship with his cousin was changing in ways he didn't want to admit. He felt angry and uncomfortable as Antipas continued.

"Of course, now that we are returning to Judea I'll put on the robe of Jewish piety, since that is expedient. But truly accept their beliefs? No! That I will not do. Not ever. I believe only in myself." With another arrogant toss of his hair he turned away. "How soon to land? Have you heard the captain say?"

Manaen realized that he was grinding his teeth as he looked at his cousin. *Yes, everything is changing. And I don't know how much longer I can put up with his attitudes. I'm going to have to tread very carefully indeed if I'm to survive when we get back to Jerusalem.*

CHAPTER 5

Back in Jerusalem the dry desert air felt good in Manaen's lungs, even if it was accompanied by the stench of sacrificial bulls and sheep at the temple, mixed with dung in the streets. It was the Jewish month of Kislev and pilgrims coming to the Feast of Dedication made the crowding worse. The census Augustus Caesar had imposed didn't help matters either, but the people were in a festive mood. Music floated above their heads and they sang and danced. It took very little to encourage these boisterous people.

They were here to celebrate the rebuilding of the temple. Herod had destroyed the one built by Zerubbabel after the Jews returned from their seventy-year exile in Syria. This one that he had rebuilt was a sight to see, because Herod had gone to great lengths to show his power and wealth. There were great stone stairs leading up to the huge porticos surrounded by tall Corinthian columns embellished with gold. His lavish use of marble in the building gave it an appearance of the celestial and was truly impressive in its richness. Manaen wondered how long this temple would last, considering the history of the Jews. An occasional whiff of food cooking made his stomach growl with hunger, so he hurried on toward the palace.

There would be a banquet tonight for the visitors from the East. Herod wanted to discover their purpose for coming to Jerusalem. If there was anything constant (one thing they could depend on to never change) it was Herod's suspicious nature. Suspicion, coupled with his fertile imagination and unquenchable thirst for power, had driven him to the brink of madness.

Just as Manaen had predicted, Herod's favorite wife, Mariamnie, and both of her sons, Alexander and Aristobulus, had fallen victim to the paranoia that drove him. They were murdered for the mere suspicion of plotting against him, although nothing had been proven against them. Oh, yes, it was safer to be Herod's pig than a member of his family.

As Manaen arrived at the palace, he realized that something was very wrong. People rushed around with the pallor of death on their faces, as if they were frightened for their lives. He realized that Herod must be in the throes of another mental attack, and he wondered whose head would roll this time. Thinking it best to stay out of the path of royal eyes, Manaen went to his apartment and shut his doors.

He enjoyed his living quarters. It was quiet in this part of the palace compound, and he could hear the fountains outside his windows in the gardens below. The songs of the tropical birds in cages added to the illusion of serenity, and even the occasional roar of one of the great cats chained there didn't disturb the peaceful setting.

Inside, nothing had been spared to make the suite of rooms comfortable and pleasant for the occupants. The heavy damask and silk curtains at the windows and doorways kept out the dust and heat during the day and the chill from the desert at night. There were huge colorful silk pillows and chairs to assure comfortable seating, and the rugs were the finest the Orient could produce. The main color used in decorating his apartment was blue, adding to the feeling of tranquility. However, Manaen knew that there was never peace in this palace, only its illusion.

Nebo was waiting for him with clean clothes and his utensils to take to the baths.

"Nebo, what's going on? Is Herod on another one of his killing sprees? Do I need to stay out of his sight?"

"You and everyone else, sir. There's talk of a new king, and he is furious. He's questioning everyone and threatening to kill all of the seers if they don't tell him what he wants to know. He seems to think that they should have the answers. Stay out of his way, or your head might roll too."

"I plan to stay as far away from him as possible. Have you seen Antipas? How is he taking all of this?"

"He's hiding in his apartments—as usual. He's always so brave," he answered with sarcasm.

Nebo was embarrassed when he realized that he had been criticizing the royal family. "I'm sorry sir. I have no right to be critical."

"No need to worry, Nebo. You know that I agree with you. He's a blubbering mess when it comes to Herod, and can we blame him? Herod would have him killed in a heart-beat, and you know it. The fact that he's his son wouldn't even cause him to pause, much less grant him any clemency. Antipas lives in constant fear. I may not know my father, but at least I don't have to worry about him killing me."

"I understand what it means to be a slave to fear."

"Why is that, Nebo? I have never mistreated you. Has someone else abused you?" Manaen could feel his anger rising as he thought of the horrible beatings he had seen some of the palace slaves receive.

"No, Manaen. But I have always known that Herod could have me sold as quickly as he could have Antipas killed."

"I would never allow that to happen, Nebo." It made Manaen angry to even think of such a thing.

"Master, please lower your voice. These walls have ears, you know. And how would you stop him from selling me or doing anything else he decided to do? We live at the mercy of his whims. Lately he seems to act on whatever enters that mad mind of his."

"Then you agree with me that he has gone mad?"

"Absolutely. His thirst for power has driven him quite mad, and it's getting worse with every passing day. Be very careful, Manaen. I don't want to lose you to his suspicions. You are the only family I have."

"I'll be careful, Nebo, very careful, indeed."

CHAPTER 6

"'Where is he that is born King of the Jews? We have seen his star in the East, and have come to worship him.' Those were their exact words, I tell you. They were talking to me, and I heard them distinctly." Herod was livid with rage and the muscles and veins in his neck stood out. His voice was shrill, and there was foam at the corners of his mouth. "Call my chief priest and all of the scribes of the people. Yes, bring me my wise men, idiots that they are."

His contempt was obvious.

"Bring them here immediately. They will tell me where this child is to be born, or I'll kill them all. King of the Jews indeed! I, Herod, am king of the Jews. The only king they will ever have."

Two hours later, the hastily-assembled chief priest and

scribes were as pale as ghosts, shaking with terror as they stood before the demented man who held the power of life or death in his hands.

"Oh, king, who lives forever," they whined. The sweat of fear began to make rivulets down their taut foreheads and into their bulging eyes. "We have searched through the ancient, sacred Scriptures of the nation. In them we found where Micah, the prophet of old, says, 'It's you, Bethlehem, in Judah's land, no longer bringing up the rear. From you will come the leader who will shepherd-rule my people Israel.' That's all we know, oh mighty king who rules forever. We didn't say it, great king. The ancient prophet did!"

They covered their heads with their hands. Their words grew clipped, and their voices reached a shrill crescendo in their fear.

"Enough! Send those fools who call themselves wise men to me. They will be no more than tools in my hand to lead me to this so-called 'King of the Jews.' King, indeed! I am the king! Do you hear me, you ungrateful Jews?" Herod shook his fist into the air as a terrible light gleamed from eyes that squinted through rolls of fat.

• • • • • • • • • • •

The men from the East were in another room of the palace talking to some of the local scholars, not realizing what a storm they had set into motion. The scholars asked them to explain why they had come to Jerusalem.

"We were on the roof of the School of Astrology at Sippar when we observed a phenomenon. Near the end of the month of Shevat, the planets began to cluster. Jupiter moved out of Aquarius toward Saturn, which is in the constellation of Pisces. It could not be seen because the light of the sun was also in Pisces, and its light covered it. But we tracked it and knew that it was there.

"In the month of Nisan both stars rose visibly at daybreak. In Zif it occurred again for a short period, and then again on the day of your atonement, the third day of Tishrei. We decided that this was an omen, and we began our journey."

"On the fourth day of Kislev," Gaspar continued, "we saw his star rise in the first rays of dawn, and we have come to worship him who we believe this great occurrence announces."

Melchazar stepped forward.

"Doesn't your Jewish tradition record that Pisces, which we in the East say represents this western area around the Great Sea, the Mare Nostrum, is the sign of Israel, the sign of the Messiah? We believe that this is the end of an old age, and the beginning of a new one, and that this king will lead us into it. Jupiter is a lucky star, a royal one. We have come to worship the one that all the heavens seem to be proclaiming as king and—" He was interrupted by the arrival of Chuza, the king's personal steward.

"King Herod has sent for you to return to the throne room."

• • • • • • • • • • • •

A strange light shone in Herod's eyes as the party entered the great hall.

"Ah, there you are. I have good news for you. My scholars have searched ancient manuscripts, and they tell me that you have almost reached your destination. The One you seek is nearby in Bethlehem. Go, leave no stone unturned.

It is only a short journey from here. But, my honored guests, I have a request of you. When your quest is complete, come back and spend some time here. I want to know where you found him so that I too can go and worship this One of whom the heavens speak."

His voice sounded like a serpent hissing, and he appeared to slither as he moved forward to take the hand of the spokesman for the group.

"This Bethlehem is such a small village and cannot offer you the amenities that men of your position deserve. We will see to your every comfort here. I'm famous for my hospitality, you know. Make haste; we will be anticipating your return. There isn't much in Bethlehem to hold your attention for long. Be swift to return and report to us what you find."

The Magi bowed respectfully and left the room.

CHAPTER 7

In the first hours of the new day, a small child's cry was heard. People were sleeping. It was hours before they would stir from their slumber and rise to begin another day. They didn't realize what had happened in their little town of Bethlehem. Few of them noticed the brilliant star, the shepherds who came, or the large caravan bearing wise men from the East. In the Jerusalem palace Herod was agitated, pacing the cold marble room like one of the tigers chained in his garden. Neither the damask tunic with its silk lining nor the thick wool of his robe could ward off the chill that pierced to his bones. Madness glistened in his eyes. They darted restlessly to see if some enemy was lurking in the dark shadows, listening as he murmured.

"I will kill him if it is the last thing I do." Over and over he hissed the words through lips that stretched in a thick, ugly line over tightly clinched teeth.

Something was happening. He sensed it. There had been too much talk about a new 'King of the Jews.' The people were restless, tired of being taxed and bullied. The incident with the eagle above the temple hadn't gained him any popularity, and his likeness on the standard the troops carried through the city had added to the growing unrest. Rome was pressing him for more control of this populous land. What did they really know about these stiff-necked Jews? Arrogant, religious, pious, intolerant, stinking Jews! How he hated them. And now, all of this chatter about a new king. He was the only king they would have and he would prove it to them. He would have this new "king" killed immediately.

Even Manaen has been talking about the star and what it meant. When he and Antipas arrived at the palace from Rome yesterday and heard the seers' reasoning, he agreed with the wise men that the planets were in position; and now, the brilliance of the star! He began muttering to himself.

"No, I've never seen such a star, never heard such talk from astronomers and seers, never been so angry and uneasy. Yes, I will have this baby killed immediately. I know that it's in Bethlehem. The people's chief priests and teachers of the law that I questioned told me about the prophecy of the child's birth. I can still hear their words ringing in that cold, still room. 'In Bethlehem of Judea,' they answered, 'for this is what the prophet Micah has written.' In Bethlehem Ephrata, that insignificant place! One who will be ruler over Israel, indeed!" He recalled their whimpering little voices quoting Micah, "He will stand and shepherd His flock in the strength of the Lord, in the majesty of the Name of the Lord His God. And they will live securely, for then His greatness will reach to the ends of the earth. And He will be their peace."

His lips curled back in a sneer as his thoughts raced. *His greatness will not reach the ends of the earth! Not if I can help it. He will be their peace, indeed! When I am finished with them they will wish they had never heard of this King of Peace! King of the Jews, indeed. I am king of the Jews.*

"Be their peace, indeed," Herod hissed again through clenched teeth.

Oh, yes, I know how to put an end to this whole nonsense. No one is going to take my place. No one! I am Herod the Great, and I will remain Herod the Great, King of all Judea. Rome gave me this land and these miserable people to rule. I am the one who has taken an ordinary country of sand and brick and rebuilt it into one of gold, marble, and beauty. I have shaped it. I will keep it. The Jews be hanged, his thoughts raged on.

Then and there the wheels were put into motion that would carry out Jeremiah's prophecy: "Rachel could be heard crying for her children and they were no more."

CHAPTER 8

The blood pounded in his ears as Manaen considered what he could do to stop this terrible slaughter. He didn't feel the desert cold as he rushed out into the night. He had to catch that caravan and warn those men not to return to Jerusalem, but to return home another way. His horse, a gift from the mad Herod himself, was the fastest around and would now carry him on an errand against the giver of the gift.

Many will die; many innocent babies will die if I don't stop him. Herod has gone totally mad at last. Manaen didn't know how he knew the babies would be killed. He only knew that it was true. Many innocent babies would die, and he had to try to stop it from happening. Deep within he feared that there was no stopping this terrible thing, but perhaps he could save the visitors from the East. He had to try, even if thwarting Herod's mad scheme cost him his relationship with the royal family, or his very life.

There is already so much blood on the king's hands. Faces of people that Herod had killed began to flash before his eyes. *No one is safe from the madness—no member of his family, no member of his court…no one living under his tyrannical rule. Antipas was right. He's not safe from his own father's sword. Herod must be stopped.*

The hooves of the horse seemed to hammer out an echo to Manaen's frantic thoughts as the great beast thundered south and then west through the clear desert night. The horse lathered with its effort, but did not slacken its speed. The animal seemed to understand the urgency of this mission.

Manaen had no concern for the cold or the thieves and zealots that frequented these roads. Neither his future nor his own life meant anything to him now. Singleness of purpose drove him in desperation and futility. In his madness, Herod would again have the stain of blood on his hands if he wasn't stopped. He had to try to save the babies, the Wiseman, and his friend from the King's madness.

Into the bitter night Manaen followed the light of the star.

• • • • • • • • • • • •

"Have you seen a caravan this evening?" Manaen shouted to the boy he passed on the road into Bethlehem. Sweat, dirt, and gravel flew as he reigned in the lathering horse and turned back toward the boy.

"Yes, most honorable one. They're at the stable behind the inn. I just left there. Do you want me to show you where it is?" Before he could jump out of the way an arm had reached down, yanked him up, and placed him in front of the rider of the huge horse. The horse pranced and shied, doing a stiff-legged dance as the boy began to struggle.

Fear gripped the boy, almost choking him. He started to struggle, twisting and fighting to get away.

"Settle down, boy. You're spooking my horse. I'm not going to hurt you. You said you'd show me the way, and the quickest way to do that is for you to ride with me. Now, how do we get there?" He brought the horse under control and the boy relaxed as he began to give directions, but Manaen could tell he was watching him out of the corner of his eye.

Shortly, they turned a corner, and the caravan came into view. Manaen saw the signs of wealth. Well-tended camels and horses sported rich trappings, and the attendants were well-dressed. Yes, this was the caravan of the Magi from the East.

"Where are your masters?" he asked the closest servant as he dismounted and lifted the boy down.

"In the stable, sir."

"In the stable? What in the world are they doing in a stable?"

"They came looking for the new king, and that's where the star directed them, sir."

Manaen was amazed. *These are not just wise men. They are kings in their own countries. They have left the splendor of King Herod's palace in search of a new king, and they have come to a stable? What kind of "king" is this? Oh, well. I must warn them not to return to Jerusalem,* he thought.

As Manaen and the boy entered the stable he was even more amazed to find the three kings bowing in obvious worship before a simple peasant woman holding a child. He was struck with awe and felt his own knees begin to bow.

Through the haze of a soft, golden glow from the oil lamps set in niches around the wall, he watched as the kings placed gifts before the child.

The first king was dressed in a flowing, white robe edged with a gold Grecian key design. He wore a white turban that was generously wrapped and clasped with a large gold pin, centered with a dangling pearl the size of a small pear. His face, which was notable in its serenity, was almost hidden by the folds of the turban. The burnoose that flowed from the turban wrapped around his lower face and was tucked into the back of his robe. It appeared to be seamless. He extended a small, gold, heavily-embossed dispenser on a matching saucer. In it was enough myrrh to perfume a large household for years. The king gazed lovingly on the baby, and his beautiful face became washed in tears. He reached up, unclasped the pin, and unwound the turban, handing the yards of fine silk to the mother, indicating that it could be used to line the bed for the baby.

The oldest king had a long white beard and was dressed in a red, flowing robe. On his bald head he wore a kaffiyeh that was held in place by a wide circle of embossed gold. The burnoose was held in place at the waist by a thick rope of finely spun gold with large tassels on the ends. His only other adornment was a heavy gold ring set with a round polished stone of red coral the size of a man's thumb. He humbly offered frankincense in a tall alabaster urn inlaid with lapis lazuli. He folded his hands in prayer as tears streaked his wrinkled, weather-worn face.

The third and youngest king appeared quite arrogant. He wore a fitted purple tunic with a gold papyrus leaf design, which was overlaid by a lavish gold collar thickly studded with rare stones. A narrow purple kaffiyeh covered his head, the back heavily embroidered with gold thread in the shape of an eagle. He appeared to be looking down his long, hawk-like nose as he held out a large onyx and gold lock-box which he opened to show that it was filled with gold. The key that he used to open the box was in itself a valuable work of art. As he presented his gift and gazed into the face of the tiny baby all of his arrogance seemed to melt away and to be replaced by an expression of wondrous love. Here too tears flowed freely.

Such costly gifts—gold, frankincense, and myrrh. Who are these people receiving these gifts and why? Manaen wondered. The young woman was quite beautiful in a simple, refreshing way. The man looked older than the woman and hovered protectively over her and the child as he watched with an expression of awe, acceptance, and amazement. His face was finely chiseled, and Manaen could tell that his hands were the hands of a laborer.

They wore simple peasant robes and no adornment. *Of course, they may not be as poor as they appear,* Manaen's thoughts wandered on. *If this is the king that the monarchs from the East were seeking, they could be in disguise. The crowded conditions caused by the census could be the reason they are in this stable. These could just be their traveling clothes. But where are their servants and guards?*

The woman beckoned for the boy who had led Manaen to the stable to come over and stand beside her. He couldn't hear their conversation, but he could see the wary expression on the boy's face change as he smiled and leaned toward her. She whispered in his ear, and the boy turned to look in the crude bed where the baby had been placed. It was a manger where the animals were fed. It had been chiseled from a large rock, filled with clean straw and hay, and was now lined with the finest silk. She placed the baby in the boy's arms, holding them both close as she did, so that the boy held the baby without realizing that she was holding him too. Tears began to make furrows in the boy's cheeks as a smile broke the crusty layers of dirt.

Manaen marveled that the mother allowed such a filthy child to hold this newborn King. He had never seen such expressions of love, joy, and peace as he saw on the faces of the woman and boy. Softly and gently she sang a song that she had obviously sung before.

"My soul magnifies the Lord and my spirit rejoices in God my Savior…"

Peace entered Manaen's spirit, and he was soon lost in it. She continued singing. "He has performed mighty deeds with His arm; he has scattered those who are proud in their inmost thoughts. He has brought down rulers from their thrones, but has lifted up the humble. He has filled the hungry with good things, but has sent the rich away empty."[1] *What does it all mean?*

After some time, how long he didn't know, the kings rose from their worship. As they prepared to leave, Manaen stood and followed them out of the crudely hewn stable that was such inauspicious housing for a king.

One of the men saw Manaen and called to him.

"What are you doing here, my friend? Did you too follow the star to find the new King?"

"I followed the star to find three kings and give them warning," Manaen returned quietly as he approached the men. He looked around for listening ears and, hoping that they could not be overheard, continued.

"Please take heed of what I tell you."

"What is it? Are we in danger?"

"You must not return to Jerusalem. Herod has no desire to worship this infant. He's in a jealous rage, and I overheard him plotting to kill the babe. Please, don't go back to the palace and give him the information he wants from you. He'll have my head if he knows I betrayed his plans and warned you, but I can't stand by and let this happen. There's too much blood on his hands as it is. Please go back another way."

There was compassion in his eyes as Melchazar looked at this earnest young man. He knew that it had taken a great deal of courage and conviction for him to go against Herod and warn them.

"It is as you say; but don't overly concern yourself. You haven't betrayed your king. I've been warned of this in a dream. He does indeed seek the life of the child, so we are returning to the east by a different route. Joseph will also be warned by an angel to take Mary and the child and leave. Your coming has, however, confirmed the truth of my dream. I thank you for caring enough to come."

Manaen realized that this man shared his ability to foresee the future, and he wanted to ask him about the strange gift. Instead he asked, "Who is this child, Melchazar? Will he truly take Herod's throne?"

"Oh, no. His will be a kingdom like no earthly kingdom. I don't understand it all, but I do know that he's destined for true greatness. He will have a people, but be no threat to any earthly king. He will rule, but in love and kindness. His great power will come from his very meekness."

"How can this be? I don't understand. Is he a new god, like Jupiter, Juno, or Apollo? What are you saying?"

"Neither do I comprehend how this will be; I just know that it will be. But, no, he's not a pagan god. Who or whatever he is goes far beyond what the mortal mind can fathom. You're a young man. Watch carefully as history unfolds. I'm an old man, and we must return to our own country. I envy you, that you will be here to see all that will happen. Watch carefully and learn well, my young friend. And don't be afraid of your abilities. Use them wisely."

With this, the majestic man strode away, mounted his camel and gave the departure signal to his lead man. Waving to Manaen, he rode away.

Afraid of my abilities? How did he know? Manaen felt a tug on his sleeve and looked down to see the small boy who had led him to this place.

"Yes, boy, what is it?"

"Where to now, sir?"

"Well, I suppose I need to pay you for your services and take you home. Your family will be worried about you. It is, after all, the middle of the night! What are you doing out so late?"

"Oh, I have no home or family, sir. I'm an orphan. No one worries about me. I take care of myself and come and go as I please."

Manaen remembered the family in the stable and wondered if they would take the boy. A feeling of compassion washed over him as he remembered how he had been without mother or father to care for him, even though Herod was his uncle. Had it not been for a kind woman present when his mother died in childbirth, he could have been homeless. As it was, that same woman had cared for him in Herod's palace when she was sent there to serve as wet nurse to Herod's son Antipas, his cousin. He didn't know why she was sent from Antioch to Jerusalem, but he suspected his father had something to do with it.

Fortunately, he had been raised in the palace as a companion to Antipas and had been treated as a son by his uncle, King Herod. He shuddered to think how his life could have been so different, or if he would have survived to have a life at all. His own father had refused to look at or acknowledge him because his birth had caused the death of the only woman his father had ever loved.

"What's your name, boy?"

"Joachim, sir."

"Would you like to come with me?" *What am I saying? Have I lost my senses? I can't take this filthy, homeless waif back to the palace with me.*

"Go where and for what, sir?" The boy eyed him suspiciously.

"Well, I suppose you could go home and live with me. I could take care of you."

"I'm not one of those boys who hire their bodies out to evil men!" The boy glanced around as he backed away, looking for a way of escape.

"Nor am I one of those vile men who hire boys for pleasure! You are right to avoid that style of life. Who warned you about such things if you have no family?"

"I may not have a family, but I have eyes. I see what happens to those boys when the men are finished with them. I'm an orphan, but I'm not stupid."

A rich laugh escaped Manaen's throat as he observed the boy.

"You're a wise one all right. I like a man who sees things as they are and plots his course accordingly. No, Joachim, you have nothing to fear from me. However, if you agree to come with me, you must never, ever tell anyone that I found you in Bethlehem tonight."

"I didn't think that you looked like that sort, but I can't be too careful. What about my money, sir? You said you were going to pay me for showing you the way." His eyes grew large with wonder as Manaen handed him a denarius.

He pocketed the silver coin quickly, fearful that Manaen would change his mind.

"Well, sir, when are we leaving, and where are we going?" The money quickened his decision about going with this man.

"We're returning to Jerusalem right now."

"Jerusalem! You mean you live in Jerusalem!" His excitement was obvious as Manaen lifted him onto the horse and mounted behind him.

He's a stinking little beggar, Manaen thought as he wrapped his cloak around them to protect the boy from the cold night air, *but a bath will cure that. What am I going to do with him? Oh, well, the palace is large. Perhaps I can hide him with the servants.*

Looking back Manaen realized that the star was no longer there. *How strange,* he thought. He looked down when the boy's head dropped and saw that he was already asleep. *What responsibility have I taken on? What is this compulsion that has caused me to want to care for this boy? It has something to do with the baby in the stable, but what?* A sense of something bigger than he was came over him, and he knew that his life was destined to change.

• • • • • • • • • • •

"Where are we, sir? Is this Jerusalem?" Joachim murmured, groggy with sleep.

"No, we are at the Jericho palace…"

"The Jericho palace?" Joachim shrieked and stiffened with fear. "Why are we at the Jericho Palace? Am I going to be a slave? They beat slaves here!"

"There is no need to be afraid, Joachim. You will never be a slave and no one will beat you. We're here because we can rest better here. It's quieter and there's a bath that you'll enjoy. Can you stay awake long enough for that?" The boy's trembling lessened, and he relaxed, deciding to trust his new friend.

"Yes, sir. I'll try." Joachim was asleep before the words were hardly out of his mouth. Manaen was thankful that exhaustion could defeat fear. He wondered how much this waif knew about the household of Herod. Too much, it seemed.

"Well, I guess that bath will have to wait." Manaen wrinkled his nose as he chuckled at the sleeping boy.

"Nebo, we'll be staying here a while," he said to the elderly slave that held his horse. "Bring a cot to my quarters for the boy. And do you think that you could find something small enough for him to sleep in? Tomorrow he gets a thorough bath, but for tonight clean clothes might help. Phew, he's a stinking little bugger."

"Who is he, sir?"

"Just a waif that I found on the street. It seems that he's

an orphan. I'll be keeping him with me," said Manaen with more bravado than he felt.

"I'll be right back, sir. Don't put him on your clean linens." Nebo looked shocked at what he had said. "Sorry, sir. I'll be glad to change your linens after we get the boy in bed. Put him on your bed for now, sir." The old slave left to do as he had been asked. Manaen sat on a chair as he continued to hold the boy, unwilling to create more work for this man who had served him faithfully for so many years.

Nebo was an old man when he was placed with Manaen as his personal servant, but he had shown great patience and fortitude in his duties. He had also shown a lot of bravery on several occasions. Palace life was full of intrigues and plots, most of which were evil. In an effort to protect him, Nebo made it his business to keep his master informed about covert affairs. He had been instrumental in saving Manaen's life on more than one occasion.

Manaen was weary from the long ride. He had decided to come to the Jericho palace rather than return to Jerusalem and face the royal family with this filthy little boy. It was farther, but Nebo was here. *What explanation can I make for my behavior? Well, they're accustomed to strange behavior from me. At least, Antipas might understand.*

Manaen was almost asleep when Nebo returned with a pallet, clean linens, and a shirt for the boy. They made him comfortable across the room from Manaen, and then Nebo helped his master into bed.

"What would I do without you, Nebo? Don't wake me in the morning. I may sleep all day...can't do that...the boy

needs a bath! I could use a dip in the tepidarium myself."
He could feel sleep rushing in.

Nebo shook his head as he left the room, wondering what his young master could be up to now. One never knew what Manaen might do. He was a kind man with a quick mind and a heart as big as all outdoors. Shaking his graying head, he quietly shut the door, for he was also a man full of love; and if this boy was to be part of his master's life, then he was part of his life too. He could sense in his spirit that he would be a welcomed and much-needed source of joy and new life for him and his master. Chuckling, he made his way to his cot and looked forward to the morning.

Before sleep came, Nebo remembered the years in Rome while Manaen was being educated. He regretted much of the education the young one had received—the introduction in the ways of a corrupt society, men thinking they knew more than the God who created them, and, more often than not, denying his very existence. They worshiped strange gods who satisfied their flesh in orgies of lust and debauchery. Men were willing to do anything in their quest for power and self-exaltation: lie, ruin another's reputation, murder, or anything else to fulfill their own agenda.

Yes, I suppose they would have to deny the existence of a just and holy God in order to go their way and do as they pleased. What fools they were, these men who thought themselves so wise and esteemed themselves so highly. Thank God my master has seen the foolishness and recognized it for what it is, but how will he be able to survive this corrupt society he has been born into? Only God has the answer for that. Then he spoke aloud.

"It is too much for the mind of an old servant. I can only

trust him into your hands, my Lord and my God. Please continue to keep your angels encamped around him and keep him safe from the hands of the evil one." With this prayer, peace came and sleep soon followed.

CHAPTER 9

What is that odor? What woke me? Manaen heard it again. A small sigh and a slight rustle of cloth. He forced sleep away as he opened his eyes to the full light of day. A small face with large brown eyes and a mop of curly black hair was watching him from the side of the bed.

"What in thunder?" he gasped as he struggled up in his bed. *That's the source of the odor!* Then he remembered the night before and smiled at Joachim.

"Good morning, Joachim. Did you sleep well?"

"Where are my clothes? Someone has stolen my clothes, and I'm stuck in this ridiculous thing! And it's too big! I want my clothes!"

"Good morning, Joachim. Did you sleep well?" Manaen repeated his question, unwilling to let the boy's bad manners pass unchallenged.

"Yes, Master. Now where are my clothes?" It was obvious that the boy was highly indignant to find his clothes missing.

"Your clothes are being cleaned, or replaced, or whatever. They'll be ready for you when you're finished. Come with me." Manaen shrugged into his robe as he talked to the boy. He picked up his brushes and motioned for the boy to accompany him.

"I'm not leaving the room in this ridiculous thing." Manaen was hard put to choke back the laughter bubbling up at this show of affronted dignity.

Manaen reached for a scarf to tie the boy's gown at the waist, but as he did, Joachim ducked and threw his arm over his head as if to deflect a blow.

"Whoa. Joachim, I'm not going to hit you. Why would I do that? I'm your protector now. I am going to take care of you, not harm you. I'm sorry I startled you. Come here to me." He held out his arms to the boy and slowly Joachim dropped his guard and came to stand in front of Manaen. Manaen reached out and took him in his arms, wondering how often this boy had endured beatings.

Joachim shuddered and then began to relax.

"Now, let me tie your night shirt for you and we'll go to the baths. Have you ever been in one? We'll go into the tepidarium first. It's warm. When we are good and clean we'll go into the frigidarium where it's cold. You'll like it.

"You see, to supply water for the Jericho fortress here, Herod had an enormous aqueduct built which carries water from Ein Kelt." Manaen realized that the boy looked puzzled. "Oh, you don't care about all of that, do you?"

Joachim shook his head as Manaen chuckled.

"Well, we'll bathe ourselves, and by then your clothes will be clean and ready for you. Then we'll eat before we see about getting you more clothes later today. Is that all right with you?" Manaen realized that he had rushed the boy earlier. He would need time to adjust to his new life. There was a lot for him to learn. It would take time and patience on both their parts as they learned each other's ways.

Joachim nodded his agreement without saying a word.

When they reached the tepidarium, Joachim reacted with awe at the beauty of the baths. After some initial objection to the necessity of removing his clothes, he was the first one into the water. With all of the abandon of a small boy, he jumped into the warm water, splashing and laughing with glee.

Manaen was glad there was no one else around to complain about the ruckus. He remembered a time when he and Antipas were splashing in the pool, and one of the people there complained. Herod happened to be there too, and he gave the man an evil look. "If you don't want to get wet, stay away from the water!" he said.

As he stepped into the water and relaxed at the side of the pool, Manaen laughed again at the memory of the man's outraged expression. He floated for a few minutes before he began the bath ritual. Then, taking the brushes and strigil, he scraped the dirt from his body. It felt so good to be clean again that he began to laugh.

"What is it, sir?" Joachim asked.

"It just feels so good to be clean. Come, let me show you how to use the brushes."

"What are the brushes for?"

"To clean your skin."

"Won't the water do that?"

"Yes, somewhat, but the brushes brush off the loose dirt and the strigil scrapes off the dead skin and gets all of the dirt off. You'll see." He took one brush in each hand and taught the boy how to brush his body. Joachim didn't like it, but he did as he was told. Then they scraped their skin and brushed again.

When they had finished, Manaen showed Joachim how to stand on the side of the fountain and rinse with the fresh water.

"I want to stay in the water," Joachim said.

"We're going back into the water in the frigidarium. Just follow me."

When they reached the frigidarium, Joachim ran to the edge and jumped in. The shock of the cold water was plain on his face; after a few seconds Manaen couldn't help laughing as he eased himself into the water. Joachim tried to be brave, but Manaen took his hand and led him from the water. The boy shook and his teeth chattered. Manaen toweled him dry and showed him how to rub the warm fragrant oil into his skin.

"Now doesn't that feel better, Joachim?"

"Yes, sir. I don't think I have ever been this clean. Can I have my clothes now?"

As if on cue, Nebo approached with clean clothes for the boy.

"Thank you, Nebo. You are always right on time. Can you thank Nebo, Joachim?"

"Thank you, Nebo, but I can dress myself," he said a little indignantly.

Nebo stopped and turned away to hide his smile.

"I think you have found a game one, sir."

CHAPTER 10

*O*h, God, the blood! I've never seen so much blood! Never heard such screaming women, babies, children, and men! People running; horses' hooves thudding; the clash and clatter of swords; men cursing and yelling! Will the madness never end? Bodies of bloody babies! Screams! Women running, screaming, with the mutilated bodies of their infants clutched in their arms. Women being decapitated when they refuse to give up their babies to the sword. Men murdered when they try to protect their wives and children. The streets running red with the blood of the infants. Sounds of the anguished screams tear the air. Manaen awoke drenched with sweat, tears streaming down his face.

Jupiter's priests, will I never stop dreaming of the things I saw? Will the torment never end? I tried to stop it, but I was helpless in the face of Herod's madness. No, I can not stay here any longer. It's time to go to Antioch.

Antipas is furious because I'm spending time with Joachim instead of spending all of my time catering to his every whim. He hates his new "dung heap of a wife" as he calls her, so much that he's acting as demented as his father. He's terrified of her father and convinced that the man is plotting to come from Idumea and kill him. And he wants me to move back to the palace and protect him!

His fear of his brothers isn't helping his state of mind either. I should have broken his neck yesterday when he threatened to have Joachim killed if I didn't come back to the palace, stay with him, and be his body guard. I should have told him that I've had about all I can take of his arrogance, narcissism, and paranoid fear. What a deadly trio. I think I'm beginning to hate him, jackal that he is, and I hope I never have to see him again!

Manaen was jerked from the cot by the sound of a scream. Rushing to the next room, he found Joachim thrashing on his pallet. As gently as possible he took the boy in his arms.

"Joachim, wake up. It is only a dream."

The boy awoke with a shudder.

"No, no," he sobbed. "It's not a dream. It really happened. We saw it."

Manaen still didn't understand how Joachim had followed him to Bethlehem that night; he refused to tell him, but what he had seen had nearly destroyed the boy. Only his knowledge of the streets of Bethlehem and his uncanny ability to hide had kept him from being killed as well. He was terrified of Herod and the royal family.

Taking a blanket and straightening it as best he could, he wrapped the boy, picked him up, and took him to the window.

"Look, Joachim. We're in Jerusalem, not Bethlehem.

You're safe here with me. I won't let anyone hurt you; not ever! Do you understand?"

"Yes, most honored master. I'm sorry that I woke you, sir." The boy's voice sounded old and tired. Manaen was angry that the boy had been so cruelly robbed of his childhood. Would he ever again be that bright, strong, confident boy he had found in Bethlehem? It was time to take him to a place of refuge where perhaps they could heal.

"You didn't wake me. My own nightmares did that." He felt the boy shake again. "Joachim, you've done a good job of keeping the secret about my being in Bethlehem to warn the wise men. Can you keep another secret?"

"Oh, yes sir, with my life." Again he shuddered, as if seeing his own blood being spilled.

"I am leaving here, Joachim. It's no longer safe for anyone in the palace. I'm going to Antioch, but no one must know." He heard a sob escape the small boy.

"Oh, most honored sir, I'll never tell anyone where you have gone. No matter what they do to me. Your secret is safe with me."

"No, no, you don't understand. I'm taking you with me. I would never leave you here or anywhere else. Do you believe me, Joachim?" He felt the small head nod against his chest.

"Do you really understand? I'm not sure you do, but I'll try to explain. Do you remember the night in Bethlehem when we went to the stable and saw that family?"

"Yes, your honorable sir."

"Something happened that night. May I tell you a story?" Again he felt the head nod, and he went on.

"In Jewish history there was a shepherd boy named

David who was destined to become a great king. When he met Jonathan, the son of Saul, who was king at that time, we are told that God knit their hearts together.

"Jonathan loved David as he loved his own soul. I think that's what happened to us. I believe the God of David and Jonathan, if he is real, knit our hearts together for some purpose of his own, and I'm to care for you as my very own son. Can you understand that? Can you look to me as your father? Can you trust me to take care of you?"

Manaen felt the thin shoulders shake and realized that the boy was crying.

"It's all right. Let those tears cleanse all of the hurt. You'll never be alone again. I'll do everything in my power to protect you from men like Herod. You see, I somewhat understand how you feel." Manaen explained about his own birth and how he was brought to the palace as a baby. "Still, even though I had more protection than you have had, I have never really had a family of my own. Now you are my family."

He let the boy cry a while before going on.

"We're leaving here, and I need your help to plan and prepare for our trip. Can you do that for me? Are you strong enough to make this trip?" He felt the boy straighten his spine as if to strengthen it.

"Yes. I'll be able to do all that you ask."

"Then do you think that you could call me something besides 'most honored sir' or 'master?'" Manaen chuckled. "And will you start eating again so that you'll have strength for our journey? It will be long and hard."

"Yes, Mas…Father. I'll eat all that you put before me. I promise."

Manaen felt his own tears streaming down his face. Gazing up at the stars he marveled at all the word "father" could mean. Being called that for the first time opened something new in his heart and the wonder of it amazed him. *Father … protector … provider … loving … caring … sharing. In such a short time this boy has come to mean so much to me. What does it all mean?*

Gently he put the boy on his own cot, covered him, and went to get the boy's pallet. He would sleep on the floor by the cot so that if the boy woke up, he would be there for him. Joachim would not be alone. Manaen remembered what it was to feel afraid, alone, and lost.

"He will not have to go through that anymore if I can help it," he murmured.

CHAPTER 11

The early morning desert air was biting cold as they left the old Turkish wall and passed through the Valley of the Cheesemakers. Everyone else was still asleep as they passed Solomon's pool, went through the Tekoa Gate, crossed the Kidron Valley, and made their way up Mt. Olivet. They stayed in the shadow of the olive trees growing there, hoping to avoid the eyes of thieves. Bands of thieves, as well as zealots, used these hills as hide outs.

It felt strange to be leaving Jerusalem, but Manaen decided that it was best for Joachim. It was time for him to rejoin his father's people in Antioch. His father's recent death left him with a terrible grief, although he had not really known the man. *I had always hoped to be reunited with my father and know a father's love. Now all I have is an inheritance of land and great wealth.* He felt strangely empty. However, having to attend to his father's estate had given him a valid reason to leave Jerusalem with Herod's blessings. *Antipas is furious with me for leaving, but I don't care what Antipas thinks anymore. I've had it with him, and I'm just glad to escape his growing suspicions and madness.* It felt so good to have the boy sleeping with his head resting against his shoulder as they rode along. Yes, it was good to have someone who trusted him completely.

Manaen signaled to stop as they reached the pass leading into the desert. He wanted time to look back at Jerusalem one last time. It was a beautiful city with its temple the focal point. Jerusalem, City of David, the city set on a hill, the one place of pilgrimage for Hebrews from every tribe. Although it was now under Roman occupation, they still came to sing their songs and offer their sacrifices. Why did they risk their very lives to come here? Oh, yes, he had studied their religion and attended the temple or synagogue when it was expedient. He had read *The Pentateuch, the Torah,* and *The Talmud,* but he knew there was something much deeper that drew these people, though he had never experienced it or understood it.

Who is this Yahweh they stand in awe of? Why all the rules and regulations? Why has their God not protected them from the Romans or from Herod? If he's such a great God, why has he allowed the Hebrew babies to be slaughtered like he allowed the Egyptian firstborn to die all those years ago? What kind of capricious God do they serve?

The boy began to move.

"Look, Joachim. Watch as the sun touches Jerusalem with its golden light. Try to remember her like this, in the first light of dawn, looking clean and beautiful. Don't hold on to the memory of the evil and corruption within her walls. She is beautiful from a distance. Can you see the temple there? What a grand structure. Herod did a few good things."

"Yes, it's beautiful from here."

"Ah, but wait until you see Antioch. I haven't been there since I was a young boy, but I remember, Joachim. I remember." Manaen smiled as he realized the boy had gone back to sleep. He motioned for his caravan to start again. They were soon swaying with the loping motion of the camel's awkward gait.

CHAPTER 12

For weeks they battled marauding nomads, sand-storms, and sea sickness. As they crossed the desert they stopped at an oasis to rest and water the live-stock. Manaen told Joachim to stay close by and was helping water the camels when a tribe of Bedouins attacked. "Attack, attack!" he heard the boy yelling and looked up to see him running toward him from the top of a dune. Joachim tumbled down the dune just as the band of Bedouins crested the hill, then he disappeared. An awful fear almost overwhelmed Manaen when he realized that he had lost sight of Joachim. Manaen drew his sword and rushed toward the marauders. Sure that the Bedouins had captured the boy, he fought the battle with a fury he had never experienced before. His sword and those of his men whistled through the air. They slashed and chopped, each swing producing more blood and destruction. The out-maneuvered Bedouins were soon defeated, and three of them had been killed.

"Where is the boy?" Manaen asked one of the captured tribesmen. He held the man by the throat with one hand and held his knife to his throat with the other hand.

"What boy? I haven't seen a boy!"

"Tell me where the boy is, or I'll cut your black heart out! Where is he?" Manaen screamed into the man's face. He shook the man until his head looked like it would fly off his neck as he tried to force an answer, but the terrified man continued to deny any knowledge of a boy. He was ready to kill the man when he continued in his denial. Just as he drew back his arm to run his knife into the Bedouin's heart, he heard Joachim calling to him. Turning without releasing his hold on the man's throat, he saw the boy running toward him, covered in sand from head to foot. Thrusting the limp Bedouin toward one of his guards, he ran and grabbed up the sand covered boy. Hugging him and swinging him around and around, he laughed with relief.

"Where have you been? I thought you had been taken captive."

"Oh, no, sir, I was hiding." The boy clung to his neck, and his legs were locked around his waist like a vise.

"Hiding where?"

"I hid in the sand at the edge of a dried-up bush. The bush hid my face so that I could breathe, and the sand covered the rest of me enough, I guess. One of the Bedouins almost stepped on me, but I didn't move. I was afraid you would be killed," he said, hugging Manaen even tighter. "What were you doing with that man?"

"I was about to cut his heart out!"

"Why?"

"I thought he knew where you were and wouldn't tell me. I thought I had lost you. I was furious with myself and the Bedouins. Come on. Let's get some of that sand brushed off and see to the men. Some of them have been injured."

Manaen was relieved that so few of his men had been injured and that what injuries they had were not severe. They left the oasis the next morning with three captives in fairly good condition. At the next oasis, he traded them back to their tribe for a small herd of goats. He knew that the men would never leave their nomadic roots; he couldn't keep them in captivity even though they would have made good herdsmen if they could have been trusted. The only way they could remain was in chains, and they couldn't tend his herds unless they were able to move about freely. As long as there was breath in their bodies they would probably try to escape and return to the desert and their tribe. Also, they were violent men, and he didn't want them around his people.

Manaen was glad that the trip was almost over, and the danger was behind them. The desert heat, lack of water, and danger from thieves, along with the storms while they were at sea, had taken a toll on everyone in the party. They had lost some of their stock in the desert and more overboard during a severe storm, but there had also been some births to replace the losses.

They came through a pass in the steep, rocky, bare mountains, and the vista changed completely. Instead of dry, barren rocks there was a green, heavily forested valley with a river flowing through it. A large city sat on the banks of the river.

The leader of the caravan came to speak with Manaen about the route they should take. The two men and the boy got down from their camels and walked to the edge of the pass.

"Look, Joachim, there is the Orontes River; Antioch rests on the banks. I had forgotten how grand and beautiful it is, and how large. I wonder if the city has grown that much, or if my youthful memories have failed me. This city is more beautiful than Athens, Alexandria, and Rome all put together. I think Antioch makes Jerusalem look like a dust bowl filled with cinders," Manaen said.

I wonder what else I've forgotten. Is it as corrupt as Rome? As piously stiff-necked as Jerusalem? How could I have stayed away for so long?

"What do you think, Joachim?" he asked aloud.

The boy was very still and quiet for a moment before he spoke.

"Big! I think it's big!" His eyes were large and filled with wonder as he looked at the phenomena spread out before them. "Can Herod find us here? How about the zealots and nomads? Do they have sandstorms here? And I never thought I would say this, but can we take a bath here?"

Manaen wanted to laugh, but knew he had better not. He took the boy's hand and pulled him away from the edge of the mountain. After speaking to the leader about the route, he and the boy remounted their camel. He struggled to get the excited boy settled before he continued their conversation.

"Yes, Herod could find us here; he knows where we are, but why would he want to? He has no reason to come after us. He knew that I had to come here to take care of family business. There are people like the zealots and nomads everywhere, but you're safe with me."

"Yes, I know; but it's still scary." Joachim bounced up and down with excitement even while he spoke of fear.

"I didn't let them get you outside Jerusalem, or in the desert, and I won't let them get you here. 'No' to the sandstorms. 'Yes' to the baths. And I can hardly wait myself. I haven't felt this filthy since I lived in Rome. There's a bathing facility in my villa, along with servants to help you—if they're still there after my father's death. Sit still now and quit bouncing. You're making the camel skittish." They were going down the steep trail at a good clip and making good progress down the treacherous mountain pass. However, camels were not as sure-footed in these mountains as they were in the sands of the deserts, and Manaen didn't want any mishaps.

Manaen gestured around them with his hand as he talked to the boy, trying to keep him still.

"I had forgotten the forest, Joachim, and just look at the orchards and the rose gardens. Antioch is famous for the perfume made from roses. See the villas within the gardens? If I remember correctly, ours is just as fine. There will be plenty of room for you to run and play; many things for you to do. You're a fine horseman. You and Nebo will get along fine."

"What about you, Father? Are you leaving us here alone?" Manaen could hear fear in the boy's voice as he pulled back close against him.

"Oh, no, son. I told you that I would never leave you, and I won't. But I will have things to take care of, and you won't always be able to be with me. At those times Nebo will be with you. You know, he has grown quite fond of you on this trip. He sees what a fine young man you are. I'm proud of the way you have kept your head and proved yourself as we have traveled. Your early warning saved the caravan when the Bedouins attacked. Your quick thinking gave us time to prepare for the attack. What would I do without you?"

"Look, Joachim, there's Mt. Silpius. There is a theater up there on one of the slopes, and we'll go there to see plays and musicals. Olympic games and Roman festivals are held here. We can go swimming, fishing and hunting; there's plenty for us to do." They had reached the base of the mountain, and Manaen relaxed his hold on the boy.

"What else? Tell me more!" Excited, he began bouncing up and down again.

"Oh, we'll plan a trip to the Springs of Daphne. That's the source of our water. We aren't far from the Mare Nostrum either, so you'll get to ride on ships and see the whales and sea birds again. I think I'm getting excited. How about you?"

"Why are there Roman festivals?" Joachim sounded anxious as he went on. "Are there Romans here too? I hate the Romans."

"I understand, Joachim, but it's different here than it is in Jerusalem. The people are different, so the Romans are different. Here the people don't resist the Romans like the Jews in Jerusalem do. In fact, they enjoy the benefits of the Roman way of life and welcome the Roman citizens and troops, so it's not as violent here. There is no need for you to be afraid. You'll see."

"I don't have to be afraid of the Romans here?" Joachim sounded amazed.

"No, son, it's peaceful here in Antioch. Pax Romana is a way of life. It's mostly the Jews in Jerusalem who hate the Romans and the changes they've brought. The Jews see the Romans as a threat to their religion; that's the problem. The people here don't care much about that. Even the Jews here get along with the Romans. Hard to believe, I know, but it's true."

Manaen signaled the leader of the caravan and the long line of camels snaked to the right. The camels snorted and bellowed as if they knew they were at the end of their journey.

"We're here," he said. "This is the entrance into the estate. It's only a couple of miles farther, and we can get off of these plagued camels and let the animals rest. I know they're ready to get rid of their loads." He felt the boy's muscles tighten in anticipation. "This is a cedar forest we're passing through. Then we'll go through the olive groves, the rose gardens, and on to the grounds of the house."

Joachim looked around him, his eyes wide with wonder. All at once he began to sound like a chirping bird as the questions rolled out.

"Where are the horses? Are there other boys and girls here? Will Nebo be the only one I have to ride with? When will we sail on the ships again?"

"Whoa! Please, one question at a time, though the answer is the same to all of them. The only honest answer I can give you is, 'I don't know.' Remember, I haven't been here in twenty or more years, and things will have changed. Right now I don't know if any of the people I knew as a boy are still here, since my father died. We'll just have to see. If any of the old families are still here I would think they would have children or grandchildren about your age. Maybe some pretty little girls, hum, Joachim?"

"I wouldn't mind a girl. I miss my sisters sometimes … but she would have to ride as well as a boy and shoot as straight. Well, I guess I could teach her."

"You never told me that you had sisters. Did you have brothers too?"

"Yes, one; there were two girls. I was the oldest. My baby sister was only a few days old when the sickness came. Why didn't it take me too? I was the only one who didn't get sick. Even the servants died." His throat was thick with tears. "I tried to take care of them," he sobbed. "I really did."

"Knowing you, I'm sure you did your very best, but who knows why some die and some don't?" He held the boy and let him cry.

"It isn't manly for me to cry," Joachim sobbed.

"Am I not manly when I cry?"

Joachim gave a shuddering hiccup.

"Oh, yes, Father." Surprise was obvious in his voice, as though he had never heard anything so strange.

"Well then, why are you any less manly to cry? We have certainly had occasion to shed a tear lately, and you don't need it bottled up inside. But I am glad to see that smile coming back. Look." Manaen pointed to a break in the olive trees. "Do you see the roses over there? The villa isn't far now."

"Is that it?"

"Yes, that's your new home."

"Why, it looks like a palace, Father. Why didn't you tell me? You're a wealthy man too!" Awe caused the boy to almost whisper.

"I've done nothing to earn this, Joachim, so why should I take any credit for it? My father deserves the credit for all that you see. I wasn't even allowed the pleasure of helping him build this small kingdom. Now it's up to me to take charge of businesses that I know nothing about and try not to lose all that my father has built. I have much to learn, my son. We'll both need tutors. I admit that I'm looking forward to the challenge. How about you?"

"I'm not looking forward to being stuck in a classroom, but I'm looking forward to learning everything that I can about the horses and ships and…who is that?" Amazement came into his voice, and his eyes widened to take in the full measure of the giant of a man coming around the side of one of the outbuildings. He had a head and beard full of long curly red hair.

"Patrobas! Thank the gods you're still here!" Manaen was shouting, and his pleasure at seeing the man was obvious.

The giant reached them, took the lead rope of their camel, and spoke softly to the obnoxious beast. When he tapped the back of its knee with his huge hand, it immediately rocked itself forward on its knees and back on its haunches. It settled in the road and its passengers clambered off.

The man bowed slightly, his eyes moving back and forth between Manaen and Joachim.

"Sir, we are glad to have you here safe at last. Now which of you is Manaen?" he spoke with a grin.

"It's as though time has been arrested, sir. I haven't seen you since you were about the size of this lad. And who might you be?" he said, speaking to Joachim.

"Joachim, sir. Was my father truly my size last time you saw him?"

"Your father?" Patrobas spoke, turning to Manaen. "We weren't aware that you had married, sir. Is your wife with you?"

"There's no wife, Patrobas. I adopted Joachim. He's no accident of birth. I've chosen him to be my son. He was an orphan, but now he's my son." The boy smiled as he paid close attention; he couldn't hear this story enough.

"You have chosen well, Master. He appears to be a sturdy lad."

"Yes, sturdy and brave as well. We were set upon by Bedouin bandits and his quick warning is all that saved us. Let him tell you about it sometime. And be sure to ask him how he saved his own hide. You can add quick thinking to his list of attributes."

Patrobas gave a slight bow and smiled as he spoke. "We'd better start unloading this caravan and let these miserable beasts rest. Do you have things for the warehouses or household items, Master?"

"Both. The lead man will show you what is what. And we need to talk."

"Yes, sir. Do you want me to supervise the unloading before we talk?"

"Please. Well, *shalom*, Dorcas." Manaen turned his attention to the woman approaching them, bowing to her slightly. "Is all well with you and with my household?"

"Yes, Master, all is well." Manaen noticed the wary look in her eyes as she answered, and she didn't look directly at him. Something was not right.

"Would you have someone show us to rooms, please? And we will want baths as soon as possible." Turning, he realized that there was a line of naked people standing in a line by the entrance to the house. Taking a case from one of the camel's loads that contained fresh clothes, one for him and one for Joachim, he turned back to Dorcas.

"Why are they lining up like that? Are we being inspected?"

"Oh no, Master. They are waiting to be inspected."

"By whom?"

"By you, Master."

"By me? But why? Who are they, and why are they naked?"

"They're your servants and slaves, my lord. They once belonged to your father. Now they belong to you. They hope that you'll not sell them away from their families, sir, and that you will be pleased with them and keep them. Your father kept them naked to keep them humble."

"Kept them naked to control them, you mean!" There was an edge of anger in his voice.

"Well, yes, that too."

"That is an atrocious practice, and it will stop! Dorcas, have they served you and Patrobas well?"

"Yes, Master, just as they served your father before you."

"Then dismiss them. They have been faithful to my father and you, and if they remain faithful to me, they have nothing to fear. And I want them clothed. Is there clothing available for them?"

"Yes, my lord. I will do as you ask, but…"

"What is it, Dorcas? Why the hesitation?"

"If you don't inspect them, they'll think that you are not pleased with them, and they'll be frightened."

"Frightened? Of me?"

"Yes, my lord."

"Very well. If it can't wait, we'll do it now. I'm meeting

with Patrobas as soon as possible. Please be there if you can arrange it."

"As you wish, my lord."

Yes, we must have a meeting as quickly as possible, he thought. As they approached the line of people, Manaen sensed their apprehension. Their eyes followed him without really seeing him. They reminded him of birds in a field, watching for the hawk, and, too late realizing that the hawk is among them.

CHAPTER 13

Refreshed by a bath and a fine evening meal from which the dishes had been cleared, Manaen sat quietly observing Patrobas and Dorcas. They didn't appear to be comfortable sitting at the table with him.

"Patrobas, Dorcas, what's happening here? Why are you so uncomfortable around me? What is it that you fear?" The young man couldn't keep the keen disappointment from his voice. "What evil have I committed that causes you to distrust me?"

"We don't understand your meaning, Master."

"I don't think that my meaning was veiled in any way. My questions are quite clear. You're afraid of me, and I want to know why. When I left here you were my friends. Now you seem to almost regard me as your enemy. I want to know why. And I want to know why the servants are afraid of me."

"You are our master, and we are your servants."

Manaen's voice grew sharp in his exasperation.

"Why should that make you afraid of me?" Noticing the quick glance of fear that passed between Patrobas and Dorcas, Manaen was sorry that he had let his frustration show. "I'm sorry, my friends. I'm simply trying to understand what's happening here. I don't like the feelings of fear and distrust that I sense. Won't you explain?"

After a short pause and many glances toward her husband, Dorcas spoke softly.

"Talk to him, Patrobas. What harm can it do? Perhaps he isn't like his father."

"Not like my father? What do you mean? And, yes, Patrobas, what harm can it do?"

"Well, Master, no man likes to taste the whip."

"Taste the whip?" Manaen felt anger boiling up in him like hot water. "What do you mean? Who would dare to whip you and for what?"

"Your father would have us whipped for any imagined failure, Master."

Manaen felt his stomach muscles tighten with disgust.

"My father would have you beaten with a whip?" His words were clipped and tight with anger. "Patrobas, I didn't know my father, but I never imagined him to be a tyrant. What happened to him?"

"He was a very unhappy man, sir. As he aged he grew more and more bitter and angry. He died cursing the gods and vowing to change his will so that you would not inherit. He had violent mood changes toward the end and only his inability to travel to Antioch prevented him from changing the will. He demanded that we send for the scribes, and we pretended to do it, but we never did. Our only hope was in you, sir, that you would return and not be a master like your father. We hoped that you would be an honorable man."

"Not like my father? An honorable man? Tell me, Patrobas, did my father lose his honor and standing in Antioch?"

"Your father was always a man of his word. It was only in the matter of his violence with the servants that his honor ever came into question. He was a very miserable man and could not handle his disappointment."

"What reason did he have to be disappointed? I look around and see great wealth. And you say he maintained his standing in Antioch. What did he have … oh, yes—the matter of the death of my mother. Is that what you mean?"

"Yes, it is, sir," Dorcas answered. "He never recovered from the death of your mother. People who knew him all of his life say that she was the only human being he ever loved. You know the story, sir. And not only did he not love anyone, but he learned to hate everyone very well."

"I knew that he hated me, but I didn't realize that the poison had spread to reach so many."

"Yes, I'm just so thankful that he sent you away, or you would have lived your life at the very gates of Gahanna. It wasn't that he hated you. He just lost his perspective when he lost her. He really blamed himself, but he couldn't admit that; so he placed the blame on you."

Manaen struggled to control the pain those words caused him.

"That's all very well. Now understand me clearly. As I said earlier, all the servants have to do is perform their jobs to the best of their ability. And most important of all, there will be no beatings. Is that understood?" He saw tears in the big man's eyes as he nodded in reply.

Manaen continued.

"I have high standards and will dismiss any servant that creates a problem. If there is a problem with one of the slaves, it will be sold, along with any family, with the stipulation that they will be kept together. I will not be responsible for splitting up families. No child is going to miss their parents because of me. Do I make myself clear?"

"Yes, Master," Patrobas replied.

"Thunder of Zeus, Patrobas. Have you forgotten my name?" He saw the big man flinch and softened his tone. "I'm sorry, my friend. Please address me as Manaen, especially in private. I'm not some Roman dictatorial ogre who has come here to take over the reigns and push you out. I recognize the fine job you've done. I would be a fool to usurp your position."

He watched for Patrobas' reaction as he spoke, hoping to see that he understood, but he still felt tension in the couple.

"But, Manaen, you're the master now. You are in charge."

"Patrobas, I know nothing about running this place. You're my foreman, and I want you to continue doing what you've always done and to teach me as we go. Can I depend on you for that?" Patrobas began to nod his big head. "And you, Dorcas? I haven't seen a home managed better, not even in Imperial Rome. Can I still depend on you?"

The man and woman looked at each other and simultaneously took a deep breath. Manaen felt their tension dissipate as they nodded to each other. Patrobas spoke.

"Mas … Manaen, you have our continued loyalty."

"And your friendship, Patrobas?"

"Yes, I can promise you that too."

Manaen reached out and pulled the big man into a fierce hug and kissed him on both cheeks. As he released him, he turned to Dorcas. She immediately stepped back from him. Manaen threw back his head and laughed.

"No hugs, Dorcas. I just wanted to thank you and ask you to help Nebo look after Joachim."

"You know I will. What woman can resist such a fine boy?"

"Thank you, Dorcas. Now, Patrobas, I want every whip destroyed. Make it clear that no person or animal will be whipped on this estate."

"What about the box, Manaen?"

"The box?"

"Yes, where men were put to sweat it out before they were whipped." Once again Manaen saw tears in the couple's eyes. "The men were often weak from dehydration when your father brought them out to be whipped. He said it stopped them from struggling."

"Where is the cursed thing?"

"It's in the middle of a field in the direct sun."

"Burn it; but first saturate the field so that the fire won't spread."

"Yes, sir, I'll take care of it first thing tomorrow."

"No, Patrobas. Let's do it tonight. I want everyone on the estate and for miles around to see it burn. I want them to know that things are going to be different. I'll help, and I want Joachim to help too. I'll call him." The men's voices faded as they moved down the hall.

Manaen's thoughts were on how Herod's servants were treated. He had seen slaves almost killed at the hand of their overseers. Men, women, and children alike had been whipped until their flesh hung in shreds for the slightest offense. That had been one of the reasons he had come to almost despise Antipas.

On more than one occasion he had seen Antipas laugh at the people's torment and tell the overseers to whip them again. Everything in him knew it was wrong to treat people that way, and the *Torah* the Jews loved so much taught that it was wrong. He had always known that the same thing could happen to him at some whim of Herod's. Worse things had happened to other family members, even death. He put his arm around the shoulder of his friend and servant, glad to be back home.

Dorcas couldn't stop the tears that bathed her cheeks as she watched the men leave the room. These tears were born of hope—a hope that the awful times were over, and they didn't have to live in fear any longer.

"I have never known which I feared most—the whip or being separated from my family. Thank God it's over. Yes, thank you, God," she whispered. Brushing the tears away, she hurried after the men. She wanted to watch it burn too. Her oldest son had almost died in the box because he had misunderstood an order. Lifting her hands in thanksgiving, she almost shouted.

"Thank you, God. It's over."

# CHAPTER 14

It took almost three hours for the men to cut brush back and haul enough water to soak the field surrounding the infamous box. Manaen instructed the men to bring enough wood to stack around and over the dreadful thing to make a bonfire large enough to be seen for miles.

Manaen and Joachim worked along with every man, woman, and child that was capable of carrying the buckets of water from the canal. Manaen watched the oldest people, slow though they were, carrying whatever they could: skins, urns, and vats of water; large or small branches; even twigs. He almost wept as he watched one elderly couple, the man stooped and walking with a cane, sharing the load of a skin half-full of water. They would walk awhile and then rest awhile, but they were determined to participate in the destruction of the dreaded chamber of torture.

People laughed, sang, and shouted in their joy. Those who couldn't carry water or wood stood at the edge of the field and joined the singing, encouraging those who were doing the hauling.

As they worked, they brushed their hands over their clothes and fingered the fabric as if they couldn't believe that they were no longer naked. The women no longer hung their heads as they walked, and the men walked with long, proud strides. Manaen could tell that they were already experiencing and accepting the changes he was making. In fact, he could see their new pride.

"Joachim, never forget this night and what you're seeing and taking part in here," Manaen told the boy. "These people have been vilely mistreated, but we are giving them hope and restoring their dignity. Never treat human beings as if they were chattel. My father treated his animals better than he treated his people. I'm sorry that you have to know that, but please let it be a lesson that you never, never forget. Always treat people with all of the respect and dignity that they deserve."

"Like you treat me, Father?"

Joy filled Manaen's heart as tears filled his eyes.

"Exactly. You learn quickly, Joachim. I'm proud of you."

"I just watch you, Father, and try to act like you do."

Manaen was almost overwhelmed by the sense of responsibility he felt at the boy's words. He choked back the tears, but before he could reply he saw Patrobas approaching.

"The field is ready, Manaen. Do you want to do the honors, or shall I?"

"Let's both do it as a symbolic gesture of our unity, ending the old evil ways and beginning a new day and way of life. Can you get me a torch?"

"Yes, there's one ready."

"Then let's do it. Joachim, I want you to wait with Dorcas."

"Please, can't I help too?"

"Yes, if you'll let me carry you. That way, you can help me hold the torch."

In reply the boy simply lifted his arms to the man that he had come to trust completely as his father. His feet almost drug the ground, but he laughed as he was lifted into the strong arms. Together they put the torch to the hut as the people wept, danced, and shouted with joy. Whoops and victory chants erupted all around them.

Never again on land belonging to me, Manaen thought. *Never again will men be treated with anything but dignity. My son will grow up with respect for people, regardless of their station in life. He'll learn to treat the things entrusted to him with care. I'm ashamed to learn that my father was like Herod. Perhaps it's a family failing, but it stops here with me and my family. I saw too much in Herod's household and in Rome to allow tyranny to rule in my household. There are better ways, and Joachim will learn them,* Manaen purposed in his heart.

Hugging the boy, he turned away from the fire and headed toward the villa. The boy's head fell against his shoulder as sleep overcame his excitement. The journey had exhausted them.

Tomorrow will open a new chapter, learning and adjusting to a new way of life that will allow me to use my education. I'll take the reins that have been passed to me, and I will learn to manage the properties and people that my father acquired. There are people here to teach me and to help me. I only hope that I am equal to the task. And, I hope that I'll be the example this boy can follow. What a responsibility.

CHAPTER 15

Nothing brought more pleasure to Manaen than the sight of his son and the daughter of Patrobas and Dorcas riding together across his fields. He laughed when he remembered Joachim saying that he would not mind a girl to play with if she could ride and shoot like a boy. Well, he had certainly met his match!

He watched Joachim trying to outride this daring young woman. Manaen had watched their friendship blossom over the years.

"I wonder if it will ever become more than friendship," Manaen spoke to himself as the two approached.

He marveled at the beauty of the two youths: Joachim's hair was the color of a raven's wings, while Lydia's was a riot of red curls like her father's. With her father's fire and fierce pride, balanced by gentleness and graciousness inherited from her mother, she was becoming a fine young woman. Manaen chuckled as he thought how gracefully and accurately she could wield a sword. Joachim had tasted its tip more than once.

Joachim had also tasted of Lydia's fist. He had learned early on not to push her past her limits of endurance. Manaen actually felt sorry for him at times because he knew better than to hit a girl, and she had no compunction against popping him if he made her angry. It didn't seem to matter how often Dorcas punished her for it, she still thrashed the defenseless boy on occasion.

While Patrobas taught Lydia to ride and shoot as well as any man, Dorcas was careful to see that she was also trained in the running of a home. Lydia had an excellent knowledge of science and mathematics, learned under Nebo's tutelage. She had been Joachim's match in the schoolroom. Again Manaen laughed at the way they had competed as they grew up together.

"Where have the years gone?"

"What, Father?" Joachim and Lydia had reached him in time to hear his remark. Dust swirled as the horses came to a standstill, but they continued to toss their heads and snort. They loved a good romp as much as Joachim and Lydia did and didn't want it to end.

"Oh, I was just standing here, realizing that you two have grown up so quickly. You'll soon be a grown man, and I'm not sure that I'm ready for that to happen. Well, go put the animals away, and come to the house. I have news. Not welcome news, I'm afraid. Hurry and let me get it off of my chest." With that he turned and strode to the villa.

. . . .

"Joachim, I understand your fear of returning to Jerusalem…"

"But, Father—"

"No 'buts' about it, son. As you well know, I don't have a choice. Antipas sent for me and that's that. No questions asked; I must do as he says. You know that he became king of Galilee when his father died. He was furious when his father split the kingdom between him and his two brothers, Archelaus and Phillip. He had been promised the whole kingdom. He also lives in constant fear that his brother, Agrippa, will take his kingdom, even though he's in prison in Rome. That is one reason he's such a tyrant. Now, more than ever, I am forced to obey him."

"Can't I stay here?"

"I know that it's hard for you to leave, but we have to go. He has ordered us to Jerusalem to attend to some business. Then we are to go to the royal palace at Tiberius to report to him. I'm truly sorry, son. I don't want to go either."

"But what about finishing my education, Father? And I don't want to go without Lydia."

"Joachim, Nebo's in charge of your education, and he'll travel with us. As to Lydia, she's a young woman and has to stay with Patrobas and Dorcas. You know that."

"Why can't we take her with us if you're going to make me go? Nebo can look after her too—like she needs looking after!" Joachim laughed at the thought.

"We'll ask Patrobas, but you know what he'll say, so don't be disappointed. He isn't going to let his only daughter, even a brave and capable girl like Lydia, leave home. She's too young."

"Thank you, Father. That's all I ask—that you try."

"Joachim, Lydia won't always be with you. In a few years she'll be betrothed and married. Then she'll leave us to start her own family. In fact, I'll provide her dowry. You have to understand that, son."

"No, she won't. We'll marry each other when the time is right. We'll always be together," Joachim shot back with a look of such calm certainty that Manaen was astonished.

"Joachim, you're young. How can you say what your future will be? You haven't even completed your education." Manaen was frustrated as he realized how quickly time was passing. Joachim had grown from a frightened little boy to a young man who felt that he was ready to choose his life's companion.

Well, he thought, *he certainly couldn't make a better choice than the spirited, beautiful Lydia. She would certainly run him a merry chase and make life interesting, just as she has here at the villa.*

"Nevertheless, my son, I'll see what her parents say. I promise you."

"Thank you. When do we leave?"

"As soon as we can get packed and on the move. The message was urgent. Of course, everything is always urgent to Antipas when something he wants is involved. I shudder to think what it might be!"

CHAPTER 16

As their caravan made the turn around the low, sandy hillside, the first view of Jerusalem was astoundingly beautiful. The low evening sun lit the city with a flaming glow. Lights from lamps set in windows twinkled like embers. Palm fronds tossed in the evening breeze and sounded like crackling flames, adding to the overall effect of a city on fire. Dust rising from the many caravans entering the city looked like smoke.

I almost wish it would burn to the ground. Manaen hated returning to this place that held so many bad memories.

"Manaen," Patrobas roared, "Jerusalem is as beautiful as you said. Is it also as vile?"

"Oh, yes. Just as vile and as holy, as stinking and as pure, as ugly and as beautiful…all of that, and much, much more. Jerusalem is the center of the world, but you would never get Rome to admit it! All of the major trade routes pass through here—north to south, east to west, and all points in between." He grew still and quiet. "I fear for our children, Patrobas. I fear for us! Don't be fooled by this beauty. Beneath the loveliness she is a wanton harlot just waiting to get you into her clutches.

"Politics here are ugly and ruthless. People are ruined or killed on the whims of mad men! Wealth is gained or lost in the same way, without regard to lives that are left devastated. People don't matter here, not even to the men in charge of the religion here. Only wealth and position matter!"

Manaen shook his head and went on.

"I don't know why Antipas has called me back, but I do know that it won't be for my good, only for his. And, it isn't from the goodness of his heart; I can guarantee you that. This summons is to further his own cause and serve his own purpose!" He felt the bile of anger rising in his throat as he warned Patrobas. "Don't ever forget that. Don't be taken in by any goodwill gesture on his part. I have watched as my only friend turned into a bitter, greedy, angry tyrant. Fear for his life and selfish ambition have turned him into a man that I hardly recognize. He has sunk into madness as frightening as his father's. He has no regard for anyone or anything unless it will be for his own benefit. He hates his wife with a passion and is terrified of his family and hers. He trusts no one. Not even me! Never trust him!" They dismounted their camels to view the great city and were joined by their children.

"Well, we won't know why we're here until we get to the palace, and that won't be today if we don't get moving. Will we be there soon?" Patrobas put his arm around Manaen's shoulder, hoping to comfort his friend.

"Too soon, Patrobas, too soon. I would say within the hour, which is entirely too soon for me. Joachim understands completely. But Lydia," he turned to face her to stress the seriousness of what he was saying, "Do you fully understand that you must never trust anyone in this city except the three of us? Don't even trust our servants except for Nebo. You can trust Nebo with your life, as I have so many times in the past. The others could easily get involved in palace intrigue and misplace their loyalty. Can you remember that, Lydia? You're only safe with us. Your life could depend on it."

When the girl nodded, Manaen turned to his son, "Joachim, talk to her! Tell her the perils she faces here. You've experienced them! Make her understand, and try to get her to promise you that she will always be on her guard."

"I've told her, but she won't listen to me!" Joachim's fear for the girl was obvious in the tone of his voice. He turned to take her hand.

"I'll try to remember. I promise. Of course, with four men around I'll be completely protected." Lydia's green eyes twinkled, and her smile hinted that she was teasing. Then, just as quickly, she became serious.

"I'm not frightened, but I do promise that I'll remember all that you've told me. I promise. And I promise not to go anywhere alone, even if it kills me! And I promise to keep my knife hidden in my girdle, just in case I need it!" Again she laughed, and as she tossed her head, the red curls bounced from under their covering, but they knew she would keep her word.

As quickly as they had stopped, the caravan was on the

move again. Soon the Gate Beautiful came into view, and they could see huge throngs of people. Delays along the route had kept them from arriving before Passover began as planned, and they would have to contend with thousands of people.

Here I go again, Manaen thought, *back for another festival of religious fervor!* He felt suffocated by the dust and the push of the crowds. The people were singing, and he recognized the music, but found no comfort in its familiarity. It bothered him that he knew the words as well as the tunes. He knew they were the psalms that King David had written, and the people had been singing them ever since.

"What a legacy that king left for his people."

"What, Father?"

"I was thinking out loud, son, about the musical and poetic legacy of King David."

"King David? Oh, I remember…Jonathan's friend."

As the caravan passed the temple, Manaen made a mental note to return for a visit when the crowds thinned after the Passover celebration.

They were soon settled in a suite at the palace. Their rooms shared a common courtyard. The servants had comfortable quarters close by, and everyone felt safe with the arrangement.

When several days passed quietly without a summons from Antipas, Manaen decided to visit the temple. He spent several hours walking around, listening to the teachers, and viewing the grandeur of the building. It was still magnificent, and he was amazed at what his uncle had created.

As he was leaving he stopped on the steps near a young boy who was surrounded by a group of elders from the temple. He answered their questions with respect, wisdom, and complete assurance. *What is this! A boy teaching the temple scholars?* Manaen was amazed not only at the boy's knowledge, but that these arrogant men would listen to him. After a few minutes of listening he was jostled by a man and woman who rushed past him. In amazement, he recognized the couple from the stable all those many years ago.

Moving closer, he heard the woman speak.

"Young man, why have you done this to us? Your father and I have been half out of our minds looking for you."

"Why were you looking for me? Didn't you know that I had to be here, dealing with the things of my Father?"[1] the boy replied.

Manaen realized that this boy was the infant in the manger, and he could tell by their puzzled expressions that the parents had no idea what he was talking about. He smiled as he thought about how time had flown since that day so long ago. So much had happened! The one who had been an infant would soon be a grown man.

"I wonder what he meant 'being about his Father's business,'" Manaen wondered aloud as he stood there. "His father has the hands of a common laborer."

Just then the boy turned and looked at him and the world's wisdom seemed to spring from his eyes. Manaen smiled at him. The parents followed the boy's gaze and recognized Manaen; the three approached him.

Manaen spoke, trying not to show how the boy's calm, steady gaze affected him. "Shalom. The years have certainly served you well, young man. You were an infant when I saw you for the first time, and now you are almost a man." Turning to the parents he went on. "I thought I recognized you. Are you here on pilgrimage, or do you live in Jerusalem?"

The boy's father returned his greeting and explained.

"We were here for Passover and had started our journey home when we realized that our son was not with us. We came back to find him. And you? It appears that the years have been kind to you."

"Yes, they have. My son and I have been living in Antioch, but have returned for a short time at a friend's request."

"Was that your son with you in Bethlehem?"

"Yes, but he wasn't my son then. He was an orphan that I had asked for directions that night. I have since adopted him. He too is a fine young man, although about six years older than your son. I'm thankful for my decision to adopt him. He has been a comfort to me as I grow older. Would you accept an offer of shelter for the evening in our accommodations? I know that Joachim would like to see you again and our sons could get acquainted."

"Thank you for your kind offer, but we left our other children with relatives and they'll be expecting us. We have to get back for tonight."

"Could I arrange transportation for you?"

The man bowed graciously before he spoke.

"Again, I must refuse your kindness. We have many things to discuss with our son regarding his responsibilities to others. We will need the time while we are walking for that."

Manaen saw the boy glance toward a donkey tethered nearby.

"Can you wait one minute, please?" He left the three and went to see if he could buy the donkey from the man who was standing beside it. It didn't take long to strike a bargain. When he returned he handed the rope to the father.

"I am Manaen, and I would like to present you with a token of my regard. This would make the journey easier for your wife. Please accept it," he said.

The man looked surprised, but after a moment he nodded and spoke.

"I am Joseph bar Jacob, and your kindness will not be forgotten. My wife is Mary, and my son is Jesus. We need to rejoin our people now and return to Nazareth. Perhaps we will see you next year during Passover."

"I hope to have returned to Antioch by then. But, if the gods will it, I am sure we will meet again." He saw the boy smile and look toward the ground.

"We will meet again," Jesus said, looking up with a level gaze.

Somehow, Manaen knew that he was right.

"Until then," he replied as he walked away. He felt shaken to his inner core and wondered how it had happened. Then he turned back to Joseph.

"Joseph bar Jacob, may I ask you a question before you leave? There is something I've wondered about since that night in the stable."

"If I can answer you, I will." Again he saw the boy's deep, penetrating gaze and the ghost of a smile, but he seemed to be focused on something far away.

"The Magi that brought your son gifts had indicated that he is a king. I know that the Magi are wise men and trust their wisdom. Yet I have seen no indication of a king's trappings surrounding you or your family."

"I don't have the answer you seek. Only Yahweh knows. I am a simple carpenter from Nazareth who is trying to raise an extraordinary young boy. There are many things that my mind cannot understand. I only know that neither Caesar nor Herod has anything to fear from my son."

Manaen watched Joseph gently lift Mary to the back of the donkey, nod again to him, and walk away with his family. When they were out of sight, Manaen realized that he was experiencing a strange emptiness, a loneliness that was unfamiliar to him. He rushed back to be with his family.

It had been several days—days spent showing his family around Jerusalem—when he was summoned to the palace. When he entered the throne room, he could tell from the scowl on his face that Antipas, now Herod the Tetrarch, was in a foul temper, but his greeting to Manaen was pleasant.

"Greetings, cousin. How are you faring?"

Manaen had to laugh at his cousin's posturing.

"You know very well how I am faring, cousin. Your spies keep you well informed. And you, cousin? I'm not privileged to such a vast network to keep me informed."

Antipas laughed derisively and replied.

"I'm in need of information. Other than that I fare very well. What do you know of Agrippa?" He motioned for Manaen to take a seat.

Manaen remained standing, anger rising in him like a wave.

"I only know that he's in Rome. He's deep in debt, and Tiberius has had him put in prison. Is that why you had me return to Jerusalem, to check on my knowledge of Agrippa?" He struggled to keep the anger out of his voice, knowing that it could put him in a precarious position.

"Yes, he has become a threat, just as you said he would. Is that all that you know? If so, you are useless to me. I already knew all of that."

"That's all I know. You could have learned that by messenger."

"Perhaps I just wanted to see you. How are things in Antioch? Never mind. You are beginning to bore me! Leave me now! You are useless!"

Without another word, Manaen left the room, packed his family, and returned to Antioch.

The years passed swiftly between trips to Jerusalem. It had been many years since the last trip. Manaen was a grandfather now to Joachim and Lydia's children, and he resented this latest intrusion of Antipas that had pulled him away from his family. True to his word, Joachim had married Lydia as soon as they were old enough, and they seemed to be extremely happy. Manaen loved being around them, and they allowed him full access to the children, who seemed to love spending time with him.

The summons to the palace in Tiberius had finally come after three months of waiting in Jerusalem. Herod preferred to spend most of his time in Tiberius where his lifestyle was not under as much Jewish scrutiny as it was in Jerusalem. Now Manaen had to go to Tiberius. During his wait, Manaen had heard the talk about Herod's divorce from his Nabataean wife and his adulterous life with Herodias who was his niece as well as his brother, Phillip's wife. He had also heard the people complaining about the war with Nabatea caused by the divorce. The people were being heavily taxed to pay for the war, and they were grumbling.

The audience had not gone well from the beginning. Manaen was furious and knew that it must show in his face and actions.

"Antipas, tell me that I didn't hear you right! You didn't seriously think that you could just divorce your wife and take Philip's wife for yourself with no repercussions. Philip is your brother, and your wife was a princess of Nabatea! She is one of the most beautiful women I have ever seen and as kind as she is beautiful. Why did you do this? Have you inherited your late father's insanity as well as his name?"

Antipas grew livid in typical fashion, his eyes evil slips behind folds of fat in his bloated face. His life of debauchery was more obvious than ever.

"Watch what you say, cousin," he snapped. "I am Herod the Tetrarch now, and I answer to no one! I told you from the beginning that she was a Nabataean dung heap and that's what she is! I'm tired of her sniveling and whining. Besides, I wanted Herodias! She makes me feel alive, and I will have her," he snarled with an ugly sneer.

"Antipas, your ex-wife's father is the most powerful man in all of Nabatea. He's the King of Arabia, for all the god's sake! They are a wild warrior tribe. This has caused a war. Were you prepared for that? Is Herodias really worth what this will cost you?"

"I don't care what it costs! If I want her, she's worth it! I have her, and I'll keep her!" Antipas shouted.

Manaen was furious to realize why he had been summoned away from his home and family in Antioch. He didn't care what this idiot before him thought!

"And what about Philip?" he snapped. "Did you imagine that he would just sit idly by and let you take his wife? He's threatening you in Rome now, and Caesar is listening to what he says. Did you take into account what his response would be when you did this evil thing?"

He struggled to remain calm.

"Is this what you ordered me to come from Antioch for, to grant my approval for your self-destruction? Well, be assured, cousin; you have it!"

"No, cousin, I need your help," Antipas sneered with contempt. "You're the only person I can trust. You've always been loyal to me, just as you were to my father."

"What do you need?" Manaen heard the sarcasm in Antipas' voice, but he knew that nothing he said would change the course his cousin had chosen. He was more willful and self-centered now than he was as a child. Neither time nor position had brought Antipas wisdom.

"I need you to watch someone for me," he sniveled.

"You mean spy on someone? Is that why you called me back?" Manaen was shouting now.

"Watch, spy, whatever you want to call it! Yes!" Herod shouted back. "That's why I need you here. There's a rabble rouser in the desert preaching against me! He says that it isn't lawful for me to have Herodias." Then, in one of his constant mood changes, he sounded like a whining child as he went on. "I would have him killed, but the people consider him a prophet, and I'm afraid there'd be trouble."

"Are you saying that you're more afraid of this man than you are afraid of a Nabataean army? What strange hold does he have? Didn't you just say that he's just a prophet? What is that compared to the King of Arabia who could and would have you killed in an instant?" Herod was starting to snivel like a weak, spoiled child, so Manaen threw up his hands in disgust. "Okay. Who is he, and where will I find him?"

"They call him John the Baptist because he goes around baptizing people for their sins." The haughty sneer was back on Antipas' face; it showed his contempt for his adversary, but Manaen also sensed his cousin's fear. His face was coated with a sheen of sweat, and his huge jowls trembled as he spoke.

"You'll find him somewhere in the desert near the river Jordan. That's where he dips his followers in dirty water to cleanse them from their sins." A nervous laugh erupted from the thick lips, and he licked them nervously. "Just find him and report to me. And don't be long about it. I want to know exactly what he's saying to the people about me and how they are responding. Go! Now! You are really beginning to annoy me! And call me Herod in the future!"

Without a word, Manaen turned and left the chamber, feeling that he was being sucked back into the madness of Herod's palace. He dreaded what lay before him.

CHAPTER 18

True to his word, Manaen followed the crowds to Bethany on the other side of the Jordan River and found the wild-looking man called John the Baptist. His long, bushy hair didn't appear to have ever been cut, and he wore a long beard. He was dressed in camel skins, and a leather belt cinched his waist. Manaen sensed strength in the man and saw the apparent fanaticism in his eyes.

Manaen understood Herod's fear as he listened to the man's words. His message was simple and clear.

"Change your life. God's kingdom is here."[1]

When John realized that a lot of Pharisees and Sadducees were showing up for a baptismal experience because it was becoming the popular thing to do, he exploded: "Brood of snakes! What do you think you are doing slithering down here to the river? Do you think a little water on your snake skins is going to make any difference? It's your life that must change, not your skin! And don't think you can pull rank by claiming Abraham as father. Being a descendant of Abraham is neither here nor there—children of Abraham are a denarius a dozen. God can make children from stones if he wants. Descendants of Abraham are cheap. What counts is your life. Is it green and blossoming? Because if it's deadwood, it goes on the fire." The crowd asked him, "Then what are we supposed to do?"

"If you have two coats, give one away," he said. "Do the same with your food."

Tax men also came to be baptized and said, "Teacher, what should we do?"

He told them, "No more extortion—collect only what is required by law." Soldiers asked, "And what should we do?"

He told them, "No shakedowns, no blackmail—and be content with your pay."

"I'm baptizing you here in the river, turning your old life in for a kingdom life. The real action comes next: The main character in this drama—compared to him I'm a mere stagehand—will ignite the kingdom life within you, a fire within you, the Holy Spirit within you, changing you from the inside out. He's going to clean house—make a clean sweep of your lives. He'll place everything true in its proper place before God; everything false he'll put out with the trash to be burned."[2] Then he began to rebuke Herod the Tetrarch for taking Herodias, his brother's wife. He was obviously unafraid or unaware of any danger he was in from such a rash action.

Manaen watched the people for their reactions, but he didn't see any signs of sedition or insurrection. They just seemed intent on hearing all this itinerant preacher had to say. He was intrigued to hear people in the crowd whispering about John being a prophet sent from God.

Several days later, Manaen returned to the Jordan. John talked about a Light that was coming into the world so that all men might believe through him. He explained that he himself was not the Light; he came only as a witness. The true Light that gives light to every man was coming into the world. He said that he was in the world, and though the world was made through him, the world did not recognize him.

John went on to say that the Light came to save those who were his own, but his own didn't receive him. Yet to all who received him, to those who believed in his name, he gave the right to become children of God—children born not of natural descent, nor of human decision or a husband's will, but born of God. He talked about the Word becoming flesh and making his dwelling among us. He said that we have seen his glory, the glory of the One and Only, who came from the Father, full of grace and truth. Manaen's thoughts tried to keep up.

What is he talking about? Who came into the world to make his dwelling among us? Full of grace and truth? What does it all mean? Then his thoughts returned to a scene from his childhood when he had warned Antipas about a dancing girl. *I don't understand what it all means, but this man, John, is a part of that somehow. Something terrible is going to happen to him. He will be beheaded! I'm beginning to understand it now.* He shivered as he remembered the premonition.

As if reading his thoughts, John pointed to a man that Manaen recognized as the boy, Jesus, now a grown man. He wondered why Jesus was there.

"This is the One! The one I told you was coming after me but in fact was ahead of me. He has always been ahead of me, has always had the first word. We all live off his generous bounty, gift after gift after gift. We got the basics from Moses and then this exuberant giving and receiving, this endless knowing and understanding—all this came through Jesus the Messiah. No one has ever seen God, not so much as a glimpse. This one-of-a-kind God-Expression, who exists at the very heart of the Father, has made him plain as day,"[3] he cried.

When Jews from Jerusalem sent a group of priests and officials to ask John who he was, he was completely honest. He didn't evade the question. He told the plain truth: "I am not the Messiah."

They pressed him.

"Who, then? Elijah?"

"I am not."

"The Prophet?"

"No."

"Who, then? We need an answer for those who sent us. Tell us something, anything, about yourself!" they said, exasperated.

"I'm thunder in the desert. 'Make the road straight for God!' I'm doing what the prophet Isaiah preached."

Those sent to question him were from the Pharisee party. Now they had a question of their own.

"If you're neither the Messiah, nor Elijah, nor the Prophet, why do you baptize?"

"I only baptize using water. A person you don't recognize has taken his stand in your midst. He comes after me, but he is not in second place to me. I'm not even worthy to hold his coat for him,"[4] John answered.

The next day Manaen was back at the Jordan. John saw Jesus coming toward him and yelled out, "Here he is, God's Passover Lamb! He forgives the sins of the world! This is the man I've been talking about, 'the One who comes after me but is really ahead of me.' I knew nothing about who he was—only this: that my task has been to get Israel ready to recognize him as the God-Revealer. That is why I came here baptizing with water, giving you a good bath and scrubbing sins from your life so you can get a fresh start with God."[5]

Jesus came and stood before John. He wanted John to baptize him, but John tried to deter him, saying, "I'm the one who needs to be baptized, not you."

The man insisted, "Do it. God's work, putting things right all these centuries, is coming together right now in this baptism." So John did it.[6]

Manaen asked a man standing nearby if he knew who the newcomer was. He wanted to find out if Jesus was well known here. He replied that he had heard John call him "Jesus." He said that he had also heard that the man was actually John's cousin.

As soon as Jesus was baptized, he burst from the water laughing in pure joy. Manaen was astounded at the scene he was witnessing. He had never seen such joy in another human being.

The moment Jesus came up out of the baptismal waters, the skies opened up, and he saw God's Spirit—it looked like a dove—descending and landing on him. Along with the

Spirit, a voice: "This is my Son, chosen and marked by my love, delight of my life."[7]

Manaen couldn't take it all in. *What have I just witnessed? Who are these men? No, who is this man; simply another itinerant preacher? This man is only the son of Joseph bar Jacob and Mary. He's the baby in the manger, the boy in the temple. Surely he's no threat to Herod; although, the Magi and Herod's wise men did call him a king. Well, I'll keep watch and perhaps time will sort it out.*

As fate would have it, the next day Herod sent for him.

"What have you learned?" he demanded. "Have you talked to the baptizer? What are the people saying?" His voice was petulant and sarcastic.

Manaen was cautious with his answer.

"I have seen him and heard him, but, no, I haven't talked to the man. He seems harmless enough."

"Well, he isn't harmless! What are the people saying?" The strident voice was rising.

"Calm down. They're just asking if he is a prophet or Elijah, but he denies it."

"And what is he saying about me?" Antipas was shouting now.

"Only what you've already heard him say, that it wasn't lawful for you to marry Herodias. But you already knew that, didn't you?" Manaen snapped.

"Careful, cousin, or I will shut you up permanently!"

"You are your father's son, all right." With that, Manaen turned on his heels and left the room, fully expecting to be recalled or arrested.

CHAPTER 19

Several weeks passed quietly with no further word from Herod. Manaen was tense, knowing how unstable his cousin was and fearing the worst. An invitation to a wedding in Cana of Galilee came, and he decided to attend. Things went well, and Manaen was intrigued to find Mary and her son, Jesus, at the reception. He watched as Jesus laughed, danced, and enjoyed the other guests. It was as if he made everyone around him just as happy as he seemed to be. It was obvious that people enjoyed his company. They jostled each other in their attempts to be near him and get his attention.

Even the children begged Jesus to come outside and play with them. He took them into the yard and swung them around until they were dizzy. Then he would pick them up and ride them on his broad shoulders as he danced around the garden in a circle with all of them, throwing back his head and laughing. He even taught them the simple dance steps.

Manaen went over to talk to Mary and together they watched Jesus. When he asked her what had brought them there, she told him that the bride was her niece. They discussed the lavish wedding flowers and the beauty of the bride, groom, and attendants. As they talked about all of the coincidences that had brought them together over the years, the wedding host interrupted and told Mary that he had run out of wine.

"Don't worry," Mary replied. "I'll take care of it." Excusing herself from Manaen, she went over to speak to Jesus.

Jesus shook his head as she was speaking. "Is that any of our business, Mother? This isn't my time. Don't rush me," he said.

Mary spoke to Jesus again quietly, approached the servants, and told them to do whatever Jesus instructed them. Jesus spoke to the servants, and Manaen saw them gather six stone water jars that were standing nearby. Then Jesus told the servants to fill the jars with water, so they filled them to the brim.

"Now fill your pitchers, and take them to the host," he told them.

They did what he said, and the master of the banquet tasted the water that had been turned into wine. He didn't realize where it had come from, but the servants who had drawn the water knew. Then he called the bridegroom aside.

"Everyone brings out the choice wine first and then the cheaper wine after the guests have had too much to drink; but you have saved the best till now."[1]

Manaen tasted the wine and realized that he had just witnessed something rare. This was the best wine he had ever tasted! *Who is this man and what is this unusual ability that he possesses? Is he some sort of conjurer? I'll be keeping an eye on him for sure. Herod will have a fit when he hears about this!*

• • • • • • • • • • •

"Antipas, oh, excuse me, I'm to call my exalted cousin Herod now," Manaen said sarcastically. "How can I keep an eye on a man that you have thrown into prison? Are you going to toss me into Machaerus so that I can continue to watch him?"

Manaen had been called in for another audience with his cousin, and, in spite of his bravado, he did not relish the idea of joining John the Baptist in prison.

"The Black Fortress is not were I want to spend any time, thank you," he continued sharply.

"No, I just want to know all that you've learned. Are you sure that you're not holding anything back?"

"I only saw him one more time before you had him arrested."

"What garbage was he spewing that time?" Herod's tone of voice was contemptuous, but Manaen could see fear in his eyes.

"He was baptizing at Aenon near Salim, because there was plenty of water, and people were coming constantly to be baptized. Some of his disciples were arguing with a certain Jew about the matter of ceremonial washing. They came to John and said to him, 'Rabbi, that man who was with you on the other side of the Jordan—the one you testified about— well, he is baptizing, and everyone is going to him.'"

"Well, well, go on. And what did he say?"

"He told them that a man can receive only what is given to him from heaven. He reminded them that he had said that he was not the Christ, but sent ahead of him. He talked about the bride belonging to the bridegroom and about the one who must become greater; and he must become less. I don't think he was talking about you and Herodias, but who can be sure?"

"Indeed! And what else?" Herod's usual uneasiness and sarcasm were obvious as the crafty eyes darted around the room. "I know there is more!"

"Well yes, but it was just some talk about the one who comes from above. He said that he speaks the word of God, and there was some talk about eternal life. He said that, 'Whoever believes in the Son has eternal life, but whoever rejects the Son will not see life, for God's wrath remains on him.'"[2]

"And what is that supposed to mean?" Herod snapped. "Oh, who cares? Just watch him for me!" He waived his hand in dismissal before going on.

"Report to me in a month and watch yourself! I don't like your attitude."

CHAPTER 20

"Hello, Chuza, old friend! It has been years since we last met. How are you?" Manaen was elated to see his friend from his earlier years at the palace. "What are you doing in Galilee? I heard that you were living in Capernaum." Manaen realized that Chuza looked troubled.

"Are you well, Chuza? And how is Joanna?"

"I'm well enough. And so is Joanna…now. That's why I'm here. I've come to find the healer and thank him for what he has done for her. I heard that he has arrived here from Judea."

"The healer? Who is that, Chuza?"

"Surely you have heard of Jesus, the healer from Nazareth!"

Manaen's shock was evident in the tone of his voice.

"Are you talking about the son of Joseph bar Jacob, the carpenter?"

"Yes, but Joseph is no longer with us. He died some time ago."

"Yes, I know, and I was sorry to hear that, but I am familiar with his son, this Jesus. In fact I was there the night he was born. I know his mother too. Not well, but well enough to make an introduction for you. I didn't realize that he's a healer." Manaen chuckled. "In fact, I thought he was a maker of fine wine and a housecleaner at the temple."

"Yes," Chuza laughed. "He did run the merchants and money changers out of the temple recently. What a sight! Tables were crashing, money was rolling all over the place, and doves were flying through the temple. What a ruckus! That really endeared him to the priests! He'll make more enemies if he isn't careful; but I must find this Rabboni, Manaen. I promised Joanna I would. She's sent him a gift from the both of us."

"Rabboni? Well, yes. I do remember hearing him teach, I just didn't realize that he had that title." Manaen laughed and saw the expression on his friend's face. "I'm sorry, Chuza. I wasn't making light of your situation. I was just remembering a wedding in Cana. Come on. We'll find him. I'll have my servants help locate him."

It wasn't long before the servants found Jesus surrounded by a welcoming crowd who had seen him earlier in Jerusalem. Many of the people had followed him to hear him teach, and, perhaps, witness a miracle. When the servants reported back, Manaen and Chuza went to see Jesus.

As they worked their way through the crowd to Jesus, a nobleman that Manaen knew during his days at the palace also approached Jesus. They heard him beg Jesus to accompany him and heal his son, saying that his son was near death.

Jesus quietly replied, "Go your way; your son lives." Manaen and Chuza heard the man thank Jesus and walk away.

"Chuza, you stay here and talk to Jesus. I want to see this sick boy."

"So, your curiosity has been aroused, Manaen?"

"Call it what you will, my friend. I will find you later. Tell Joanna hello for me."

"Come take the evening meal with us."

"Thank you. I'll see you at your table." With a clasp of their hands, Manaen hurried away.

Later that evening Manaen joined Chuza and Joanna at their home for a bountiful meal. "I hear that you witnessed a miracle today, Manaen. Tell us what happened," Joanna said.

"I can't say that I saw a miracle, but before we arrived at the nobleman's home, a servant met him on the road. He told him that the boy was very much alive. And, yes, he said that it happened at the very hour when the father was talking to Jesus.[1] But you know children as well as I do, Joanna. In fact, I'm sure you know them much better since I only had the one adopted son. And I've had to spend too much time away from my grandchildren, thanks to Herod. However, the fact is that a child can seem near death one minute, and be up chasing around and playing the next."

"Ah, a true skeptic," Joanna chuckled. Looking deep into his eyes, she went on.

"I'm not a child, Manaen, and I can tell you that I was near death. The physicians had given up on me when the

Master healed me instantly. I'm not trying to convince you of anything. I am just telling you what happened to me."

"Very well, Joanna. I will keep that in mind, but it doesn't change my mind. We have seen too many fakes and impostors for me to simply believe everything I hear. Please forgive me; but I was there in the stable where he was born. I understand that he's supposed to be a king of some kind. Jupiter's priest, I heard him teach the priests things they didn't know when he was only a boy!"

"Don't swear, Manaen."

"Sorry, Chuza, but it is just too much for me to take in. I know that Herod is keeping a watchful eye on him. I don't know how many others are watching him, and John, for that matter; but I do know that Herod hates John and is looking for any excuse to silence him permanently. Now he has me watching this Jesus too! It's enough to make any man swear!"

He and Chuza chatted, but Joanna was quiet as she put oil in the lamps and lit them. Manaen enjoyed her graceful movements as she circled the room. He realized that he had missed having a wife to care for his home. Now it was too late.

When she finished, she spoke.

"Manaen, please be careful. Don't get yourself caught in the web of Herod's deceit! There's a good reason why people have begun to call him 'the Fox'! Frankly, I think that to call Herod 'the Fox' is an insult to every fox in the world, but I understand the analogy. Herod is sly and tricky. Don't let him entrap you too."

Manaen marveled at the woman's wisdom and discernment.

"Don't worry, Joanna. I've known 'the Fox' most of my life, and I learned at an early age to watch my back when

I'm dealing with him. I've always loved my cousin, but it is evident that madness as well as the crown was passed down to him from his father."

"I tend to forget that you're related."

"I wish I could forget it," Manaen replied sourly. "I'm afraid that my love for him is turning to contempt very fast. In fact, I almost hate him at times. It gets a little tiring being his errand boy, especially when it involves spying on innocent people. I only hope that my spying isn't what got John thrown into prison."

"No, Manaen," Joanna replied softly. "It was his preaching against Herodias that landed John in prison."

"Thank you, Joanna. But it isn't over; John will lose his head over this."

"What do you mean?" Joanna looked shocked.

"When we were boys I remember trying to tell Antipas that this was coming. It would really frighten him when I told him that he would be king one day in his father's place and be called 'Herod the Tetrarch.' I also remember something about a dancing girl, but I can't recall all of the details. It has been too many years; but I do know that John will be beheaded."

"Chilling fact, isn't it, knowing that your cousin could do such a thing?"

"Yes, Chuza, but as I say quite often, it's all in the hands of the gods. Why do you look so unhappy, Joanna?"

"Manaen, you know our beliefs."

"Oh, yes, you good Jews believe your Yahweh is the only God. Well, you haven't convinced me yet, and from the way he allows his people to be trampled on by Rome, I'm not sure that I will ever believe in such a weak god. Pardon me, dear lady, but I think I should leave now. The wine is beginning to affect my good manners. I hope that you'll forgive the ramblings of this cynic."

"You're forgiven, but you are in our prayers, Manaen." Then they asked him about his ability to foresee the future. They called it a gift but to him it was a curse, and he refused to discuss it.

Manaen shook his head as he left the home of his friends. *How can people insist on this "one God, this Yahweh?"* he wondered.

CHAPTER 21

The audience with Herod at his palace in Tiberius deteriorated rapidly. He was angry that Manaen couldn't give him a reason to kill John. Any trumped-up charge would have put him in a better mood, but Manaen wouldn't cooperate.

"Herod, I don't understand why you keep up this relentless pursuit of a man that you have locked up in the Black Fortress. What does it matter what his 'followers' are saying or doing? You have divorced your wife and taken Herodias. You do as you please, so what is driving you?"

"I'll tell you what's 'driving' me, my dear cousin!" he replied with an ugly sneer. "John has a cousin that seems to be taking over where John left off!"

Anger gleamed in his eyes.

"Is that what you plan to do? Take over where I leave off?" Herod screamed.

His head thrust forward, and his hands gripped the arm of his chair so tightly that his knuckles were white. Madness was obvious in the king's eyes.

"Antipas…excuse me, Herod, what are you saying? When have I ever been disloyal to you? I am as loyal to you as I was to your father!" Manaen was so angry that he could have gladly smashed his fist into the arrogant face. "Was I ever disloyal to your father? No, I was not; and I will never fail in my loyalty to you! Whether I agree with you or not, you are still my cousin and the king of Galilee."

"Yes, yes, I know," Herod responded petulantly with a swift change of mood, "just as you predicted all those years ago!"

He started to chuckle.

"I don't suppose that you will ever let me forget that you were right, and I was wrong," he said.

Manaen was relieved to see that Herod had put aside his anger so easily.

"What difference does right or wrong make? You're the king, and I'm still your faithful lapdog. Who is John's cousin?"

"Jesus of Nazareth. He and his people are baptizing more people than John did. And crowds follow him everywhere he goes. I think he is a greater threat to me than John."

Manaen struggled to hide his surprise and alarm.

"Are you going to imprison him at Machaerus with John?"

"Yes, if you can find me a reason. And I expect you to do just that," he ordered, suddenly angry again. His moods seemed to change more quickly than the tides. He pointed toward the door.

"Now go see what he is doing," he shouted. "I want you to watch his every move for me! Go! Now! You bore me more every time I see you."

As Manaen left the throne room he studied the palace at Tiberius. His cousin had certainly done what he said he would. Manaen felt that Antipas had built a city more beautiful than his father ever had, even if it was built over an old Jewish cemetery. At least it was located on the Via Mare and the Sea of Galilee, which made it easily accessible. The surrounding mountains also made it easy to defend.

Right now I just want to go relax and wash off the stench of that interview in one of the hot springs, Manaen mused. *I feel dirtier every time I come away from talking with 'mighty Herod the Tetrarch.' I want to go home to Antioch, and I just might do it! No, not even the distance from here to Antioch can free me from his insane clutches. His reach is getting too long for my comfort.*

CHAPTER 22

ord had spread that Jesus was preaching by the Sea of Galilee, so Manaen made his way to where the crowd was gathered. The harp-shaped lake was calm today, but Manaen knew how quickly a storm could change things. The winds would come howling through the breaks in the mountains that encircled the lake and cause real turbulence.

Manaen located Jesus and was able to make his way through the throng of people in time to see him talking to two fishermen. They had left their boats to come ashore and tend their nets. Jesus climbed aboard one of the boats and asked the owner, whom Manaen later learned was Simon Peter, to take him a little way off from shore. From there Jesus sat down and taught the people.

When he finished teaching, Jesus instructed Simon to go

out into the deep water and let down his nets. Simon replied in frustration that they had fished all night and hadn't caught a thing, but he would do what Jesus commanded. Manaen had already heard the other fishermen grumbling about not being able to catch any fish, so he was amazed when the nets were hauled up with so many fish that the nets broke.

Simon yelled for another boat to help them. There were so many fish that both boats were in danger of sinking. Manaen saw Simon fall to his knees and say something to Jesus. Back on land both owners walked off with Jesus, leaving their boats, the fish, and everything else they owned on the beach. As they passed by, Manaen heard Jesus say something about becoming "fishers of men."[1] He wondered what it meant.

Several days later Manaen met Chuza and Joanna in Capernaum and accompanied them to the synagogue, where Jesus astonished everyone with his teaching. His words held such power and authority that Manaen couldn't help but contrast his teaching with that of the priest. Things that he had never understood were becoming clearer to him, but why the women were separated during worship at the synagogue remained a mystery to him.

Just as he started to ask Chuza a question a man screamed, "Ho! What business do you have here with us, Jesus? Nazarene! I know what you're up to. You're the Holy One of God and you've come to destroy us!"

Jesus shut him up: "Quiet! Get out of him!"[2]

The man fell to the floor writhing and screamed at the top of his voice, but the demon left and didn't hurt him. Then the man jumped up and threw his arms around Jesus, weeping, laughing, and thanking Jesus for setting him free from the demon. Jesus hugged him and laughed with him as they danced around the men's section of the synagogue.

That set everyone back on their heels, whispering and wondering what was going on. Everyone talked at once, asking what had happened, and the women's section seemed to be in a complete panic.

"What is this?" "What new doctrine is this?" "What kind of authority does he have that even unclean spirits obey him?" people asked.

Manaen found himself wondering the same thing.

"Chuza, what is …"

"Wait, Manaen," Chuza interrupted quietly. "Let's go meet Joanna. She's leaving the women's galley now."

They made their way to Joanna and quietly left the synagogue. As soon as they were on the street Manaen asked Chuza to explain what they had just witnessed.

"Jesus cast an unclean spirit, a demon, out of the man. Now the man is free to live his life without its influence."

"All right, I'm familiar with demonic activity. I have certainly seen enough of it in the pagan temples, especially in Athens, but what did the man mean when he called Jesus the 'Holy One of God'? And how could Jesus 'cast out' a demon?"

"Let's go to our house, Manaen," Joanna spoke quietly. "It is time for the noon meal."

Their home was gracious and inviting. The rooms surrounded a central open court with a fountain in the center. Not only did the fountain provide water for the running of the household, but it also helped to cool the area. Large palm trees and vines that covered arches provided shade. The scent of flowers in large, well-tended gardens filled the air. There were also large containers of flowers placed all around, spilling colors and scents into the area and covering the stench of the streets.

After a servant removed their sandals and washed their feet, the three friends went into a small inner room. Chuza was the first to speak.

"Joanna, you are better at this than I am. Explain all of this so Manaen will understand."

"Manaen, as you well know, Chuza and I have never been really religious. We only performed enough religious practice to maintain our position in the spiritual community while we continued with our social activities. Our social standing was very important to us, and we did thrive, both financially and socially. But we were never truly happy. In fact, nothing seemed to satisfy us. Then I became seriously ill, and the doctors could do nothing to help me. Actually, they gave up on me and left me to die! That is when Chuza heard about Jesus healing people."

Chuza spoke up.

"I can't say that I believed in his ability to heal, but I was desperate and would have tried anything at that point. I'm sorry I interrupted; go on, Joanna."

Joanna smiled and her gaze seemed to focus on something far away.

"I have to confess that I felt the same way. But, praise be to God, Chuza sent two servants to find Jesus, and then took me to him. I knew as soon as I looked into his eyes that he was different, special somehow. He smiled at me and said, 'Your sins are forgiven.' Instantly I felt health return to my body. It was the most amazing, defining moment of my life, and I have been totally healthy since that day. Even more important is the peace and joy that I have now."

"How can a man say, 'Your sins are forgiven'?"

Joanna looked deeply into his eyes. Manaen felt like she was reading his mind. What she said next shook him to his core.

"Because, dear Manaen, he is the true Son of God—our promised Messiah."

Manaen was astonished and his voice was heavy with sarcasm.

"What? You truly believe this? The Jews have waited for years, and there have been many men that claimed to be their long awaited messiah. They all proved false!" In aggravation he went on. "You are two of the most intelligent people I know. Chuza, you are the steward in Antipas' court as you were in his father's! How can you believe this?"

Manaen's voice was tight with frustration, and he felt angry.

Chuza replied calmly.

"Because we have listened carefully to his teachings and have seen the miracles that he does. Isn't Joanna proof to you that he is not a fake? The proof is right here before your eyes. Didn't you see the demons leave that man today? Couldn't you see the change in him after they left? His countenance was completely different."

"Yes, Manaen," Joanna added. "He didn't look like the same man, but you know that he was. His face and body changed from that of a madman, to one who is completely sane. Even his speech was different, and the sound of his voice changed. He's no longer insane. Doesn't that tell you something?"

Manaen's eyes became slits in his face, he was so angry.

"Oh, I see that Jesus has some kind of strange power, but

there are sorcerers and soothsayers everywhere! How can you say that this man is the Son of God? I was there the night he was born to Mary and Joseph! For that matter, how can you be so convinced that there is only one God?"

Joanna was calm in the face of his anger as she answered.

"Faith, Manaen, simple faith. For example, we live in a world of order. How did that happen? Not by accident, I can assure you. We have met a man that has the ability to completely transform lives. Have you ever seen a soothsayer or sorcerer who could do that?"

"I'm trying to understand what you're saying; it's hard to take it all in." Manaen tried to relax and push his anger aside. He didn't want to offend his friends, and he wanted to keep an open mind to what they were saying. The entire concept just seemed ridiculous to him.

Joanna seemed to glow as she replied.

"Manaen, this man, this Jesus, brings such peace and joy into the lives that he touches. I think that is the biggest miracle of all. The joy is incredible."

"I remember seeing the light of joy on Jesus' face after he was baptized by John. That gives me the impression that John has that same ability."

"No, that had nothing to do with John. It was Jesus' connection to his Heavenly Father. He was obedient to be an example to all of us in water baptism, and his joy was just that feeling of connection that comes with obedience. He also heard his Father say, 'This is my beloved Son in whom I am well pleased.' That alone would be enough to bring unspeakable joy."

"Ah, Joanna, you do put forth a convincing argument, but …"

"But what, Manaen?"

"Listen, you know where I stand with all of this. I am the world-weary cynic. You both know that. And to make matters worse, Herod sent me to monitor this situation and report to him. What am I supposed to do? Go dancing into the throne room singing 'I have found the long-awaited Messiah'? Wouldn't that just make Herod the happiest of men?"

"Don't tell him anything!"

"Chuza, you know better than that! He hears talk about a new king and demands information from me. Have you forgotten what happened when his father heard about a new king? I don't want to remember that carnage! Joachim still has nightmares! And, as I have told you before, Antipas is exhibiting more of Herod's madness every time I see him. I'm thankful that I don't have any of my family here with me for him to harm. I'm afraid that he is as mean and crazy as a Nile crocodile and just as ruthless!"

CHAPTER 23

As the days and weeks passed, Manaen watched events unfold shrouded in many rumors. He heard that the people of Jesus' hometown of Nazareth had tried to kill him because of what he had preached in their synagogue.

Jesus told them that he had been sent to fulfill Isaiah's prophesy, that the Spirit of the Lord was on him, and that he was anointed to preach good news to the poor. He might have escaped their wrath if he had stopped there, but he added that he had been sent by God to proclaim freedom for the captives, recovery of sight for the blind, to release the oppressed, and to proclaim the year of the Lord's favor.

To make matters worse, Jesus rebuked them openly and said that no prophet is accepted in his own country, and that God couldn't send Elijah to any of them, but sent him to a widow in Zarephath in Sidon. Digging himself in deeper, he reminded them that there were many people in Israel that suffered with leprosy when Elisha was the prophet, yet not one of them had the faith to be cleansed of leprosy. It was only the Syrian captain, Naaman, who believed Elisha and was healed.

That stirred up a furor in the synagogue, and the people drove him out of town.

"They took him to the edge of a cliff to throw him down and kill him, but he walked right through the crowd without them even seeing him and went on to Capernaum."[1] Chuza said.

Manaen was visiting with Chuza and Joanna, and they confirmed the rumor about Jesus healing Simon Peter's mother-in-law, who was at death's door from a fever. He still didn't believe it. Now he had to endure it as they discussed what Jesus taught in Galilee.

"Manaen, you should have heard him," Joanna said. "He teaches about love and a better way of living than we have ever thought possible."

"How is that, Joanna?" He was bored, but he didn't want to appear rude.

"Chuza, you may have to help me get it straight. Where did he start? Was it with the poor in spirit part?"

"Yes, he said that theirs is the kingdom of heaven and that those who mourn are blessed because they will be comforted." Chuza paused as if thinking about what he had just said. He smiled as if he were hearing Jesus teaching the concept again.

Joanna took up the story where Chuza left off.

"The meek are blessed because they will inherit the earth. It was amazing! He taught that the ones who hunger and thirst for righteousness are blessed because they will be filled and the merciful for they will be shown mercy.[2] Oh, dear, Manaen, I wish you could have heard him!"

Joanna's eyes sparkled with unshed tears, and Manaen saw that same glow of joy on her face he had seen earlier when they had spoken about Jesus.

"I did, Joanna. I was there when he was teaching. I'm sorry I didn't see you. Where were you seated on the mountain?"

"Near the top so we could hear every word. Isn't it amazing the way he can stand at the bottom of the mountain and the sound can travel all the way to the top! Did you hear it all?" When Manaen nodded she went on. "Then what did you think of his teaching? Did you see the zealots? And the priests?"

Chuza laughed.

"Whoa, Joanna. Ask one question at a time. So what is your opinion, Manaen?"

"I found his teaching to be radical and unbelievable. No one could live by it. What kind of foolishness was that 'love your enemies and do good to those who persecute you?' And what about 'Give to those who ask you and don't turn away from those who want to borrow from you?' Frankly, I think the man has lost his mind if he thinks people will abide by that kind of drivel!"

Now it was Joanna who, unperturbed, was laughing at him.

"You are absolutely right, Manaen. You are a true cynic. But I can tell you from personal experience that people can indeed live by his 'drivel,' as you call it, and be completely happy doing it. In fact I have never known such peace and happiness before; money and position certainly didn't give it to me. I don't always follow his admonitions as I should, and when I don't, I lose that peace. I know his ways are true and right."

"My experience has been the same," Chuza spoke up, rejoining the conversation. "When I live according to Jesus' teaching I am at peace with myself and everyone else. When I try to live any other way I am miserable and, as Joanna would probably agree, very hard to live with."

"Drivel! Total drivel! Listen, I've studied your Law! In fact, I know your laws! I have a pretty thorough knowledge of your religion, and it doesn't teach this foolishness. The law teaches 'an eye for an eye and a tooth for a tooth.' Now this man comes along and says that if someone smacks you on one cheek, you should also turn the other around for him to smack? I don't think so, Joanna!"

"Manaen, I'm not talking about our religion. I'm talking about a relationship. There is a difference, you know. Religion is about law. Relationship is about love."

"And now I suppose that you are going to explain that difference to me, whether I want to hear it or not!"

"No, but when you want to know, I will be glad to discuss it with you."

"I'm sorry, Joanna, Chuza. I didn't mean to sound so rude and ungrateful. I wouldn't hurt you for anything, but you're talking about things I just can't grasp. I feel like an untrained runner trying to win an Olympic race!"

Chuza put his arm around his friend's shoulder.

"It's okay; we understand how you feel. Just promise us that you will keep an open mind and come to us if you have any questions," he said.

"You have my word on it, but right now my biggest problem is what to tell Herod. He will demand answers from me, and I certainly can't tell him what I know. If I did he would have me killed along with Jesus."

"You are probably right, my friend. You are going to have to be very careful about what you say to Herod. You are walking a fine line indeed."

"I'm glad that you understand. You work for him! How do you manage?"

"I watch my words very carefully and spend as little time in his presence as I can."

"Then you do understand. I live in dread of his next demand on my time and am always looking for ways to avoid being at either his Jerusalem palace or the one in Tiberius."

"Well, I have a way for you, at least for the evening. I've been invited to a banquet tonight at the home of Simon the Pharisee. Please join me. He would welcome you."

"If you are sure it won't be an inconvenience."

"Not at all; I'm sure. Be here at dusk and we will walk over together."

• • • • • • • • • • • •

They arrived at the Pharisee's house at the appointed time.

According to custom, their shoes were removed, their feet were washed, and their heads were anointed with oil. Then Simon greeted them, giving them a kiss on each cheek, and they were placed in positions of honor to recline at the triclinium.

Manaen saw Jesus enter with several men. They were escorted to their places. Manaen realized that Jesus and the men had been intentionally insulted: no one removed their sandals, and their feet were not washed. They acted as if nothing had happened and slipped their sandals off before coming to the table.

Manaen wondered if they had even been invited, and he also wondered how they could so completely ignore such an insult. Not having a servant wash a guest's feet was rude. Guests' feet were washed out of concern for their comfort and health. It wasn't just a luxury that was done for the sake of hospitality. And not anointing a guest's head with the customary oil was not only discourteous, but it was an insult in this wealthy home.

Jesus and the men with him simply took their seats and prepared to join the conversations at the table. The other people seemed to welcome them.

Almost immediately, as the food was being served and conversation flowed, there was a commotion at the door. Manaen saw a woman who was known as the town harlot entering the room, carrying a bottle of very expensive perfume. He heard angry remarks and saw the woman stumble.

"What is she doing here? Get her out of here!" one of the women serving the meal said quite angrily.

"She has some nerve coming in here with decent people!" another said. Her words sounded harsh and ugly as they left her mouth.

Even the men were making ugly remarks as they sneered at the woman. Some of the more religious people turned their backs and wouldn't even look at her.

The woman's face was flushed with shame and tears streaked her face, but she walked straight to Jesus and dropped to her knees at his feet, still weeping, her tears bathing his feet. There was an audible gasp around the room as she removed her head covering, loosened her hair, and used her hair to dry his feet. Then she kissed his feet, opened the bottle of valuable perfume, and poured it over them. She continued to weep as she rubbed the perfume into his feet and dried them with her hair.

As Simon the Pharisee watched this, his shock and displeasure were clearly evident on his face. He said to himself, *"If this man were a prophet, he would know who is touching him and what kind of woman this is falling all over him."*

Jesus turned to his host and said, "Simon, I have something to tell you."

"Oh? Tell me, Rabboni," he replied arrogantly.

"Two men were in debt to a banker. One owed him five hundred pieces of silver, the other fifty. Neither of them had the money to pay him back, so the banker canceled both debts. Now which of them will be more grateful?"

Simon replied smugly, "I suppose the one who was forgiven the most."

"That's right," said Jesus.

Then he turned toward the woman and said to Simon, "Do you see this woman? I came into your house. You didn't give me any water for my feet, but she wet my dirty feet with her tears and she has wiped them with her hair. You did not give me a kiss, but this woman, from the time she got here, has not stopped kissing my feet. You didn't put oil on my head, but she has poured perfume on my feet. In view of that, I tell you, her many sins have been forgiven—for she loved much. But he who has been forgiven little, loves little."

Then Jesus said to her, "Your sins are forgiven."

The other guests were indignant and began to say to each other, "Who does he think he is, forgiving sins?"

Jesus ignored them and said to the woman, "Your faith has saved you; go in peace."[3]

Jesus stood, reached down, took her hand, and helped her to her feet. As she left the room her face was radiant with joy.

In amazement, Manaen had watched as the woman's face completely changed. When she came in she had hung her head and seemed fearful and ashamed; now she carried her head high and walked confidently. He saw that same look of peace and joy on her face that he had seen on Joanna's and Chuza's faces.

What is going on here? How can this happen? Surely I didn't just see the transformation on that woman that I thought I saw. Am I losing it? And who was that woman? Manaen didn't know what to think anymore.

Manaen wanted to ask Chuza who she was, but Chuza stood to leave and merely nodded to their host. Manaen was astounded at this show of rudeness. It was almost unheard of to leave before the meal was over, especially without thanking the host, but Manaen followed Chuza from the house.

"What was that all about?" he asked when they were outside.

"Simon deliberately insulted my Lord. If he is not welcome, then I don't want to stay."

"Chuza, Jesus is still there. He didn't leave."

"I know, but I don't want to participate in the religious posturing that I know is about to take place. It would sour the food in my stomach."

Manaen laughed at his friend's sincerity.

"It seems to me that you are being pretty pious yourself."

Chuza snapped.

"You're probably right, but there was no place in that room for my anger."

"I'm struggling with what we just witnessed. I can't imagine any woman uncovering her hair like that in public, much less letting it fall loose like she did. And then to wash Jesus's filthy feet with it! Why, you know that since his feet hadn't been washed, they must have had camel and sheep dung on them. There is no way to walk these streets without stepping in it! How could she do that? And to lower herself to the position of the most humble servant in the home…"

"Yes, it was humble and an act of selfless devotion and pure love. And that vile Simon was making it look dirty and sinister. Don't you do the same thing! He should love the Lord as much as she does, and you should too, for that matter!" His anger was evident in every word he spoke.

"Who was that woman, Chuza?" He ignored the implied insult, hoping to calm his friend by getting his attention away from Simon.

Chuza's voice did become calm as he replied.

"She's Mary, the sister of Lazarus and Martha. She has always been the wild one in that family. After their parents' death she took it pretty hard and blamed God. Then she left the family and … well, you saw."

"I know Lazarus and Martha, but I have never heard them speak of this sister."

"Now you know why."

"Chuza," Manaen spoke almost angrily, "If I had a sister, I would never deny her. I wouldn't care what she had done."

"You weren't raised in a Jewish household, Manaen. You were raised in the permissive culture of the palace. Things are different with us. We have strict laws that must not be broken, laws put in place for our own good. But Jesus has come to teach a better way, a way of love and forgiveness."

They walked past the beautiful Capernaum synagogue with its tall pillars and stonework gleaming in the moonlight. The fronds of the palm trees rustled softly in the breeze, seeming to play a melody. The air was heavy with the sweet fragrance of flowers and the spicy twang of dates ripening on the trees, but none of this softened Manaen's mood.

"Oh, yes, I forget about you pious Jews and your all-consuming religious laws. What I do remember increases my doubts about this Yahweh of yours. I could never keep all of your laws and regulations!" Manaen snapped angrily.

"Please keep an open mind, Manaen," Chuza replied, softly, oblivious to his anger. "Jesus says that he has come to fulfill the law. He also says that he has come that we might have life and that more abundantly. Can't you see from what we just witnessed that he is not like the Pharisees and Sadducees? He doesn't posture and prance around and puff himself up like the priests and scribes do. He's humble in thought, word, and deed."

"So who is he, Chuza? Will you answer that for me?"

"No one can answer that for you, Manaen. You either believe, or you don't. You must decide for yourself."

"But you and Joanna believe that he is the long-awaited Messiah!"

"Yes. We do."

"I have heard people say that he quieted a storm that would have sunk the boat he was in. And they say that even the wind and waves obey him. This is ridiculous rubbish, Chuza. Impossible! You know that as well as I do!"

"I know nothing of the sort, Manaen. I know that, as the very Son of God, Jesus can do anything. Nothing is impossible for him. If he created the wind and rain, then they must certainly obey his bidding. It's simple to me, probably because I believe."

CHAPTER 24

Joanna turned to Chuza and Manaen with a face no longer weary from their traveling to see Jesus, but radiant with joy.

"There he is, Chuza. There is the Master."

Manaen thought that she was going to break and run from them, but she maintained her composure. His thoughts stirred as he watched the way women looked at this man. *What is the hold he has over women?* Then he looked at the faces of some of the men seated nearby. *Why, the men are looking at him with the same blissfully happy attention.*

An elderly woman fell to the ground at Jesus' feet. She was twisted, groaning, and moaning as if she was in great agony. Jesus looked at her for a moment, and then he cast out seven demons from her. The demons tried to tear at the woman and cause a scene, but Jesus commanded them to be quiet and come out of her. It happened so quickly that most of the crowd couldn't really understand what happened. Then Jesus bent down and lifted the woman.

"Go your way, daughter. Your sins are forgiven,"[1] Jesus said. What Manaen saw was astonishing. The "old" woman who had fallen at Jesus's feet was transformed into a beautiful, radiant, young woman. The woman began to sing, laugh, and dance. Then she fell at Jesus's feet again, thanking him and worshiping him.

"Who is that, Chuza?"

Chuza beamed.

"That's Mary Magdalene. She owns quite a prosperous fishing business in Magdala. No one could understand her fall into immorality, until today. Now we know the answer. She was controlled by those demons that Jesus cast out. Watch and see the change in her life now, Manaen," he said.

"Where will I see her again?"

"Oh, she will probably be like the rest of us that Jesus has touched," Joanna answered.

"Do you mean following him around, hanging on to his every word?"

Manaen's sarcasm was so obvious that it shocked Joanna, and she was quiet for a moment before answering.

"Yes, just like you; but for a different reason."

"Oh, I've made my last report to Herod. At least I think I have. Or, should I say, I hope I have?"

"Hope, Manaen. Never give up hope," she answered. Suddenly she grabbed Chuza by the arm, a look of astonishment on her face.

"Chuza, isn't that Jairus, the ruler of the synagogue?"

Manaen recognized the priest from the temple, who had fallen prostrate on the ground at Jesus' feet. He begged Jesus to go to his house because his only daughter, a girl of about twelve, was dying.

Jesus went with him, making his way through the pushing, jostling crowd. Suddenly Jesus stopped and asked, "Who touched me?"

Everyone nearby denied touching him. Then his disciple, Peter, said, "But Master, we've got crowds of people on our hands. Dozens have touched you."

Jesus insisted, "Someone touched me. I felt power discharging from me."

A woman came trembling, falling at his feet. She told him that she had been bleeding for twelve years and physicians couldn't help her. She believed that if she could just touch the hem of his garment, she would be healed. That was why she had crawled through the crowd and touched him. She said that she was instantly healed.

Jesus said, "Daughter, you took a risk trusting me, and now you're healed and whole. Live well, live blessed!"[2]

While he was still talking, someone from Jairus' home came and told him, "Your daughter died."

He said, "No need to bother the Teacher."

Jesus overheard and said, "Don't be upset. Just trust me and everything will be all right."

Manaen looked at Chuza and shook his head in disbelief. "How can he say that and give him false hope?"

"Just wait and see what happens," Joanna replied.

At Jairus' house, Jesus turned to the people and told them

to wait outside. Then he took Peter, James, and John, along with Jairus and his wife, and went inside.

On their way in, they passed the mourners sitting on the ground. The people in their black mourning garb were wailing and mourning for the daughter. The men were on one side with their hands over their beards; the women were on the other side with their hands over their heads and their heads hanging over their knees. Jesus told them to stop because she was not dead, but asleep. When he said it the mourners starting mocking and laughing; they knew she was dead! Manaen laughed with them, but Joanna and Chuza were silent. Anticipation showed on their faces.

There was a swelling crowd of people who had come to see what Jesus would do. Manaen was pushed to the side of the house behind the stairs leading to the roof. The flickering of an oil lamp caught his attention. He realized that he could look in through a window just to his right. That window looked in on the room Jesus had entered. He saw Jesus take the young girl by the hand and tell her to rise. When she sat up, Jesus told the parents to give her something to eat. Her parents were ecstatic, but Jesus warned them to keep quiet. "Don't tell a soul what happened in this room."[3]

It can't be that simple. No one can have that power! Manaen thought.

"No one can raise the dead!"

Manaen didn't realize he had spoken aloud until he heard Joanna's soft reply. "Evidently Jesus can."

CHAPTER 25

Manaen was annoyed to be summoned to the royal palace again, even if it did mean he was going to get to see Chuza. He always dreaded going to that vile place.

There was going to be a party to celebrate Herod's birthday, and he couldn't think of anything he dreaded more. But from the look on Chuza's face, Manaen's feeling of dread deepened. He hadn't seen Chuza since they had been in Capernaum several days before.

"What is it, my friend?" he asked.

"Herod's in a very festive mood, perhaps too festive. I suspect that there's going to be trouble ... a lot of trouble."

"That's always a possibility when Herod is involved."

"How well I know, but this seems different. Herodias is up to something, and I can't find out what."

"She is always up to something!"

"Not like this, she isn't. She has been laughing like a maniac all day!"

"She always laughs like a maniac … or a demoniac!"

"Manaen, please listen to me. She has spent the entire day holed up with Salome. She has kept the palace staff busy, dancing in attendance, grooming that young filly for something. I just know that there is going to trouble, big trouble. Everything in me says that something terrible is about to happen. I know you are the one with the prophetic gift, but I'm telling you I can just feel it! You had better take this seriously." Manaen had never seen his friend in such obvious distress.

"I hear you, Chuza, but Herod, Herodias, and her daughter are going to do what they want to do, and there is nothing we can do about it. And it isn't unusual that they should be spending time getting ready for tonight's orgy, is it? They always keep the slaves running. What else do those two have to do? They take long baths. Their eunuchs pour perfumed oil over their bodies and massage it in. Their clothes and jewels have to be unique, and the kohl around their eyes will have to be applied over and over until it is perfect." Manaen pretended to apply black kohl around his eyes, posturing and mimicking the women as he did it.

Chuza laughed and joined him in the little drama.

"And that is just the beginning! I know how these things are done. I'm thankful that Joanna is not that foolish! She's so beautiful that she doesn't need that mess."

"Yes, you're a blessed man," Manaen replied quietly. "Before I met Joanna I didn't realize how much I have missed not having a wife. She doesn't need jewels because she is a jewel."

"Careful, Manaen," Chuza responded. "Remember the law."

"Oh, you Jews and your plagued law!" The men laughed together as only comfortable old friends can, and proceeded toward the banquet hall.

"Manaen, why did you never take a wife? You're a handsome man. I know that from the way women look at you. And I know you have a great deal of wealth. You could certainly have afforded to take a wife, and you could have had your pick of any number of fine candidates."

"Joachim was my life. He brought me so much happiness and taught me so much about love and family. Without Joachim and Nebo I would probably have not been much different than Herod. That may sound smug, but I do know that I'm a better person because of their influence. There was also the matter of palace intrigue hanging over my head, and I would never have wanted to expose a wife to that life. Also, I never met a woman that I trusted to be good to Joachim. Now I have Joachim and his family. It has always been enough." He chuckled. "Besides, I was waiting for Mary."

"Mary? Lazarus' sister?"

Manaen laughed at the thought of Lazarus' alarm if he thought such a thing.

"Or Magdalene," he answered as a diversion to Chuza's question. He continued to laugh as he thought of Lazarus' reaction to the thought of him with his sister. *Why am I laughing? I'm beginning to wish I did have a woman to share my life with. Loneliness is a miserable bed fellow! God, how I miss my family.*

Chuza threw him a quizzical look as they entered the banquet hall. The noise stopped their conversation. The music was loud and raucous and dancing girls were everywhere. They gyrated their hips and spun to the music as they played their castanets. These small brass discs that were attached to their thumbs and middle fingers tinkled and jingled, adding to the wild rhythm as they snapped them together.

Herod and Herodias were enthroned on a dais at the center front of the hall. Their beautiful robes and the pillows they lounged on were of the richest damasks and silks. Yards and yards of the same fabrics hung overhead, forming a brilliant, opulent canopy. Cascades of the fabric were braided and draped, wrapping up and around palm trees and columns all around the hall. At places it was draped in swags and twisted into knots that had ropes of jewels entwined.

On the balcony that circled the hall, lengths of wide ribbon of various colors were woven into a basket weave that made the hall look like an inverted bowl. There were cages of exotic birds suspended from matching ribbons all around the bottom. The ribbons were also woven into the bird cages. The birds were singing and flying around in their cages, hitting the bells suspended there with the same type ribbons. The effect was stunning.

Every column, corner, and nook contained huge alabaster urns of fruit stacked to the ceiling. The apples, limes, pomegranates, citron, grapes, and figs were artfully arranged and held in place by the garlands of flowers and ribbon that wound around them.

A lavish table was loaded with food of more varieties than Manaen had ever seen, and he had attended some of the finest banquets in Rome. Even the Caesars had not provided such a spread at any banquet he had attended. There was everything from roasted hummingbirds to roasted boar; savory meats, fish, and cheese; onions, melons, cucumbers; whole heads of roasted garlic; apples stewed with raisins, almonds, pistachio nuts, and cinnamon; corn and lentils. The aroma of saffron, butter, and honey floated on the breezes.

The food was served in vessels that rivaled even those in the temple: silver plates, platters, and bowls with gold trim that were studded with beautiful gems in various patterns. The wine goblets matched the serving plates.

The brilliantly-hued fabrics around the hall were used again in the table covers. The covers were tucked up and tied with bouquets of flowers and ribbon to reveal contrasting underskirts of damask.

There were wild animals in cages in the corners of the hall. Their growling and shrill yells mingled with the birds and added to the wild atmosphere in the hall.

Wine flowed from a many-tiered fountain at the center of the hall. By the time the two men arrived, it was evident that the guests had made good use of the fountain. Inhibitions and good manners had been cast to the wind, and couples were wrapped together like animals on the couches around the hall.

Manaen was disgusted by what he saw. He had attended orgies in Rome, but they had seemed to have, at least, a tone of civility and class. This was just base and bawdy. He saw Chuza's shocked expression.

"Is this your first orgy, Chuza?"

"No, just the worst." His face was pale. "How can people behave like this? Are they taking lessons from the animals? Do they have no sense of morality?"

Manaen laughed cynically.

"Morality? These people don't know the meaning of the word. In fact, Chuza, they don't even know there is such a word. Why do you think Herod and Herodias surround themselves with this type of people? Water seeks its own level, you know!"

They found a seat and immediately they were approached by writhing, twisting, dancing girls who tried to join them on their couch. Manaen dismissed them with a wave of his hand. They pouted and begged as they displayed their bodies, but they left when they realized he was serious. Manaen thought he had seen it all in Rome, but this was the most debauched, revolting show of depravity he had ever witnessed. He felt nausea rise in his throat.

Chuza leaned over to him.

"Can we leave? I am not comfortable with all of this. It's sickening!"

Manaen was thankful that Chuza wanted to leave. He felt like he couldn't get out of this hall and away from these people fast enough. *What has happened to me? This actually makes me nauseated!*

Just as the men started to rise, the music changed, and the most beautiful dancer of all came twirling into the room and blocked their exit. She was clothed in layers of colorful, translucent, transparent skirts and veils. Her body was clearly visible in the light that shone behind her. She had tiny golden bells sewn around the hems of her skirts, and more dangled from gold cords around her ankles and wrists.

The gold cords around her forehead were strung with precious stones that hung down over her cheeks and eyes like falling water. Her gold neck chains were entwined with pearls, coral, and precious stones that were separated by half-moon-shaped gold pieces. A huge ruby on a heavy gold cord hung between her breasts and the gold bracelets that circled her arms from her wrist to her elbows were studded with magnificent precious jewels. Bracelets fashioned like snakes with emeralds for eyes circled her upper arms. Gold chain belts with more bells hung around her waist and hips, adding to the undulating effect of her dance. She wore a huge diamond in her navel to keep the watchers' eyes riveted there.

So this is the provocative Salome, Manaen thought as he watched the girl writhing and twisting in front of Herod. Over and over she undulated around and around, and then gyrated toward Herod. She teased him into a frenzy, then twirled away and stripped off a layer of cloth that she would then use to entice him even more. When he would start to pant she would twirl back to him, undulating and writhing at him as she spun around and around. When Herod tried to reach for her, she would spin away and strip off another layer until she was dancing before him with only one layer of the thin fabric covering her naked body.

Manaen remembered the boyhood day by the sea when Antipas had said the girls would dance in only one layer of the cloth and nothing more. *By Medusa's snakes, it's happening!* Then the music stopped abruptly.

Manaen had watched Herodias during all of this, and her face looked like a snake waiting to strike. *So that is what made me think of the myth of Medusa!*

Manaen wondered what this sly-eyed woman was thinking. She seemed pleased at the spectacle before her, as if she was waiting for something—some precise moment. There didn't seem to be any jealousy as her daughter enticed Antipas. There was only a sinister, impatient waiting.

Herod was wet with sweat, and the lust on his face was obvious. *The old fool is absolutely panting,* Manaen thought. Then he heard Herod make an oath to Salome. He said that he was so pleased with her dancing that she could have anything she wanted—up to one-fourth of his kingdom. The girl threw back her head with a wild, demonic laugh and went over to her mother; her eyes never left Herod.

After Herodias whispered in her ear, Salome went to Herod and said something Manaen couldn't hear. Herod turned pale, and his eyes took on that wild look of fear that Manaen was so familiar with, only worse.

Manaen tried to make his way to Herod but was stopped by his guards. He and Chuza left in disgust and defeat.

Chuza spoke first.

"What was that all about?"

"I don't know, but I could tell he didn't want to do what she asked. I think Herodias has put her up to something, which means it is probably some evil scheme."

"Do you think he will do it?"

"Probably. I could tell that he regretted his oath, but I know him all too well. Besides, he is probably hoping to bed the beautiful Salome!"

"Herodias' daughter?"

"Don't sound so shocked, Chuza. And don't act so innocent! These things go on all the time and you know it!" Manaen regretted his outburst. "Sorry, Chuza. I'm returning to my rooms. What are you going to do?"

"As his steward, I have to stay here at the palace until it is over. Then I'm going to the baths before I go home and try to wash off this filth!"

CHAPTER 26

Several hours later, Manaen woke up to the sound of someone pounding on his door like they were trying to break it down. He went to investigate. A servant had already admitted Chuza, who was standing there and appeared to be in shock. He was white as a specter from the grave and tears were streaming down his face.

"What is it, Chuza? Has something happened to Joanna? Forgive my manners; come in, my friend, come in. Go get water to wash his feet," he told a servant as he pulled the stricken man into the shelter of his room.

"Forget the water, Manaen. It's John," Chuza sobbed.

"John the Baptist?" Manaen waved the servant away.

"Yes."

"Well for the gods' sake, Chuza, tell me what happened!"

"Herod had him beheaded."

"What did you say?" Manaen was stunned to realize his premonition had actually come to pass.

"Beheaded; he had John beheaded!"

"When?"

"Tonight!

"Why?"

"That was what Salome asked him for—John's head on a silver platter! It was horrible. They actually brought it in, uncovered on the platter with blood dripping, leaving a trail on the floor as they walked. His eyes were…"

Manaen interrupted, shaking with anger.

"I knew that Herodias was up to something as totally evil as she is," he snapped. "Where is John's body?"

"His disciples took it and buried it. Then they went to tell Jesus."[1]

"I knew Antipas had gone crazy, but this is the end!"

"Careful what you say to him, Manaen. He has indeed completely lost his mind!"

"How well I know." Manaen was angry and sad at the same time to think of all the years he had wasted trying to help his cousin. He was also horrified to think that someone so close to him could do such a despicable thing.

"Do you want me to go with you to tell Joanna?"

"No, but I had better go tell her before someone else does."

After his friend left, Manaen couldn't sleep. All he could think about was the horror of what had taken place that night and the fact that the same blood flowed in his veins that flowed in Antipas.' *Will I go mad too and become a killer?*

Two days later he was called to the throne room.

"Well, my mighty Manaen, what have you learned for me?" Herod asked smugly.

Manaen took a deep breath before he allowed himself to speak.

"Herod, do you remember when we were by the Mare Nostrum as children, and I told you that you would be king in your father's place?"

"Of course I remember your mad ranting!" Herod smirked. His huge jowls and extra chins made him look like a giant pig. "Of course you were right, but so what?"

"Yes, everything I ever told you has come to pass, including what I tried to tell you about the dancing girl who would bring great grief to your life! How could you have done this horrible thing, Antipas?" Manaen could see the fear and evil fighting for predominance in Herod's eyes.

"Because I am Herod, and I do as I please!" He was shouting now.

"Well, don't ask me to do anything else for you. It is over! King or no king, cousin or no cousin, I will not be a part of your scheming any longer." With that Manaen turned and left the throne room, fully expecting to be drug back and thrown into prison. But as he left the room, Chuza was waiting. He took Manaen's arm and escorted him out of the palace unharmed.

"I heard that you had been summoned. What happened, Manaen?"

"I told him that I won't spy for him anymore. I reminded him of all of the things that I had told him would happen, and now they have all happened. I am through, Chuza. I won't be a part of his evil schemes anymore!"

Several days later Manaen was eating with Chuza and

Joanna when Chuza asked him what he meant about telling Herod what was going to happen. He went back as far as he could remember and told them of all the things that he had known about and how they had all come to pass.

"Do you mean that you even knew John would be beheaded?" Joanna asked.

"I remember that I knew that a beautiful young girl would dance for him and cause him a lot of grief. There was more, but I don't remember it all now."

Chuza was quiet for a moment before he spoke.

"Manaen, do you realize that you are a prophet?"

"No, don't be absurd!" he snapped at his friend. "I just know that I know things and they happen. Antipas used to call it a curse. He was afraid I was going to get him killed."

Manaen chuckled quietly as he remembered those long ago years by the sea.

"I love my cousin, and it causes me real pain to see how his mind has deteriorated just like his father's. I'm afraid there is no hope for him now. Depravation has taken over, and his mind is gone." He shook his head sadly. "It is also frightening to realize that we are related. As I look at his father, his brothers, and Antipas, I wonder if I'm mad too or if I'll go mad someday."

"No, you are neither mad, nor will you go mad. This ability that you have isn't a curse or madness. It is a gift from God and few have it," Chuza said quietly.

"Just stop it, Chuza! Why would your supposedly all-knowing God give a cynic such a gift? I have never believed in him and probably never will!" He stood and started to leave. Then he turned back.

"No, not even all of the teachings or miracles of Jesus have convinced me, and I have been watching him closely for a long time. Remember I have known him longer than you have—since his birth, in fact."

Chuza took his arm and indicated that he should sit back down and finish his meal. He sat, but he no longer wanted any food. Everything tasted like wood shavings in his mouth, and he wanted nothing to do with it.

"No, Manaen, you have never really known him at all. You are only acquainted with him." Joanna's soft remark shook Manaen to his very core and left him speechless. He realized the truth of what she said, and there was no reply that he could make. He sat staring at his plate.

"Then I will probably never know him."

CHAPTER 27

Manaen couldn't understand what kept him following Jesus around when he was no longer reporting to Herod. It was a compulsion within him. It was as if it was a habit he no longer wanted to indulge in, but couldn't seem to stop.

He hadn't seen Chuza and Joanna since Jesus sent his twelve disciples out. Jesus had given them authority and power to deal with all the demons and cure diseases. He told them to preach the news of God's kingdom and heal the sick. Manaen thought it strange when he told them not to take anything for their journey—no staff, no bag, no bread, no money, not even an extra tunic. Jesus told them to stay with one family in each town, and if the town didn't welcome them, to shake the dust off their feet as they left the town as a testimony against them.[1]

After they left, Manaen returned to his own home, and

while he was there, the thing he dreaded most happened. Herod sent a palace guard for him—not just a summons, but a guard to bring him back. *No, not again,* he thought. *He must be planning to arrest me and have me thrown into the Black Fortress.*

When the entourage entered the throne room, Manaen stood waiting while Herod studied his nails for over an hour before he acknowledged Manaen's presence. Just as Manaen's patience reached the breaking point, Herod spoke.

"I beheaded John. Now who is this that I am hearing such things about? People are saying that John has been raised from the dead!" he said.

Manaen felt the muscles in his jaw and stomach tighten, and he raised his chin in defiance. He had to fight to keep his eyes from turning into angry slits.

"What 'things' are you referring to, Antipas?" he asked sarcastically, using the old name to irritate his cousin.

"People are saying that there is a man preaching about the kingdom of God and that he is healing people—lepers are being cleansed and blind men can see again. Some are even saying that he is Elijah.[2] Is this true, cousin?"

"I've heard these things."

"I asked if they are true!" Herod snapped.

"How should I know?" Manaen snapped back.

"I want to see him."

"Why? So that you can have him imprisoned or beheaded?"

"Careful, cousin," his eyes took on an evil glint. "Watch your mouth. I am still your king, and you will do as I say! Always! Now, tell me where he is!"

"If I knew, I would. He means nothing to me. He is just

another itinerant preacher who moves around all the time. Sometimes he is in Galilee, sometimes in Judah or even Samaria. He just moves around preaching and healing. Your spies shouldn't have any trouble finding him, though. Just tell them to follow the crowd."

"What crowd are you talking about?"

"There's always a crowd everywhere he goes. It seems that people like his teachings and want him to heal them. Oh, he feeds them too."

"Find him for me and report back to me. That is an order, cousin." The last was said with such venom that Manaen had to double his fist and steel himself to keep from hitting Herod. Only fear of arrest held him in check. He spun on his heels and left the chamber as quickly as he could and walked through the palace searching for Chuza. Finally, a servant told him where to find him.

Chuza embraced him warmly and asked after his health.

"It isn't my health I'm worried about, Chuza. It's Jesus'. The Fox is trying to find him. Or maybe I should say 'The Snake!' That can only mean trouble for Jesus. I will have to find him and warn him."

"The Fox? The Snake? Oh, you mean Herod! Well, you are right about one thing. There are definite signs that he's up to no good again. There are rumblings among the palace staff that real trouble is brewing; but Jesus can take care of himself. Besides, he's always in a crowd."

"Crowds didn't help John much, now did they?"

"No, you're right, and a crowd won't stop Herod if he wants to strike at Jesus, either. If you are going to find Jesus, do you want me to travel with you?"

"Yes, Joanna too if she would like to go."

"Joanna's with the disciples now. She left about a week ago to take money and food."

"Do you mean that you let her travel alone?"

"No, I sent servants with her. But do you really think that I could have stopped her if she got it in her head to go alone?" Chuza laughed.

"Yes, I do."

"Well, again you may be right, but I won't be the one challenging her to find out." He was still laughing as he turned to two servants and gave them orders to prepare for the journey.

It was late afternoon when Manaen and Chuza arrived near Bethsaida. The area was swarming with people—people believing in Jesus and those who just wanted to test him or trip him up. Jesus and his disciples had just arrived. The disciples had returned from their journey, and they wanted to be alone with Jesus; but a multitude gathered almost immediately. After locating Joanna, Manaen and Chuza joined them.

As the day declined, the Twelve said, "Dismiss the crowd so they can go to the farms or villages around here and get a room for the night and a bite to eat. We're out in the middle of nowhere."

"You feed them," Jesus said.

They said, "We couldn't scrape up more than five loaves of bread and a couple of fish—unless, of course, you want us to go to town ourselves and buy food for everybody. (There were more than five thousand people in the crowd.)

But he went ahead and directed his disciples, "Have them sit down in groups of about fifty."

They did as he asked and after considerable confusion and shuffling word spread through the crowd and everyone found a place to sit. When everything was quiet, Jesus took the five loaves and the two fish and looked up to heaven. He gave thanks and broke them, and then he gave them to his disciples to set before the people. After everyone had eaten and were satisfied the disciples picked up twelve basketfuls of broken pieces that were left over.[3]

The three friends were quiet for some time before Manaen spoke.

"Tell me what just happened here!"

Chuza chortled.

"We just had the best fish supper I have ever eaten." He realized what he had just said and tried to apologize. "I'm sorry, Joanna."

She laughed heartily.

"No apology needed. I know that I'm a good cook, but it's true, I have never tasted such delicious bread and fish."

"Chuza, that man only had five small loaves of bread and two fish. How did he feed all of these people and still have twelve basketfuls left over?"

"Very well, Manaen, he fed them very well indeed. Don't you agree? Speaking of agreeing, have you seen Mary lately? I think we all three agree that she is looking quite lovely these days."

Joanna joined in.

"Have you ever seen anyone so completely changed? And to have her beauty restored is amazing. I've even heard that her health has improved dramatically too."

"Don't try changing the subject on me. You know what I'm talking about!"

"What difference does it make? You refuse to believe—

even the things that you see with your own eyes—you refuse to believe! You saw and tasted the same things that we did, and I am not going to argue with you about it. You make up your own mind, and we will discuss things that we can agree on, like the lovely Mary." Chuza's voice was soft and teasing.

"There is nothing to discuss where Mary is concerned," Manaen snapped.

"Ah, I see."

Joanna giggled at their exchange.

"I see you both have your doubts, just about different things. Well, while you two were arguing, the Master dismissed the people, so we may as well leave. He won't be teaching anymore today."

Chuza looked perplexed.

"Did you hear where he is going from here?"

"He sent his disciples by boat to Gennesaret."

"It doesn't matter. I need to get back before Herod misses me. What are you going to do, Manaen?"

"Stay as far away from Herod as I can! But I'll walk back with you two. I need to get my horse from the stable." Manaen had started walking more so that the people he was associating with wouldn't think of him as a Roman. He didn't want or need that stigma.

They walked back in the glowing peach, lavender, and yellow glow of the sunset. The beauty of the sunset and flowers growing all along the road were lost on Manaen. His friends sensed that he was deep in thought and just walked quietly with him.

CHAPTER 28

" Shalom, Manaen. Welcome to our home." Lazarus' pleasure at seeing his new friend was obvious. "I'm thankful that you could accept our invitation to the evening meal." He escorted Manaen into a gracious, well-appointed home. "We'll take our meal on the roof tonight, but first please allow the servants to wash the dust from your feet." Even as he talked, Lazarus was rubbing sweet scented oil on Manaen's head. "I'm so glad that Chuza and Joanna introduced us that day. I'm sorry that they couldn't join us here, but I'm glad that we could convince you to come alone."

"Thank you for inviting me. I've heard what a gracious host you are."

Manaen had always admired the style of houses in this area, with their outside stairs leading to a flat roof. There were openings to each floor and some of the houses had both outer and inner stairs. The roof served many purposes. Fruits and grains could be spread there to dry in the sun. People could gather to enjoy the cool evening breeze, eat the evening meal, or even sleep under the stars on their rush mats. People would talk and laugh together from one roof to the other. He also knew that these people came here at times to be alone and pray.

Manaen noticed that this home was meticulously cared for, as well as being very well-furnished. The female influence was evident. Manaen chuckled. *No wonder, with two sisters living under this roof to care for the home and the lucky Lazarus.* He wondered why the number of lamps and their placement was one of the first things he noticed about a home. Here the lamps were in every niche around the room and on every table. *I'll bet they are full of oil too.* As if on cue, a woman came into the room and began to light the lamps. She was as graceful as any of the women, simply dressed, but wearing beautiful jewelry. She seemed intent on getting the lamps lit for the evening and was ignoring the men.

Lazarus spoke.

"My sister, Martha." The woman nodded to him. "That is my sister, Mary, that you hear singing in the other room. She has been singing since she heard that Jesus is coming to join us."

"Oh, will he be here tonight?" Manaen asked as he tried to calm a sudden urgency to leave. He realized that his voice had betrayed him.

"No. You're safe." Lazarus laughed at Manaen's shocked expression. "I'm afraid your facial expression and tone of voice gave you away. He won't be here for several days, but

Mary's looking forward to his arrival with joyful anticipation, as we all are."

Manaen was glad that he didn't have to make eye contact as he was shown the way to the roof. He felt uncomfortable to have his emotions read so easily and was glad that the meal arrived almost as soon as they did. As they were eating, Manaen was again shocked to discover that the emotion churning in his belly was raw jealousy. He was jealous that Mary was so happy to know that Jesus was on his way to visit their home. *What is going on with me? Am I seriously thinking about Mary in those terms?* Manaen wondered.

As they ate, the conversation revolved around daily life at home, in the market, and at the temple. After the meal, everyone sat around the roof on reed mats and reclined on pillows. Manaen heard the conversation take an unexpected turn when those around him began talking about the exploits of Jesus. *Zeus and all his thunder, is there no rest from this man?* He realized that Mary was asking him a question.

"I'm sorry, Mary. What did you say?"

"I asked if you heard about Jesus feeding 4,000 people."

"I thought it was 5,000."

"No, that was in Bethsaida, right before he walked across the Sea of Galilee."

"Walked across the Sea…" Manaen was so shocked he couldn't speak.

"Yes! Have you not heard?"

"No. I'm afraid that I have been spared that story. However, I did witness the feeding of the 5,000 or more." He hoped he could keep his sarcasm from showing in his voice.

Mary's eyes were shining with a light like nothing Manaen had ever seen. Manaen felt the twist of jealousy again.

"Tell him, Lazarus. You tell it so well," she said softly.

"It was soon after John was beheaded, and Jesus needed a little time alone. I suppose he needed time to pray, so he dismissed the crowd, and told his disciples to take a boat to the other side. While they were rowing across, the wind kicked up, as it is so prone to do on the lake. The waves were battering the boat that was already a considerable distance from land when Peter looked up and thought he saw a ghost. All the disciples cried out because they all saw the same thing and they were scared out of their wits. But it was Jesus—walking toward them—on the water! As he neared the boat, he was quick to comfort them and said, 'Courage! It's me. Don't be afraid.'

"Then, suddenly bold, Peter replied, 'Master, if it's really you, call me to come to you on the water.'

"He said, 'Come ahead.'

"Peter got down out of the boat, walked on the water, and went toward Jesus." He stopped talking, and Manaen could only stare at the man, his mouth half-open.

"Finish the story, Lazarus. Please, I want to hear it again," Mary begged.

"Well, when Peter saw the waves churning beneath his feet, he lost his nerve and started to sink. He cried out, 'Master, save me!'

"Jesus didn't hesitate. He reached down and grabbed his hand. Then he said, 'Faint-heart what got into you?'" He paused, a gentle smile on his lips as he watched Manaen's reaction before he went on. "Can you imagine how strong

Jesus must be to be able to almost effortlessly lift Peter up like that. Peter is a big man! No, Peter is huge!"

Now it was Martha's turn to speak impatiently.

"Finish the story!"

Lazarus laughed and went on.

"The two of them climbed into the boat, and the wind died down. The disciples in the boat, having watched the whole thing, worshiped Jesus, saying 'This is it! You are God's Son for sure!'"

Mary's eyes were sparkling as she spoke.

"On return they pulled the boat ashore at Gennesaret. When the people got wind that he was back, they sent out word through the neighborhood and rounded up all the sick, who asked for permission to just touch the edge of his coat. And all who touched him were healed.[1] Can you imagine, Manaen? All they had to do was touch the hem of his cloak and they were healed!"

"No, I can't imagine such a thing."

"Well, it happened!"

"I didn't say it didn't. I just said I can't imagine it. But quite frankly, I must admit that I simply can't believe it!"

Mary looked hurt; there were tears in her eyes. Manaen wished he could take back his response, but knew he couldn't. He looked away.

"I understand," Lazarus replied. "It all seems too good to be true. But it is true! There was even a Canaanite woman who had a daughter suffering terribly from demon-possession. She came to him, crying out, 'Mercy, Master, Son of David! My daughter is cruelly afflicted by an evil spirit.'"

"A Canaanite woman?"

"Yes, someone we are not even supposed to ever speak to, but she kept on. Well, Jesus didn't answer her, so his disciples came to him and complained. They said that she was bothering them and asked him to please take care of her. They said that she was driving them crazy."

"What did he say?"

"He told them he had his hands full dealing with the lost sheep of Israel. She came back to Jesus and fell to her knees begging him to help her."

"Well, did he?"

"He said, 'It is not right to take the bread out of the children's mouths and throw it to dogs.' She was quick to reply, 'You're right, Master, but beggar dogs do get scraps from the masters' table.' Jesus gave in. 'Oh, woman, your faith is something else! What you want is what you get.'[2] Manaen, her daughter was healed instantly!"

"Lazarus, I admire your tenacity to convert me to what you obviously believe to be the truth, but it's just too much for me! I have seen the soothsayers do these same things. And not only that, but what proof do you have that these supposed miracles have any lasting effect?"

"I have myself. I'm not a strong man; never have been. That's one reason I've never taken a wife. My health has never been good, but when I am with him I'm renewed, invigorated! But, let's put the matter of his miracles aside for now and simply consider his teachings."

"Oh, yes, his teachings that go so against your old Talmudic law?" Manaen threw back his head and laughed in mockery. "Let me tell you, my friend, your priests are really appreciative of his teachings. And they certainly do appreciate his healing on your Sabbath!" Manaen's voice was heavy with scorn, and his handsome mouth was curled into an ugly smirk. "Let's see—I believe John's teachings cost him his head. I wonder what Jesus' teachings will cost him—his popularity with the Pharisees and Sadducees, I can assure you! But he'll be popular with the simpletons who believe. I'll grant you that!"

Lazarus' answer was gentle.

"Jesus isn't seeking popularity, Manaen. He is simply trying to teach us simpletons a better way to live and to help the people."

Once again Manaen regretted his words, but went on.

"Are you aware that Herod is looking for him already? He's heard the rumor that Jesus is John raised from the grave!" Shaking with anger, he continued. "Don't you see? Antipas is crazy enough as it is. He certainly doesn't need another itinerant preacher to push him over the edge and cause another bloodbath."

Mary spoke calmly, trying to cool the volatile situation.

"You called Herod the Tetrarch, 'Antipas.' Are you on such familiar terms with him?"

"I really prefer to call him 'the Fox' or 'the Snake,' but yes, I'm his cousin. I was raised with him, and we were constant friends and companions until he began to think of me as his lap dog and head of his ring of spies. I hope that I've been able to sever that tie, but with him, who knows. I live in dread of a summons to the palace!"

"I had heard that you're from Antioch. Have you considered going back there?"

"Nothing would make me happier. My family is there, and

I miss them, but for some reason, a reason that I certainly don't understand, I feel compelled to remain in this area. Perhaps it's a death wish." Manaen laughed a nervous laugh, hoping to ease the conversation into a more comfortable area.

"May I offer an observation?" Lazarus asked.

"Could I stop you?" Manaen snapped.

"Yes," Lazarus replied quietly.

"Then go ahead and offer your observation." Manaen felt like he was drowning. He just wanted this conversation to move into safer waters as quickly as possible.

"I just think that, whether you're aware of it or not, you are seeking the truth. Let me share some facts with you that Simon Peter, a personal friend, as you know, has shared with me. Simon, that hard-headed, boisterous fisherman, has come to the full realization that Jesus is the Son of God. He's even confessed it openly. Yes, I admit that Peter is impetuous, but, as I have stated, he is quite hard-headed and not easily persuaded." Lazarus paused, studying Manaen.

Manaen listened to the soothing rustling of the women in the background before he spoke.

"Go on. I know there is more."

"How much do you really want to hear? Would you believe me if I told you about a boy being healed of an evil spirit?" When Manaen shrugged his shoulders Lazarus went on. "The boy had been robbed of his speech. When the spirit seized him, it would throw him to the ground. He would foam at the mouth, gnash his teeth, and go stiff as a board. The boy's father had asked the disciples to drive the spirit out. They couldn't do it, so they brought the boy to Jesus. As soon as the spirit saw Jesus, it threw the boy into a seizure, causing him to writhe on the ground and foam at the mouth."

"I've seen such things, and even the soothsayers pretend to cast them out."

Undeterred, Lazarus went on.

"Jesus asked the boy's father, 'How long has this been going on?' and the boy's father replied, 'Ever since he was a little boy. Many times it pitches him into fire or water to do away with him. If you can do anything, do it. Have a heart and help us.' Jesus replied, 'If? There are no ifs among believers. Anything can happen.' No sooner were the words out of his mouth than the father cried, 'Then I believe. Help me with my doubts!'"

"What did Jesus do?" *Why did I ask that?* Manaen thought. *He'll think I'm interested!*

"When he saw that a crowd was forming fast, Jesus gave the vile spirit its marching orders. 'Dumb and deaf spirit, I command you—out of him and stay out.'"

"And?" Manaen asked. *I can't believe this. I did it again!*

"Well, screaming, and with much thrashing about, it left. The boy was pale as a corpse and people were saying, 'He's dead.' But Jesus, taking his hand, raised him. The boy stood up."[3]

"Again, I remind you that soothsayers can do such things."

"Can soothsayers make a mute boy talk like this one did? There was no hesitation in his voice. He started talking as if he had been doing it all of his life. Jesus also healed the sight of a beggar who had been blind from birth. Of course, I'm sure that the fact of the man's neighbors testifying that he was blind from birth wouldn't influence you; but it is true, nevertheless. In fact, it is such truth that the Pharisees threw the man out of the temple."

"Why did they do that?" *Maybe if I could stop asking questions he would hush!*

"Neither the man nor his parents would refute the healing. The Pharisees called them into the temple and tried to get them to say that Jesus is a sinner.

"The parents were so frightened of being thrown out of the temple that they told them to ask the son. The son replied that he didn't know if Jesus was a sinner or not. He said, 'I've told you already, and you didn't listen. Why do you want to hear it again? Do you want to become his disciples too?' They were furious and jumped all over him, claiming that he might be a disciple of Jesus and stating that they were disciples of Moses! You know how they posture and carry on. They told him that God spoke to Moses, but as for this fellow, they didn't even know where he came from."

Manaen threw back his head and laughed.

"I can see them now! All puffed up, strutting like peacocks in mating season. They must have been furious. What did the man say?"

"He replied that their attitude was amazing and that they didn't know where Jesus came from, but the fact was that he had opened his eyes. He went on to say that we know that God doesn't listen to sinners. He listens carefully to anyone who lives in reverence and does his will. That someone opening the eyes of a man born blind had never been heard of—ever. And that if this man didn't come from God, he wouldn't be able to do anything."

"How did they reply?"

Mary spoke up.

"They treated him like dirt. They accused him of being steeped in sin at birth and asked how he dared to lecture them. Then they threw him out!" She looked as indignant as she sounded, but embarrassed to have interrupted her brother.

Manaen smiled at her.

"Go on, I want to hear more."

"That is just the beginning of the story. When Jesus heard that the Pharisees had thrown the man out, he went and found him. He asked him if he believed in the Son of Man. The man replied, 'Point him out to me, sir, so that I can believe in him.' Jesus told him that he was looking right at him, and asked him if he didn't recognize his voice. Then the man replied, 'Master, I believe,' and he worshiped him. Jesus told him that he had come into this world to bring everything into the clear light of day, so that the blind will see; and those who see, will become blind. Some of the Pharisees who were with him heard him say this and asked him if they were blind too. Jesus said, 'If you were blind, you would not be guilty of sin; but now that you claim you can see, your guilt remains.' That stirred up a hornet's nest, let me tell you!"

"I can just imagine the reaction of that pious, self-righteous group. What do you think the outcome will be, Lazarus?" Manaen asked. *I already have a good idea what the outcome could be: death for Jesus. The temple priest won't put up with any opposition for very long. They will want to remove any threat to their grandiose positions or any that might affect their pockets. And if Jesus is teaching about sin it will certainly reflect poorly on that bunch!*

"Well, the Jews are divided. Many of them are saying that

he is demon-possessed and raving mad. Others are saying that these are not the sayings of a man possessed by a demon. They are also asking if a demon can open the eyes of the blind.[3] Only God knows how it will end, but I don't have a good feeling. The priests won't give up their control of the people without a fight."

"You are right about that. They want the … what is it you call it, the tithe?"

Now it was Lazarus' turn to laugh.

"Manaen, don't take me for a fool! You know all about the tithe. You've studied our sacred scriptures. Your reputation precedes you, my friend."

Manaen laughed and replied.

"So, I have been found out! Should I slink away in shame?" He felt his hostility slipping away.

"No, just accept our hospitality for a few days."

Before he realized what he was saying, he heard the words tumble out of his mouth.

"Thank you. I would like to become better acquainted with this man." *Now what made me say anything so stupid? I don't care about this fraud, not who he is or what he is doing! I just want to be left alone to go back to Antioch! And, for that matter, why haven't I already gone back to my home and family? My grandchildren are growing up without me. I miss them and Joachim and Lydia. I wonder if Nebo is still alive and how Patrobas and Dorcas are. Why don't I just leave this festering place and go home?* His mind would not be still as he followed Lazarus to his sleeping quarters.

CHAPTER 29

After a restless night, Manaen wasn't particularly pleased when Jesus and his disciples arrived the next day, two days early. He didn't feel like listening to the man's drivel. How stupid! How could he expect people to turn the other cheek and do good to their enemies? This man obviously didn't know Antipas!

Everyone was sitting around listening to Jesus. Manaen felt the jealousy return as Mary sat on the floor at Jesus' feet, gazing at him with rapt attention. Manaen could tell she didn't remember that he was in the room. Martha was busy, distracted by all the preparations that had to be made for their meal. Finally she came into the room and asked Jesus if he didn't care that Mary had left her to do all the work by herself. "Tell her to help me," she said.

"Martha, dear Martha," Jesus answered, "you're fussing

far too much getting yourself worked up over nothing. One thing only is essential, and Mary has chosen it—it's the main course, and won't be taken from her."[1]

Manaen wondered what he meant by his remarks, and after the meal he pulled Lazarus aside to ask him. The answer stunned him.

"Manaen, Mary is a worshiper. Martha is a worker. Both are needed, actually both are necessary, but Mary's time with Jesus will always be a part of her, something she will never forget, even after he is gone. She feels that it is better to sit at his feet and be fed by him than it is to feed him. Who is to say which one is right?"

"Not me, I am sure! What did you mean 'after he is gone'? Is he going somewhere?" Manaen hoped with everything in him that it was true!

"He predicted his death when he was in Caesarea Philippi. He has told his disciples that he must go to Jerusalem and suffer many things at the hands of the elders, chief priests, and teachers of the law. He said that he must be killed and on the third day, be raised to life. Of course Peter jumped to his defense and denied it. He said that it would never happen to him."

"That sounds like Peter—speak and then think. How did Jesus respond?"

"He rebuked him. He said, 'Get behind me, Satan! You are a stumbling block to me. You do not have in mind the things of God, but the things of men.'"

They had been leaning against the low wall of the rooftop. Now Manaen stood up abruptly.

"And how did that make Peter feel? It seems like a rather

insensitive remark to make to someone who was trying to defend him."

"Jesus doesn't need Peter's defense, Manaen. Rather, Peter needs to learn when to talk and when to keep still. He's too impetuous for his own good. That can be a dangerous thing in these days of unrest."

"I still think it was an unkind remark for Jesus to make to a man who has given up everything to follow him. Then again, that very fact proves how impetuous Peter is. Who's taking care of his family now?" Manaen had always felt that the followers of Jesus were foolish to leave their livelihood and just take off like they had. He wondered how they took care of their families and their other responsibilities. It all seemed like foolishness and foolhardiness to him.

"Since Jesus healed Peter's mother-in-law, they are all following Jesus. They still have their home in Capernaum, and the boats are still there if they ever decide to go back. I can't imagine him leaving Jesus to go back to fishing, though. Changing the subject, Manaen, why did you come to Bethany?"

"You don't waste any words, do you?" Manaen laughed at being found out so easily. "Why do you think I came?"

"To see Mary."

"Yes, that's partly true. She's very beautiful and pleasant to be around, but I also wanted to get to better acquainted with you and Martha."

"I know that you were at Simon the Pharisee's when she anointed Jesus with oil. Why do I sense there is more?"

"I have to confess that I have a strange compulsion to better understand this Jesus. Is he real or just another false prophet? That's why I stayed when you offered the invitation.

Originally I followed Jesus around, spying for Herod. As I said earlier, those days are over…I hope. The fact is, I find that I want to get to know him, but, then again, I don't."

"Why do you think that is, Manaen?"

"Well, for one thing, if I don't know anything about him, then I won't have anything to tell Herod if he asks. Yet, all I can say is that this man interests me more than anyone I have ever known. He teaches love and forgiveness, but he attacks the temple officials with a vengeance. I heard about him throwing the money changers and merchants out of the temple. That took some doing!"

"Oh, yes, he did that, and, as you say, with a vengeance! I can assure you that it was quite a sight. The money changers' coins were spilling and rolling everywhere. What a racket! The sheep that he had let loose were running around, bleating, and tripping people up. The dove cotes he was overturning were crashing to the ground, and the released doves were flying everywhere in the confusion."

"But what about the merchants and moneychangers?"

"Oh, he took a whip to the men, told them they had made his father's house a den of thieves, and ran them out of there. He does have a way of speaking his mind. But I've never heard him say an unkind word to anyone, except, of course, as in this case with the hypocrites."

"What about Peter?"

"He wasn't speaking to Peter. He was actually talking to Satan who was trying to get to him through Peter. Listen, you are a very well-educated man. Why do you have so much trouble understanding what I'm trying to say?"

"I think you've answered your own question. I am too well-educated, too much of a cynic."

"Listen to yourself, friend. A well-educated man doesn't close his mind to new ideas. Why are you not willing to at least explore the possibilities that are right before you?" Lazarus was getting a little frustrated with his friend.

"I've seen too much, too much of the hypocrites." Manaen shook his head in weariness. "I've seen too much of this world and what it has to offer."

"I'm not talking about this world, Manaen. Jesus' emphasis is on the world to come."

"Are you talking about a new power to overthrow Rome?"

"No, friend. I'm talking about eternal life—the hereafter. Were you there when Jesus talked to Nicodemus?"

"The Pharisee?"

"Yes, the same."

"No, I wasn't."

"Well, that's understandable, since he came to see Jesus at night. You see, Nicodemus is a member of the Jewish ruling council, and my guess is that he didn't want to be recognized talking to Jesus."

"Another hypocritical Pharisee!"

"I think he was just being cautious. Anyway, he called Jesus 'Rabbi' and told him that he knew he was a teacher who has come straight from God. Then he went on to say that no one could do all the God-pointing, God-revealing acts he was doing if God was not with him. Jesus replied to him, 'You're absolutely right. Take it from me: Unless a person is born from above, it's not possible to see what I'm pointing to—to God's kingdom."

"What did he mean by that?" Manaen asked, puzzled.

"That must be what Nicodemus wondered, because he asked, 'How can anyone be born who has already been born and grown up? You can't re-enter your mother's womb and be born again. What are you saying with this 'born-from-above' talk?'

"Jesus' answer was even more astounding. He replied, 'You're not listening. Let me say it again. Unless a person submits to this original creation—the *wind hovering over the water* creation, the invisible moving the visible, a baptism into a new life—it's not possible to enter God's kingdom. He went on to explain about flesh giving birth to flesh, but the spirit giving birth to spirit. He told Nicodemus that the wind blows wherever it pleases. You can hear its sound, but you don't know where it comes from or where it is going. He explained that is how it is with everyone born of the Spirit."

Manaen couldn't believe what he was hearing.

"What did he mean by that? How can that happen?"

"Manaen, that is exactly, word for word, what Nicodemus asked. Jesus talked to him about his being a teacher of Israel and that he should know these things. He said that he spoke of what he knew and testified to what he had seen, but still people do not accept the testimony. He also said that he had spoken of earthly things and Nicodemus didn't believe him, so how would he believe if Jesus spoke of heavenly things? He told Nicodemus that no one has ever gone up into the presence of God except the one who came down from that presence—the Son of Man."

"What did he mean?" Manaen was growing impatient with this talk.

"I'm not entirely sure, but then he talked about how

Moses lifted up the serpent in the desert so people could have something to see and believe. And that it was necessary for the Son of Man to be lifted up—and everyone who looks up to him, trusting and expectant, will gain a real life, eternal life. Then he said the most incredible thing of all, 'this is how much God loved the world: He gave his Son, his one and only Son. And this is why: so that no one need be destroyed; by believing in him, anyone can have a whole and lasting life.' Can you grasp that, Manaen?"

"No! Certainly not! You Jews have always worshiped Yahweh, the God of the law, justice, and judgment!"

"Jesus went on to say that God didn't go to all the trouble of sending his Son merely to point an accusing finger, telling the world how bad it was. He came to help, to put the world right again. Anyone who trusts in him is acquitted; anyone who refuses to trust him has long since been under the death sentence without knowing it ..."[2]

Manaen stood up abruptly. "Enough! It is time for me to go to bed for the night. I will see you in the morning." Manaen had listened to all he could stand about Jesus. *What is wrong with these people, and why didn't I return to Jerusalem? Now I'll have to try to find an excuse to leave without insulting my new friends. I simply can't listen to anymore about this man, Jesus!*

Lazarus shook his head sadly as his new friend rushed down the stairs to his room. He started to kneel.

"Well, I can see that I need to take time to pray. The Lord our God is one God ..."

CHAPTER 30

Aherd of sheep, driven by a Bedouin shepherd, blocked the road as Manaen tried to make his way back to Bethany from Jerusalem. He urged his horse through the sheep, trying not to scatter them. He had just gotten word that Lazarus had died. It had been quite a shock for him, since the man had seemed well enough when he was in his home less than a month ago.

He remembered when he had first seen Mary. She had washed Jesus's feet with tears, anointed them with perfume, and dried them with her hair. She had carried the fragrance of what she had done with her for months. Martha had complained about it petulantly, and Manaen had heard Mary say that the fragrance wouldn't wash off. He was glad it wouldn't. Now the sisters probably needed him, and he was hurrying to help them. Yes, they would need him in the coming days.

Women without a man to protect them were at the mercy of the world. He chuckled at the thought of someone thinking that Martha would be at their mercy. They would certainly be in for a surprise!

He urged his horse past the herd and through a field of large, white stones that looked like sheep lying on the dry ground. He wanted to rush, but he had to guide his horse carefully to prevent injury, and it was a frustrating pace.

Long before he arrived at the house he could hear the mourners and the wailing women. Their screams tore at his heart as he thought of what Mary and Martha must be feeling as they listened to these people who had been hired to mourn their brother. *What a barbaric practice! Why should mourners have to be hired for Lazarus? He was one of the finest men I have ever known. Everyone for miles around should be mourning and wailing with grief from this great loss. I feel as though I'm going to start wailing any minute now, and I haven't even know him for very long.*

He finally arrived and the first thing Mary said, even before saying hello, was that they had sent for Jesus several days earlier when Lazarus was sick.

Stifling his jealousy, he asked her if he had come yet.

"No! And if he had Lazarus wouldn't be dead now!" she said.

"Hush, Mary! You don't know that!" Martha said.

"Yes I do! He has healed so many people—do you really think that he would have let Lazarus die? Why didn't he come, Manaen? Why didn't he come?" She was sobbing uncontrollably.

As he reached out to comfort the grief-stricken woman, pulling her into his arms, Manaen thought.

Because he couldn't do anything to help, and he knew it! He didn't want to be proven to be a fraud!

"It takes time to travel, Mary. I'm sure he's on his way."

"You're here. How long did it take you to get here?"

"I was on horseback. Jesus travels by foot, and there are usually huge crowds of people following him. That slows his pace. You know that. You also know that the last time he came to this area they tried to kill him. Try to remember all of this, Mary."

"All I know is that my brother is dead, and Jesus let him die!" Mary was still sobbing as she jerked away from Manaen and ran out of the room toward the stairs leading to the roof.

Manaen started after her, but Martha caught his arm and stopped him.

"Let her go. She has to grieve. I am sorry that you witnessed this scene, though. Please forgive her bad manners."

"No apology is necessary, Martha. I understand her grief."

"She has been behaving badly, though. She is so angry with Jesus. She was saying earlier that if he could raise the dead son of the widow in Nain, then he could have helped our brother. I haven't seen her behave like this since Jesus forgave her sins."

Here we go again; her sins! Let's remind everyone about her past; never let her forget either! Didn't their precious Jesus forgive that woman who was taken in adultery and say that anyone who was without sin could throw the first rock at her? Her sins! How long am I going to have to listen to this? Controlling his emotions, he spoke. "Martha, Mary will be fine. Give her time. We'll just let her grieve in peace."

Three days later, Lazarus had been laid in a tomb, the stone rolled over the opening to seal it, and still the women wailed and cried. Manaen had just arrived to tell Mary and Martha that he was returning to Jerusalem, but would be back in a few days to help them put their affairs in order. Just then he saw a large crowd approaching the house. Then someone came in and said that Jesus was coming.

Manaen went with Martha to meet him, but Mary stayed at home.

"Lord," Martha said to Jesus, 'if you had been here, my brother would not have died. Even now, I know that whatever you ask God he will give you."

Jesus said, "Your brother will be raised up."

Martha said, "I know he will be raised up in the resurrection at the end of time."

"You don't have to wait for the end. I am, right now, Resurrection and Life. The one who believes in me, even though he or she dies, will live. And everyone who lives believing me does not ultimately die at all. Do you believe this?"

"Yes, Master," she told him, "All along I have believed that you are the Messiah, the Son of God, who comes into the world." After she said this, she went to her sister Mary and whispered in her ear. "The Teacher is here," she said, "and is asking for you."

The moment Mary heard this, she jumped up and ran out to meet him. Jesus hadn't entered the town, but was still at the place where Martha had met him. When her sympathizing Jewish friends saw Mary run off, they followed her, thinking she was on her way to the tomb to mourn there.

Mary came to where Jesus was waiting and fell at his feet, saying, "Master, if only you had been here, my brother would not have died."

When Jesus saw her sobbing and the Jews who had come along with her also sobbing, a deep anger welled up within him. He said, "Where did you put him?"

"Master, come and see," they said. Now Jesus wept.

Then the Jews said, "Look how deeply he loved him!"

Others among them said, "Well, if he loved him so much, why didn't he do something to keep him from dying? After all, he opened the eyes of a blind man."[1]

Manaen walked with Mary and Martha to the tomb. He had tried to hold Mary's shoulder, but Martha had gently removed his hand and shook her head. He realized that Martha was trying to protect the reputation of a woman who was alone now without a male's protection. *They will have my protection now, and I am going to have to protect them from this fraud, Jesus. They put entirely too much trust in that ridiculous man.* He realized that they had arrived at the tomb, and even though it was sealed, there was still the stench of death.

Then Jesus, the anger again welling up within him, arrived at the tomb. It was a simple cave in the hillside with a slab of stone laid against it. Jesus said, "Remove the stone."

"But, Lord," said Martha, "by this time there's a stench. He has been dead four days!" She looked as shocked as Manaen felt.

Then Jesus said, "Didn't I tell you that if you believed, you would see the glory of God?"

So, even though Manaen protested, they took away the stone. The stench of death swirled out to meet them. Then Jesus looked up and said, "Father, I'm grateful that you have listened to me. I know that you always do listen to me, but because of this crowd standing here, I've spoken so that they might believe that you sent me."

Then he shouted, "Lazarus, come out!" And he came out, a cadaver, wrapped from head to toe and with a kerchief over his face.

Jesus told them, "Unwrap him and let him loose."[2]

Manaen fell to his knees, all defenses stripped away. He could hear people screaming and shouting. He could hear Mary and Martha weeping with joy as they screamed, "Lazarus, Lazarus," and "thank you, Lord," over and over. But nothing mattered. He knew beyond a shadow of a doubt that he had just witnessed a man raised from the dead. He also knew that the son of Mary and Joseph bar Jacob, the baby in the stable, the boy in the temple, the cousin of John the Baptist, the man they called Rabboni, this man, Jesus, was the Son of God. He felt a hand on his shoulder and looked up into the loving eyes of Jesus. Then he was gone, and Manaen fell prostrate, weeping as joy flooded his soul like nothing he had ever known.

While he was on the ground his entire history with Jesus went through his mind like a beautiful dream. He realized that everything he had witnessed had been preparing him for this moment in time.

He didn't know how long he had been lying on the ground when he felt someone touch his shoulder again. This time he looked up into the eyes of Chuza, who spoke with concern.

"Are you well, my friend? Do you need help?"

Manaen heard himself laugh that same joyous laugh that he had heard so often from Jesus, Mary, and the others.

"It is well with my soul, Chuza. At last, it is well with my soul," he said.

Chuza reached down to help him up. The next thing Manaen knew, he was being hugged, and they were dancing around in a huddle of friends, including Lazarus, who were all laughing and crying at the same time.

"Where is he?" Manaen asked when he could catch his breath.

"Lazarus? He's right here."

"No, Jesus. I want to thank him."

"He's on his way back to Jerusalem. But, there's no need to thank Jesus. He knows your heart."

"Yes, I really believe he does. Tell me, Chuza, does every-one experience this euphoria when they realize they have been so wrong about something and finally accept the truth?"

"It seems that way. You weren't the only one to come to the truth today. Many of the Jews who were here to visit Mary and Martha saw what Jesus did and put their faith in him. But I must say that none of the others seem quite as changed as you do."

"I'm going to follow him. I'm going to Jerusalem."

CHAPTER 31

Manaen learned a great deal in the days he spent traveling with Jesus and his followers. He saw ten lepers healed as they walked away after Jesus had finished praying for them. He wondered why only one returned to thank Jesus for his healing. Jesus remarked about that too with sadness in his eyes.

It was a joy to watch this simple carpenter. While he was speaking, the wind blew in from the desert or the Sea of Galilee tugging at his robe or tossing his hair, almost as if it were caressing him. The sun appeared to sparkle brighter on the Sea of Galilee when Jesus stood on its shore teaching the people or simply enjoying being with them. His laughter, which always seemed to hover around him, was robust. It spilled out on everyone nearby, as if inviting them to partake of his joy and zest for life. He was in every sense a man's man, but he showed a great tenderness and respect toward women.

He had a happy, loving smile on his face as he taught the people and fellowshipped with them. His teachings were filled with everyday examples that the people could easily understand, and humor was often a part of it. His teaching about trying to get a small splinter out of your neighbor's eye when you had a beam in your own that would hold up a house brought gales of laughter from the crowd. But they understood what he was saying: fix your own life before you try to correct your friend's. It was obvious that he was enjoying every minute he spent with the people as he laughed, sang, and danced with them, infusing his own joy into their lives. Manaen had never seen or experienced anything like it. He'd never known anyone so happy and full of life.

Jesus was teaching about the coming of the kingdom of God when one of the Pharisees asked him when it would come. He explained that the kingdom of God doesn't come with your careful observation, nor will people say, "Here it is," or "there it is," because the kingdom of God is within the individual.

Later he explained this to his disciples. He told them that the days are coming when they will be desperately homesick for just a glimpse of one of the days of the Son of Man, days spent with him, and they won't see a thing. And men will tell them to "Look over there!" or, "Look here!" But they weren't to fall for any of that nonsense. He said that the arrival of the Son of Man is not something people will go out to see. He will simply come.

"You know how the whole sky lights up from a single flash of lightning? That's how it will be in the Day of the Son of Man. But first it's necessary that he suffer many things and be turned down by the people of today," he said.

He went on to say that the time of the Son of Man will be just like the time of Noah—everyone carrying on as usual, having a good time right up to the day Noah boarded the ship. They suspected nothing until the flood hit and swept everything away.

The people there listened intently, struggling to grasp all that he was saying. It was difficult for them to understand, and Jesus knew it.

He explained that it was the same in the time of Lot—the people carrying on, having a good time, business as usual right up to the day Lot walked out of Sodom, and a firestorm swept down and burned everything to a crisp. That's how it will be—sudden, total—when the Son of Man is revealed.

"When the Day arrives and you're out working in the yard, don't run into the house to get anything. And if you're out in the field don't go back and get your coat. Remember what happened to Lot's wife! If you grasp and cling to life on your terms, you'll lose it, but if you let that life go, you'll get life on God's terms.

"On that Day, two men will be in the same boat fishing—one taken, the other left. Two women will be working in the same kitchen—one taken, the other left."[1]

Manaen didn't understand it all, but he made a mental note to talk to Chuza and Joanna about it. He did understand the story Jesus told about the widow who kept pleading with the unrighteous judge until he granted her request.

Manaen watched Jesus and listened intently as the days passed, trying to learn as much as he could about the new way of life that Jesus taught. Things that had once seemed so foolish now seemed reasonable. He began to have a fresh understanding and appreciation of the people around him and realized that he was beginning to look for ways to help them and ways to use his wealth for good.

One day he saw people bringing babies to Jesus, hoping he would touch them. When the disciples saw this, they tried to shoo them off. But Jesus called the children back to him and said, "Let these children alone. Don't get between them and me. These children are the kingdom's pride and joy. Mark this: Unless you accept God's kingdom in the simplicity of a child, you will never get in."[2]

Now I understand! When I saw Jesus raise Lazarus from the dead, I put aside all of my inhibitions and became like one of these little children. I stopped trying to reason everything out and came to simple acceptance just like a child.

Manaen heard someone laughing and looked up to see Jesus tickling the children, hugging them, and playing with them. He joined in the laughter and felt like he had been given the gift of joy. He remembered that Jesus had said that his joy would be their joy and that it would be full. *This is what he was talking about: total and complete joy in the everyday things of life. He was talking about living a life filled with joy regardless of the circumstances. We can all be like him—filled with joy all the time and spreading it to everyone around us. Help me to be like this man, Father. Help me bring this joy to other people like he does.*

The group accompanying Jesus continued to make its way to Jerusalem, and they came to Jericho. As Jesus and his disciples, together with a large crowd, were leaving the city, a blind man, Bartimaeus, the son of Timaeus, was sitting by the road begging. When he heard that it was Jesus of Nazareth, he began to shout, "Jesus, Son of David, have mercy on me! Have mercy on me!" It seemed that all thought of pride and personal dignity was forgotten as the man realized that help was near.

People rebuked him and told him to be quiet, not to bother the Master, but he shouted that much louder, "Son of David, Mercy, have mercy on me!"

Jesus stopped and told the people to bring him over.

So they called to the blind man, "Cheer up! On your feet! He is calling you." Throwing his cloak aside, he jumped to his feet and came to Jesus rushing blindly, stumbling over everyone and everything in his path in his determination.

"What do you want from me?" Jesus asked him when he fell again at his feet.

The blind man said, "Master, I want to see again."

Jesus said, "Go ahead—see again. Your faith has saved and healed you." The healing was instant. [3]

Manaen watched Bartimaeus when he received his sight. The man looked at his hands in astonishment, looked around him at the people in amazement, and then looked straight at Jesus. He knew him instantly. With a loud shout of joy, he ran and threw himself into Jesus' arms, and they went tumbling to the ground. They laughed and rolled around together like children as the dust swirled up around them.

Manaen wanted to join them in their joyous exhibit, so he grabbed Chuza and swung him around and around while they laughed and shouted praise. They too were like young boys as they danced and celebrated. Joanna and both of the

Marys were laughing and clapping their hands. The joy and laughter spread through the crowd like a wave of glory until everyone was clapping and shouting, all dignity forgotten, like happy children, and just like Jesus. The Pharisees who were watching the crowd didn't join the happy celebration. They reminded Manaen of black carrion birds hovering over a dying man—ever watching and ever waiting, ready to pounce when the time was right.

Then Herod pounced! A servant came to tell Manaen that Herod had sent guards to his home demanding that he come to the palace in Jerusalem. The servant heard them at the door and left out the back entrance to come warn Manaen.

"Are you sure that it was palace guards and not just a messenger?"

"No, I'm sure that it was guards, and they were fully armed."

"Go back and act as if nothing has happened. If they come back, say you don't know where I am, which is true. We are always moving around. Just don't tell anyone that you have seen me. I can't stay with these people, though. It would put them in too much jeopardy."

"Where will you go? What will you do?"

"I don't know yet. I may have to make a quick retreat to Antioch, but I won't leave without you. I'll get word to you as soon as I can."

After the servant left, Manaen went to find Chuza and found him with a group of the men. He pulled Chuza to the side and told him what had happened.

"I have to leave now," Manaen explained.

"Why do you say that?"

"My life is in jeopardy. I could be arrested and killed any

time now, and my presence here would put everyone in jeopardy. If Herod is looking for me the last thing I want to do is put Jesus and his followers in peril. You know as well as I do that Herod is as mad as his father was. You have worked for both men. Which one do you think is worse?"

"Herod the son; his weaknesses makes him more dangerous!"

"My point exactly! Now I need get away from here as quickly as possible." He turned to go and then stopped and turned back to Chuza. "No! I will not run in fear from this coward! He wants to see me, so see me he will! The only way to deal with this is to trust God and confront Antipas! Please have our people praying for me. This is going to be an ordeal. I may be arrested!"

"I'm going with you, but not until we spend some time in prayer."

"No, Chuza. We could be killed and you have Joanna to think about. I can't let you risk your life as well."

"Why did you say that Chuza has me to think about?" Joanna had heard the last of the conversation when she walked up. "What is happening?"

Chuza explained the situation to her as gently as possible.

"Let's pray," was her only comment.

After an hour of intense prayer it was agreed that Chuza should go with Manaen, and the two men set off knowing that the prayers of the people would surround them. When they arrived at the palace, they were thankful they weren't arrested, but they had to wait for two days before seeing Herod. The uncertainty of their situation kept them on edge and they prayed constantly. Chuza went about his role as Herod's steward as if everything was normal. Manaen accompanied him when he could, always with his sword and a knife at hand, hoping to protect him if he needed it.

Finally the call came, and they were escorted into the lavish throne room. Herod was in one of his foul moods.

"Where have you been?" he roared.

"Traveling. Doing just what you told me to do," Manaen answered quietly.

"If you've been following Jesus as I commanded, why you have not reported back to me?" The beady eyes bored into Manaen's eyes from a face contorted with evil vengeance.

"I've been following him, and there was nothing to report. If I had come back here I could have missed something you might need to know." Manaen was praying he could control his tongue.

"That's not what I have heard. Do you think I am a fool? I've been told by reputable sources that you are one of his followers too! What do you have to say for yourself? And you, Chuza, are you one of the 'believers' now?" His tone was full of contempt, and the evil eyes had been reduced to slits as his anger intensified.

"Leave Chuza out of this." Realizing what he had said, he quickly added, "Please. I told you that I would tell you. You wanted to know if you have anything to fear from Jesus, and I am telling you that you don't. Have I ever lied to you, Antipas? Sorry, I mean Herod. I have always been honest with you. That hasn't changed. I have been watching him very carefully indeed, and he is absolutely no threat to you or anyone else for that matter."

"I've been told that this rabble-rouser is plotting to overthrow Rome! As if he could!" This was accompanied by a quick roar of nervous, maniacal laughter.

"There is absolutely no truth to that!" Manaen fought to control his emotions. *Stay calm, and you can stay in control. You know that. Lose your temper and you could quite literally lose your head.* "In fact he always obeys the law and encourages others to do the same thing. Does that sound like a rabble-rouser? No, in fact quite the opposite; he teaches peaceful coexistence, not war. How can that be a plot to overthrow Rome?"

"May I speak?" Chuza knew their lives were in peril, but he refused to allow his fear to show.

The evil eyes slowly turned on him now as if Herod had forgotten he was in the room. Then his eyes squinted, and muscles under his left eye began to twitch, but Herod nodded.

"The only plotting being done is by the temple rulers. They are the ones you need to be watching. They hate Rome and everyone connected with it, including you. They would slit your throat if they thought they could get by with it."

Herod's face turned flame red then white. "Are you saying those pious peacocks are plotting against me?"

"No, they fear you too much for that, but they are plotting against Jesus. They spread vicious lies about him, lies with no foundation to support them. As your steward I'm asking you to consider carefully what you believe."

"Don't you dare to lecture me! I'll believe what I choose to believe and when I choose to believe it!"

"Herod, consider our long history together. Again I ask you, have I ever lied to you or given you false information?" Manaen asked.

"You wouldn't dare," Herod answered haughtily.

"Then will you trust me to return to the assignment you gave me? I'll continue watching Jesus and the people following him. And I promise you that if I see or hear of any threat against you or Rome I will report it to you immediately." Manaen could read the emotions in Herod's evil eyes as he thought about what Manaen had said. *Father, please help us here. He's ready to take off our heads.* His prayer was answered so quickly it was almost confusing. The evil expression on Herod's face changed before his eyes, replaced by an expression that was almost lucid.

"Very well. I choose to release you for now, but know this, cousin; if you betray me I'll have your head, just like I had John's! Don't ever forget that. We're not boys playing by the Mare Nostrum now. I am the king and you will obey me! Do you understand?"

"Yes, I understand very well, and I have no plan to betray you." Manaen was amazed that he could answer so humbly.

"Get out of here! You bore me with your sniveling!" He roared with laughter. "However, I do enjoy watching you beg for your lives!" He laughed again, and then with an arrogant toss of his oily black curls, he turned his back on the two men and began to examine his fingernails as he chuckled wickedly.

The two men were quiet as they left the throne room and made their way out of the palace and to the market where they would be hidden by the crowds of merchants and shoppers. Then Chuza stopped and leaned against a building for support.

"Well, that went well! Are your knees shaking as badly as mine?" he asked.

"Probably, and the only reason it went so well is that God was right there with us. At one point I thought we would be arrested, and we still might. There is no telling where his capricious imagination will take him next. We need to be on our guard at all times. The others too! Should we warn Jesus?"

"He knows. Nothing surprises him."

"True."

The two made their way back to the crowd of people following Jesus, knowing the danger they were in.

Six days before the Passover, Jesus arrived at Bethany where Lazarus and his sisters lived, and a dinner was given in Jesus' honor. Martha served while Lazarus was among those reclining at the table with Jesus. Mary came in with a jar of pure nard, an expensive, highly fragrant perfume. She poured it on Jesus' feet and wiped his feet with her hair. The fragrance of the perfume filled the house and spilled out to the street.

Judas Iscariot, one of the disciples, objected. "Why wasn't this perfume sold and the money given to the poor? It was worth a year's wages."

The poor indeed! You just want the money for yourself! Manaen wanted to laugh out loud. He knew that Judas was a thief. Judas was keeper of the money bag, and he had seen Judas help himself to what was put into it. Jesus' reply kept him from saying anything.

Jesus said, "Let her alone. She's anticipating and honoring the day of my burial. You always have the poor with you. You don't always have me."

A large crowd of Jews had found out that Jesus was there and came out. They came not only because of him but also to see Lazarus who had been raised from the dead. So the high priests plotted to kill Lazarus because so many of the Jews were going over and believing in Jesus on account of him.[4]

Nicodemus had gotten word of the scheme to Cleopas, one of their fellow followers of Jesus, and Cleopas had told Chuza. Now Chuza and Manaen were trying to think of a way to save both Jesus and Lazarus. Chuza finally spoke up.

"The crowd is the only protection the two of them have."

"I think you're right, Chuza; there's safety in numbers. I don't think we have to worry too much about Lazarus, but how do we keep Jesus from going off alone to pray? He slips away at every opportunity."

"Mary and Martha keep a sharp eye on Lazarus. And they stay as close to Jesus as possible, too, but we can't warn them."

"Why not?"

"They are women, Manaen! Don't tell me that you haven't noticed!"

"These women are strong and smart. They can help us be on guard. I would trust any one of them with my life. Not only that, but if they are aware of what is going on they can help us pray about the situation."

"You are right about that! They are strong in spirit, and we definitely need their prayers. You go find Mary and Martha. I'll tell Joanna, and then they can spread the word among the other women to be on the lookout and pray."

It wasn't hard to find Mary and Martha. Manaen just followed his nose. The pleasant fragrance of the Nard that Mary had poured on Jesus feet was still strong in her hair. He drew the women aside and told them about the plot.

Neither woman panicked. They simply looked at him with wide eyes for a moment.

"We will pray and tell the other women to be praying too," Martha said.

"Isn't a crowd the best protection we can have?" Mary asked.

Manaen looked at her in amazement.

"Chuza and I were just saying the same thing."

"Then we need to keep the crowd growing. Do the disciples know about this?"

"Yes. They know and understand the situation very well," Chuza replied as he rejoined them.

"Then they'll stay close to Jesus. We'll stay close to Lazarus. There is something else that just came to mind that we can do. Manaen, tell everyone to keep talking about how Jesus raised Lazarus from the dead. The more they spread the word, the more people will come to learn about Jesus and Lazarus. Some will come just to see them out of curiosity, but at least it will mean more people around them."

Manaen had to laugh, and the spirited Mary looked as if she might hit him.

"No, I'm not laughing at your idea, Mary." He threw up his hands in defense, as if he expected her to hit him. "I am just enjoying your quick thinking. I just told Chuza what smart, strong women you are, and you have just proved me right!"

Mary laughed with him, but Martha, always the practical one, spoke.

"We need to get busy and start spreading the word to draw the crowds."

Manaen went to find Jesus and the disciples who were on their way back to Jerusalem. It didn't take long to catch up to the crowd and talk to the disciples. Rather than go back to Bethany, he decided to go on to Jerusalem with them.

CHAPTER 32

The next day, as they approached Jerusalem and came to Bethpage at the Mount Olivet, Jesus said for two of his disciples to go the village ahead. He told them that just as they entered it, they would find a colt tied there, which no one has ever ridden. He instructed, "Untie it and bring it here. If anyone asks, 'What are you doing?' say, 'The Master needs him, and will return him right away.'"[1]

When the men got there they found everything just as Jesus said they would. When they brought the colt to Jesus and threw their cloaks over it, he sat on it.

Manaen was amazed that a wild colt, one that had never been ridden, would allow a man to get on its back. The colt didn't even attempt to buck him off or try to get away. It just walked where Jesus directed. Then his amazement vanished as he remembered who Jesus really was. *Why, even a wild*

colt recognized the Son of God immediately and it took me years!
That wild colt is smarter than I was!

The great crowd that had come for the Feast of the Passover heard that Jesus was on his way to Jerusalem. They took palm branches and went out to meet him, shouting, "Hosanna! Blessed is he who comes in God's name! Blessed the coming kingdom of our father David! Hosanna in highest heaven!"

Some of the Pharisees in the crowd said to Jesus, "Teacher, rebuke your disciples!"

"I tell you," he replied, "If they keep quiet, the stones will cry out." [2]

Now the crowd that was with Jesus when he called Lazarus from the tomb and raised him from the dead continued to spread the word that he was entering the city. Many people, simply because they had heard that he had given this miraculous sign, went out to meet him. So the Pharisees said to one another, "See, this is getting us nowhere. Look how the whole world has gone after him!"

As Jesus approached Jerusalem and saw the city, he wept over it and said, "If you had only recognized this day and everything that was good for you. But now it is too late. In the days ahead your enemies are going to bring up their heavy artillery and surround you, pressing in from every side. They'll smash you and your babies on the pavement. Not one stone will be left intact. All this because you didn't recognize and welcome God's personal visit."

Then he went into the temple area and began driving out those who had set up stalls and were selling merchandise. "It is written," he said to them, "'My house will be a house of prayer' but you have made it 'a den of robbers.'" [3]

Manaen saw the godly, blazing anger in Jesus as he drove out the ungodly, greedy men who were destroying the true spiritual purpose of the temple. He also watched the ungodly, blazing anger in the hypocrites who called themselves priests of God. They profited from this business venture with the money changers and those who sold sacrificial doves and wares in the temple courtyard; Jesus was cutting into their profits. He had to go! Manaen could sense trouble coming and hoped to find a way to avoid it. But Jesus wasn't helping. He would not keep out of the public eye.

The blind and the lame came to him at the temple, and he healed them. But when the chief priests and the teachers of the law saw the wonderful things he did and the children in the temple area shouting, "Hosanna to the Son of David," they were indignant.

"Do you hear what these children are saying?" they asked Jesus.

"Yes," replied Jesus, "I hear them, and haven't you read, 'From the mouths of children and babies I'll furnish a place of praise'?"[4] His answer only made his enemies angrier and more determined to kill him.

The next morning Manaen was with Jesus and his followers as they were walking along. They saw a fig tree that Jesus had cursed the day before because it didn't have fruit on it. Now it was only a day later and it was withered and just a dry stick. Peter remembered what had happened the day before and said, "Rabbi, look! The fig tree you cursed has shriveled up!"

Jesus was matter-of-fact: "Embrace this God-life. Really embrace it, and nothing will be too much for you. This mountain, for instance: Just say, 'Go jump in the lake'—no shuffling or shilly-shallying—and it's as good as done. That's why I urge you to pray for absolutely everything, ranging from small to large. Include everything as you embrace this God-life, and you'll get God's everything. And when you assume the posture of prayer, remember that it's not all *asking*. If you have anything against someone, *forgive*—only then will your Heavenly Father be inclined to also wipe your slate clean of sins."[5]

When Manaen heard Jesus say this, he felt like he had been stabbed in the heart. Chuza, who had joined him, saw his face turn white. He took him aside.

"What is it, Manaen? You are as pale as a ghost!"

Manaen couldn't answer. He tried to turn away, but Joanna caught his arm.

"Talk to us," she said.

"I just realized that I have never forgiven my father. I haven't forgiven Herod or Antipas either. How can my sins be forgiven?"

"Because you just realized that you need to forgive them. Forgive them now, and all will be forgiven, as well as forgotten." Joanna's voice was gentle and kind.

"Is it really that simple?"

"There you go again, Manaen. Don't try to reason it out. Just do what Jesus said and forgive them. If you hold on to the anger now it will be like leprosy spreading through your soul. And remember, you won't be hurting any one of those three. You will only hurt yourself."

"Chuza, how did you ever win the heart of such a smart woman?"

"I caught her in a weak moment. But don't try to change the subject."

"Oh, I'm not! I forgave them while she was explaining. I know that I'm going to need forgiveness every day, so I'm going to do my best to keep my forgiveness account current with our Heavenly Father." Then great whoops of laughter seemed to explode from his belly. He laughed until tears were streaming down his face.

"What is so funny, Manaen? People are starting to stare."

When he could quiet his laughter, he spoke.

"I just feel like a great weight has been lifted from my shoulders. I feel totally, completely free for the first time in my life." He laughed again. "It is wonderful!" he shouted, "and I don't care who knows it! I want everyone to feel as free as I do!"

Manaen looked up, and Jesus was looking at him with the same expression of deep knowing that he had when he was just a young boy in the temple. Then Jesus smiled at him with his wonderful smile that seemed to light up the whole world. *Oh, yes, it is well with my soul!* Manaen thought.

Manaen realized that he was totally free; totally, completely free of all encumbrances. He didn't need anything except the love and acceptance of this man, Jesus.

CHAPTER 33

Every day Jesus took his place and taught at the temple. The chief priests, the teachers of the law, and the leaders among the people were trying to kill him. The people who were traveling with Jesus tried to convince him to stay out of the way of harm, but he insisted that he only had a short time left to teach the people. Manaen kept as close to him as he could while he watched and listened, his sword by his side. He wanted to learn everything he could about Jesus's teachings, but he also wanted to protect him if he should need to.

The Pharisees went out and laid plans to trap Jesus in his words. They sent their disciples to him along with the Herodians.

Manaen knew what they were doing, and it was difficult for him to control his anger. There were times when he could have gladly let them taste his sword. The only thing keeping him in check was the knowledge that Jesus could be hurt.

He had to be still and listen, ever on guard. He knew that he would defend Jesus if the opportunity came.

"Teacher," they said, "we know you have integrity, teach the ways of God accurately, are indifferent to popular opinion, and don't pander to your students. You aren't swayed by men, because you pay no attention to who they are. So tell us honestly: Is it right to pay taxes to Caesar or not?"

Jesus knew they were up to no good. He said, "Why are you playing these games with me? Why are you trying to trap me? Do you have a coin? Let me see it." They handed him a silver piece.

"This engraving—who does it look like? And whose name is on it?"

They said, "Caesar."

"Then give Caesar what is his, and give God what is his."

The Pharisees were speechless. They went off shaking their heads.[1]

Manaen couldn't help laughing out loud at their chagrin. "Chuza, he put them in their place that time! Have you ever seen people try so hard to keep their superior expressions in place? That was quite a sight. And to think I thought I had to defend him!"

"Jesus can certainly put them in their place intellectually."

"Yes, but I'm still keeping my sword close and ready for my sake as well as his. I never know when Herod will strike!"

The peace and quiet didn't last long. The Sadducees, who say there is no resurrection, came right on their heels. They asked, "Teacher, Moses said that if a man dies childless, his brother is obligated to marry his widow and get her with child. Here's a case where there were seven brothers. The first brother married and died, leaving no child, and his wife passed to his brother. The second brother also left her childless, then the third—and on and on all seven. Eventually the wife died. Now here's our question: At the resurrection, whose wife is she? She was a wife to each of them."

Jesus answered, "You are off base on two counts: You don't know the scriptures, and you don't know how God works. At the resurrection we're beyond marriage. As with the angels, all our ecstasies and intimacies then will be with God. And regarding your speculation on whether the dead are raised or not—don't you read your Bibles? The grammar is clear: God says, 'I am—not was—the God of Abraham, the God of Isaac, and the God of Jacob.' The living God defines himself not as the God of dead men, but of the living."

When the Pharisees heard that Jesus had gotten the best of the Sadducees they got together. One of them who was an expert in the law tested him with a question, "Teacher, which commandment in God's Law is the most important?"

Jesus replied, "'Love the Lord your God will all your passion and prayer and intelligence. This is the most important, and first on the list. But there is a second to set alongside it: 'Love others as well as you love yourself.' These two commands are pegs; everything in God's Law and the Prophets hangs from them."[2]

Manaen thought about what Jesus had just said and realized what he meant. *Yes, only if you truly love yourself can you truly love your neighbors. Love is something that comes from within so it has to start with your own self. Then if you love your neighbors you will never do anything to harm them. Yes, I understand what he means. That's incredible; that takes care of all of the laws. It's all about love.* Manaen was amazed at the simplicity of what Jesus was teaching. *No wonder it is so hard to grasp. The simplicity of his teaching is what trips us up and keeps us from the truth.*

Manaen walked quietly through the crowd, searching for any sign of trouble. He didn't trust the Pharisees and Sadducees or the rabble-rousers they had brought with them. He had been around people like them enough to recognize politics when they came into play. And he knew the trouble that could follow when people sought political control. He went back to stand with Chuza and Joanna.

"Chuza, Jesus is walking into a trap." Manaen was watching the crowd and saw the growing unrest.

"He knows what he's doing. Don't worry, he can handle it. Just watch."

As the Pharisees were regrouping, Jesus caught them off-balance with his own test question: "What do you think about the Christ? Whose son is he?"

They said, "David's son."

Jesus replied, "Well, if the Christ is David's son, how do you explain that David, under inspiration, named Christ his 'Master'? God said to my Master, 'Sit here at my right hand until I make your enemies your footstool.' Now if David calls him 'Master,' how can he at the same time be his son?"

That stumped them, literalists that they were. Unwilling to risk losing face again in one of these public verbal exchanges, they quit asking questions for good.

Now Jesus turned to address his disciples, along with the crowd that had gathered with them. "The religion scholars and Pharisees are competent teachers in God's law. You won't go wrong in following their teachings on Moses. But be careful about following them. They talk a good line, but they don't live it. They don't take it into their hearts and live it out in their behavior. It's all spit-and-polish veneer.

"Instead of giving you God's Law as food and drink by which you can banquet on God, they package it in bundles of rules, loading you down like pack animals. They seem to take pleasure in watching you stagger under these loads, and wouldn't think of lifting a finger to help. Their lives are perpetual fashion shows, embroidered prayer shawls one day and flowery prayers the next. They love to sit at the head table at church dinners, basking in the most prominent positions, preening in the radiance of public flattery…"

Manaen lost track of Jesus's voice as he thought about what he was saying. Then he understood—*The Pharisees and Sadducees are nothing more than strutting bullies! They are just showing off to make themselves look and feel big. How small they look!* He watched them and could see the anger growing in their eyes. *Thank God they aren't as powerful and important as they think they are.*

"Do you want to stand out? Then step down. Be a servant. If you puff yourself up, you'll get the wind knocked out of you. But if you're content to simply be yourself, your life will count for plenty."[3]

Manaen continued to scan the crowd for trouble as he thought about what Jesus was saying. *That is certainly a new concept. Or at least, one I'm not familiar with. I'm not surprised to hear him saying this, though. That is how I have always seen Jesus live his life; quietly and honorable, but with no thought of making himself look good. Well the Magi were right when...* He realized that someone was speaking to him quietly.

"I'm sorry, Chuza. What did you say?" he replied.

Chuza took Joanna's arm and lead them away from the crowd before he spoke. "I just asked why you seemed so far away?"

"Sorry, I was just remembering when Jesus was born."

"When he was born?"

"Yes. When the Magi came from the East they said that he would be a king, but unlike any earthly king. I couldn't understand it at the time, but it's perfectly clear to me now."

"I wish the zealots could understand it!" Chuza replied with a disgusted snort. "They are still trying to get him to overthrow Rome."

"Imagine that!" Manaen had to laugh at the irony.

"My point exactly! Can you imagine that? And one or two of his inner circle are some of the worst! I've even heard some of them arguing about who was going to be the greatest in his kingdom!"

"Do you ever wonder if they're really listening to what he is saying? But, like he says, we aren't to judge each other. I just hope that I understand it all so that I can share it with my family and friends if I ever get to return to Antioch."

"You do and you can understand and share this message. I had forgotten that you will leave us one day, and I don't appreciate being reminded! I hope you are not planning a trip any time soon. We haven't known each other for a long time, but now you seem closer to me than a brother."

Manaen's emotions were almost too much to bear as he spoke.

"Thank you for your kind words. You and Joanna seem like

family to me too. And, no, as long as you are in this area I'll stay here, if God is willing. I certainly wouldn't want to leave Joanna!" The good friends laughed together and embraced.

"You don't fool me, Manaen. It's Jesus you don't want to leave!"

"I hope I don't ever have to, Chuza!" They had returned to the crowd and could hear his angry words. "He's really angry at the Pharisees now."

Jesus was almost shouting in his indignation, "I've had it with you! You're hopeless, you religious scholars, you Pharisees! Frauds! Your lives are roadblocks to God's kingdom. You refuse to enter, and won't let anyone else in either.

"You're hopeless, you religious scholars and Pharisees! Frauds! You go halfway around the world to make a convert, but once you get him, you make him into a replica of yourselves, double-damned."

"Chuza," Joanna whispered, "they will have him killed! Is there no way that we can stop him?"

"Joanna," Chuza replied kindly, "Jesus knows what he is doing."

"You're hopeless, you religious scholars and Pharisees! Frauds!" Jesus said. "You keep meticulous account books, tithing on every denarius you get, but on the meat of God's Law things like fairness and compassion and commitment—the absolute basics!—you carelessly take it or leave it. Basic bookkeeping is commendable, but the basics are required. Do you have any idea how silly you look, writing a life story that's wrong from start to finish, nitpicking over jots and tittles?

"You're hopeless, you religious scholars and Pharisees! Frauds! You burnish the surface of your cups and bowls so they sparkle in the sun, while the insides are maggoty with your greed and gluttony. Stupid Pharisee! Scour the insides, and then the gleaming surface will mean something."[4]

Manaen was astonished when Jesus went on to call the Pharisees such vile names, saying that they were like whitewashed tombs—beautiful on the outside, but full of dead men's bones and everything unclean. *He really made his case clear when he said that they appear to be righteous on the outside, but on the inside they were full of hypocrisy and wickedness. I have to agree with Joanna, especially after hearing Jesus call the Pharisees snakes and a brood of vipers, asking how they would escape being condemned to hell. I wonder how Jesus can avoid being killed. I fear he has just signed his own death warrant.*

Jesus's tone changed, and his voice sounded like a funeral lament as he said, "Jerusalem! Jerusalem! Murderer of prophets! Killer of the ones who brought you God's news! How often I've longed to embrace your children, the way a hen gathers her chicks under her wings, and you wouldn't let me. And now you're so desolate, nothing but a ghost town. What is there left to say? Only this: I'm out of here soon. The next time you see me you'll say, 'Oh, God has blessed him! He's come, bringing God's rule!'"[5] With those stinging words, Jesus left the temple.

Later that day, Manaen accompanied the group when Jesus returned to the temple. Jesus sat down opposite the place where the offerings were put and watched the crowd putting their money into the temple treasury. Many rich people threw in large amounts. But a poor widow came and put in two very small copper coins, worth only a fraction of a penny.

Jesus called his disciples to him and told them that the

poor widow had put more into the treasury than all the others. They gave out of their wealth, while she, a woman of poverty, put in everything—all she had to live on.[6]

"Chuza," Manaen asked when they had left the temple, "Has the Master always been so hard on the priests? Even this afternoon it seemed that he was contrasting the giving of the Pharisees and Sadducees with the giving of the little widow woman. Wasn't he saying that their gift was less valuable than hers because she had less to give?"

"Yes, I think so. They only gave an offering that they will never miss while she gave all that she had. She gave a real gift of love."

Joanna spoke up.

"Manaen, do you remember when King David went to Araunah and asked to buy his threshing floor to build an altar to the Lord so that the plague on the people would be stopped?"

"Yes, I remember that. Didn't Araunah offer to give him the land?"

"Yes. And do you remember David's reply?"

"He told him that he had to pay for it, but I don't remember why."

"He said that he refused to sacrifice to his God with an offering that cost him nothing."[7]

"The widow's offering cost her everything that she had! What a gift to our Lord. I'm glad that he was there to see it," Chuza said.

Manaen grew quiet before he spoke.

"I'm glad I was there to see it too. Do you know the widow, Joanna?"

"No, I'm sorry, but I don't. Perhaps I could locate her through some of the other women. Why do you ask?"

"I would like to try to help her. Would that be appropriate? But, I wouldn't want her to know where the help came from. Could that be arranged?"

"I'll see what I can do," replied Joanna with a look of respect and understanding in her eyes. "You have matured quickly, dear friend."

"Manaen," Chuza said, "Do you remember when we returned to Jerusalem earlier this week and Jesus told the men to go find the wild, unbroken colt? He told them to tell the owner that the Master had need of it. At the time I thought of you. For so long you were like that colt, wild and unbroken, but the Lord has need of you."

"What are you saying?"

"Only that he needs you to do something. I don't know what it is, but you will know—when the time comes."

CHAPTER 34

Two days before the Passover, Chuza invited Manaen to the evening meal. As they ate, Chuza told them that he had been talking to some of the disciples, and they had shared some of Jesus's latest teachings with him.

"Tell us, Chuza," Joanna said excitedly.

"Well, you know that Jesus has mentioned his death often. He's said several things about the temple being destroyed and rebuilt in three days[1]. Just after we left the temple, Jesus took his disciples and went to Mt. Olivet to continue to teach them privately. It wasn't easy to escape the crowd, but they managed. He was able to teach them a great deal in a short time." Chuza grew quiet.

"Are you going to tell us what he taught, or keep us in suspense?" Manaen asked.

Chuza laughed and replied, "You are as impatient as Joanna. Okay, can you two be quiet long enough for me explain?"

When the two nodded quietly, Chuza told them that the disciples asked Jesus what he meant about the temple buildings and what the signs were of his coming and the end of the age. Jesus had cautioned his disciples to watch out that no one deceives them.

"He told them that many will come in his name, claiming, 'I am the One,' or 'The end is near.' We're not to fall for any of that! There will be wars and uprisings, but we're to keep our heads and not panic. This is just routine history and no sign of the end. There will be famines and huge earthquakes in various places, and at times it will seem like the sky is falling.

"He went on to tell the disciples that they would be arrested, hunted down, dragged into court and jail. And that isn't all; things will go from bad to worse. There was more in that vein."

"What does it all mean?" Joanna asked. She had tears in her eyes.

"I don't know. Jesus said that we are not to go chasing after him if someone tells us that he is in the desert or some such place. He said that there will be men performing false miracles and wonders; we are not to follow after them either.[2] He spoke about the sun not shining and the moon not giving light. There was something about stars falling from the sky and heavenly bodies being shaken. That is when the sign of the Son of Man will appear in the sky, with power and great glory. He will send his angels with a loud trumpet call, and they will gather his elect from the four winds, from one end of the heavens to the other.

"Jesus told the disciples to learn from the fig tree. He said that as soon as its twigs get tender and its leaves come out, you know that summer is near. When we see these things, we will know that the end is near, right at the door."[1]

The things Chuza had just told them were beyond Manaen's comprehension. He was quiet for a moment before he responded. "Chuza, Joanna, he's talking about a time in the future—following his death and resurrection."

"What? His death?" Joanna's eyes were filled with tears.

"Joanna," Manaen chided gently, "don't you remember that he has spoken many times about his death?" She nodded, and he went on, "And when Lazarus died Jesus told Mary and Martha, 'I am the resurrection and the life.' I think that the time has come, dear friends. I think that we will soon see Jesus crucified."

"How do you know that he will be crucified? How can you say such a horrible thing with such certainty? Crucifixion is the cruelest death there is and is only for the vilest of criminals. What has our Lord done to be crucified?" Chuza's voice rose, and he seemed to be indignant with Manaen.

"I don't know how I know. I just know—partly from his teachings and partly from a feeling in my spirit. It seems that all of my life I have known things about the future that I didn't want to know, and it has caused me a great deal of grief. When we were just boys I knew that someday Antipas would become Herod the Tetrarch. He stayed frightened and, I might add, angry with me about that. Every time I mentioned it, Antipas would start ranting and raving that I would get him killed if anyone overheard me. I was always surprised that no one overheard his tirades. But, you know all of that. And, like I said, I don't know how I know, I just know; and now my knowing has made you angry."

"I'm sorry. I'm not angry with you. It's just that I don't want to believe that a thing like that could actually happen, especially to Jesus."

"It's all right. I understand how you feel. But remember, we heard him say that the temple would be destroyed and rebuilt in three days.[2] Chuza, he was talking about his own body. I believe he knows that he'll be killed, but I also believe that he will be resurrected, just like he said he would."

Joanna was weeping softly when she spoke up.

"I don't want to believe it, Manaen, but I think you're right. All we can do now is pray for him."

"We have to do more than pray. We also have to believe; believe in Jesus as the Son of God and believe that, if he dies, he will be resurrected just as he has said."

"You amaze me; you have learned so much so quickly. And you're right, Manaen. We need to pray, and then trust God to take care of Jesus. That is what he has been trying to teach us to do all along—simply believe the things he has said, and trust him."

Joanna was trying to smile through her tears as Chuza gently took her in his arms, cradled her head against his chest, and spoke quietly to her.

"I believe that Manaen is right in all that he has said. And I believe that, somehow, Jesus will come out of this victoriously. If we believe, really believe, that he truly is the Son of God, which we do, then we have to believe that something miraculous is about to happen."

Forcing a show of bravery that she didn't feel, Joanna spoke.

"I choose to believe that."

CHAPTER 35

"John, where are you and Peter going in such a rush?" asked Manaen.

"Greetings, Manaen. Jesus has sent us on an errand to prepare the Passover meal."

"Where are you having it?"

"We don't know. Jesus just told us to look for a man carrying a water jug, and we are to follow him home."

"Then we are to tell the owner of the house that the Teacher wants to know where the guest room is where he can eat the Passover meal with his disciples." Peter spoke up. "Jesus said that it will be a spacious second-story room, swept and ready."

"Yes, we are to prepare the meal there.[1] Come with us. Look, there is the man with the jug. Let's go." John took

Manaen's arm and the friends followed the man together. They found everything just as Jesus had said.

Soon everyone had joined them, and the men and women worked quickly to prepare the meal. When they had finished serving the meal everyone left except Jesus, the disciples, and a few serving women who came and went about their serving chores.

Manaen was standing at a vantage point near the door and could observe what they were doing. He felt like he was eavesdropping, but he didn't want to move.

He saw Jesus get up from the supper table, set aside his robe, and put on an apron. Then he poured water into a basin and began to wash the men's feet. When he knelt before Peter and began to remove Peter's sandals, Peter was shocked and said, "Master, *you* wash *my* feet?"

Jesus answered, "You don't understand now what I'm doing, but it will be clear enough to you later."

Peter persisted, "You're not going to wash my feet—ever!"

Jesus said, "If I don't wash you, you can't be part of what I am doing."

"Master!" said Peter. "Not only my feet, then. Wash my hands! Wash my head!"

Jesus said, "If you've had a bath in the morning, you only need your feet washed now, and you're clean from head to toe. My concern, you understand, is holiness, not hygiene. So now you're clean. But not every one of you."

The disciples looked around at one another as if confused. Jesus quietly finished washing the disciple's feet, set the basin and towel aside, put on his clothes, and returned to his place at the table before continuing. "Do you understand what I have done for you? You address me as 'Teacher' and 'Master,' and rightly so. That's what I am. So if I, your Master and Teacher, washed your feet, you must now wash each other's feet. I've laid down a pattern for you. What I've done, you do. I'm only pointing out the obvious. A servant is not ranked above his master; an employee doesn't give orders to the employer. If you understand what I'm telling you, act like it—and live a blessed life. [2] "You have no idea how much I have looked forward to eating this Passover meal with you before I enter my time of suffering. It's the last one I'll eat until we all eat it together in the kingdom of God."[3]

Manaen wondered if there was any way the people with him could prevent the suffering of which Jesus spoke. Then he knew with a certainty that there was no way because this was part of the plan that Jesus had spoken of so often. His heart grieved with the knowledge that this man had to suffer.

Then he saw Jesus take bread. He blessed it, broke it, and gave it to the disciples, saying, "This is my body given for you. Eat it in my memory."

He did the same with the cup after supper, saying, "This cup is the new covenant written in my blood, poured out for you."

"Do you realize that the hand of the one who will betray me is at this moment on this table?"[4]

The disciples stared at one another at a loss to know which one of them he meant. John, who was reclining at the triclinium next to Jesus asked, "Lord who is it?"

Jesus answered, "It is the one to whom I will give this piece of bread when I have dipped it in the dish." Then he dipped the bread and gave it to Judas Iscariot[3].

As soon as Judas took the bread, Satan entered him; and

Jesus said, "What you are about to do, do quickly." That's when Judas went to the temple rulers and betrayed Jesus for thirty pieces of silver.[5]

A little later in the meal Jesus told them that he was going away to a place where they couldn't come. Then he gave them a new commandment to love one another as he had loved them. This would be the way people would know they were his disciples, by their love for one another.

Peter asked him, "Lord, where are you going?" It was as if Peter hadn't even absorbed the fact that Jesus had just instructed them in an entire new way to live. He just wanted to know were Jesus was going.

Jesus told him that he could not follow him now, but would follow later.

Peter asked him, "Lord, why can't I follow now? I'll lay down my life for you."

Jesus answered, "Will you really lay down your life for me? I tell you the truth, before the rooster crows, you'll deny three times that you even know me."[6]

No one seemed to understand what all of this meant. But Manaen was beginning to understand. It was as if a scroll was unfolding before his eyes, and he could read every word written there as he remembered the events of the last few days, events that would change their lives forever, events that they were helpless to prevent.

He could see how the sequence of events was ordered and planned by a loving Heavenly Father. He could see how the creator of the universe and all that was in it had cared enough about fallen man to step into the pages of history and make a way to be reconciled with the people he loved so joyfully.

Yes, now it was clear. At this Passover meal, Jesus had been getting himself and his disciples prepared for his upcoming death. After the Passover meal was finished, Manaen and some of the others followed as Jesus went with the disciples across the Kidron Valley to Mt. Olivet to pray in the Garden of Gethsemane. He heard Jesus ask Peter, James, and John to go deeper into the grove of olive trees and pray with him for an hour. He told them to pray so that they wouldn't fall into temptation, but they couldn't stay awake. Manaen watched and prayed as Jesus seemed to pray like a woman giving birth to a baby. He was praying in such travail that his sweat seemed to turn to blood. He came back to the disciples twice to wake them up, and he would look at them with such sorrow that Manaen felt like his heart would break for him.

The third time when he went back to them, he said that it was time. Then Judas arrived with soldiers. He went to Jesus and betrayed him with a kiss to identify him to the soldiers. At that moment Manaen was so angry he could have killed Judas with his bare hands.

Jesus asked them who they had come for and one of the soldiers said that they were looking for Jesus of Nazareth.

Jesus told them that he was Jesus, and when the words left his mouth the soldiers fell to the ground as if they were dead. This left Judas standing alone. He stuck out like a sore thumb and looked like he was looking for a place to hide.

When the soldiers finally got up and arrested Jesus, Peter, in a moment of bravado, drew his sword and cut off the ear of Malchus, one of the servants that Manaen knew. Manaen was horrified thinking his friend would bleed to death. He started forward to help the man, but Jesus told Peter to put his sword away, reached out and touched the man's ear. Instantly it was reattached and the man was healed. Manaen was so astonished that he just stood there with his mouth hanging open.

Then Jesus was arrested, bound, and taken to Annas, who was the father-in-law of Caiaphas, the high priest that year. Manaen followed them in the hope that he could intervene in some way, but he was not allowed inside and had to stay in the courtyard.

Manaen saw Peter following, but at a distance. In the middle of the courtyard some people had started a fire and were sitting around it, trying to keep warm. One of the serving maids sitting at the fire noticed him, then took a second look and said, "This man was with him!'

He denied it, "Woman, I don't even know him."

A short time later, someone else noticed him and said, "You're one of them."

But Peter denied it: "Man, I am not!"

About an hour later someone else spoke up, really adamant: "He's got to have been with him! He's got 'Galilean' written all over him."

Peter replied, "Man, I don't know what you're talking about!" At that very moment, the last word hardly off his lips, a rooster crowed. Manaen saw Jesus turn and look at Peter. Then Peter remembered what Jesus had said to him: "Before the rooster crows, you will deny me three times." He went out and cried, and cried, and cried.[7]

Later that night the men in charge of Jesus began poking fun at him, slapping him around. They put a blindfold on him and taunted, "Who hit you that time?" They were having a grand time with him.

When Judas saw that his sin of betrayal would cause Jesus's death, he was seized with guilt for what he had done. He went back to the temple and tried to return the thirty silver coins to the chief priests and the elders. "I have sinned," he said, "for I have betrayed innocent blood."

"What is that to us?" they replied. "That's your responsibility." Then Judas threw the silver coins at their feet, went out, and hung himself.

Caiaphas, the high priest, picked up the coins and decided that, since it was against the law to put blood money into the treasury, they would use it to buy the potter's field. This would give them a place to bury foreigners.[8] *What an irony that Judas was the first person buried there,* Manaen thought when he heard what happened.

Manaen saw Malchus later that night.

"Greetings, Malchus. How is that ear?"

"My ear is fine, and so is my soul."

"Your soul?"

"Yes, I became a believer when Jesus healed my ear. How could I not after experiencing such a miraculous healing? Several of the others instantly became believers when Jesus healed my ear. One moment I was in agony, with my ear on the ground, and blood pouring down my neck. I knew I was bleeding to death. The next moment Jesus had touched me, my ear was reattached, and I was completely healed[6]. There isn't even a scar! How could anyone not believe that Jesus is the son of God after experiencing something that miraculous?"

"How indeed! Welcome into the family of God and to the fellowship of believers, Malchus." Manaen gave his friend a big hug and thumped him on the back soundly, thankful that he had been spared. "Now go home and get on some clean clothes. Those are a bloody mess!" The friends laughed together, hugged again, and Manaen left to try to get some sleep.

It had been a long night with little sleep for the people who loved Jesus. They had wrestled with ideas of what they could do to help and realized that they were helpless to intervene in what was happening to Jesus. Manaen had spent the night in tearful prayer as he thought about what must be happening. He knew the Romans and the horrible things they were capable of.

At daybreak he was present when the council of the elders of the people, both the chief priests and teachers of the law, met together, and Jesus was led before them. "If you are the Christ," they said, "tell us."

Jesus answered, "If I tell you, you won't believe me, and if I asked you, you wouldn't answer. But from now on, the Son of Man will be seated at the right hand of the mighty God."

They all asked, "Are you then the Son of God?"

He replied, "You are right in saying I am."

Then they shouted, "Why do we need any more testimony? We have heard it from his own lips." They were furious at his answer, considering it blasphemy and an excuse to have him killed.

Then they all took Jesus to Pilate, the governor of the area who had been appointed by Rome, and began to bring up charges against him. They said, "We found this man undermining our law and order, forbidding taxes to be paid to Caesar, setting himself up as Messiah-King."

Pilate asked him, "Is this true that you're King of the Jews?"

"Those are your words, not mine," Jesus replied.

Pilate told the high priest and the accompanying crowd, "I find nothing wrong here. He seems harmless enough to me."

But they were vehement, "He's stirring up unrest among the people with his teaching, disturbing the peace everywhere, starting in Galilee and now all through Judea. He's a dangerous man, endangering the peace."

When Pilate heard this he asked, "So he's Galilean?" Realizing that he properly came under Herod's jurisdiction, he passed the buck to Herod, who just happened to be in Jerusalem for a few days.[9]

CHAPTER 36

Manaen was struck with fear when he learned that they were taking Jesus to Herod. He knew as well as anyone how capricious Herod's thinking could be. Herod would do anything he wanted to do without considering the consequences, including having Jesus killed. He rushed to the palace and was in time to see how pleased Herod was at seeing Jesus. Relieved, he remembered hearing from Chuza that Herod had hoped to see Jesus perform some miracle.

Herod plied Jesus with questions, but Jesus gave him no answer. The chief priest and the teachers of the law were standing there, vehemently accusing him. Then Herod and his soldiers ridiculed and mocked him. They were furious because he wouldn't answer them. Dressing him in an elegant robe like a king to mock him, they sent him back to Pilate.[1] As the crowd was leaving, Herod saw Manaen and smirked. His bloated face was filled with evil. He motioned for him, and when Manaen approached his throne fearing arrest, Herod said, "So, I was right when I accused you! You are a follower of this man too. That makes you as big a fool as he is. Perhaps you will both be killed now!"

Manaen tried to talk to him and convince him to intervene on Jesus's behalf. But with an arrogant toss of his head and a dramatic swirling of his robe, Herod turned his back on Manaen and left the room.

Feelings of contempt and disgust replaced all of the feelings he had once had for his cousin. He knew that Herod could easily have him killed now that he knew he was a follower of Jesus. He was amazed to realize how little this knowledge mattered to him. The only thing that mattered was Jesus.

Back at the governor's palace, Pilate had questioned Jesus, but couldn't find any reason to crucify him. He went to the Jews and said, "I find no basis for a charge against him, but it's your custom for me to release a criminal at the time of the Passover. Do you want me to release 'the king of the Jews'?" But, there was an angry mob at work that had been incited by the temple rulers. They were screaming for Jesus's crucifixion.

They shouted back, "No, not him. Give us Barabbas." Barabbas was a condemned robber and murderer.

While Pilate was dealing with all of this, his wife sent him a message telling him not to have anything to do with condemning Jesus. She told him that Jesus was innocent and that she had had a very troubling dream about him. But the chief priest and the elders had convinced the mob to ask for Barabbas and have Jesus killed.

Pilate tried again, "Which of the two do you want me to release to you?"

The mob began screaming.

"Give us Barabbas, give us Barabbas." The priests had whipped the crowd's emotions into a wild frenzy.

When Pilate asked what they wanted him to do with Jesus, they screamed and chanted, "Crucify him. Crucify him."

"Why? What crime has he committed?"

They screamed even louder, "Crucify him."

But Pilate answered, "You take him and crucify him. As for me, I find no basis for a charge against him."

The Jews insisted, "We have a law and according to that law he must die. He has claimed to be the Son of God!"

This frightened Pilate, and he went back inside the palace. "Where do you come from?" he asked Jesus, but Jesus refused to answer him. "Do you refuse to speak to me?" Pilate said. "Don't you realize that I have the power to either free you or crucify you?"

Jesus answered, "You would have no power over me if it were not given to you from above. Therefore, the one who handed me over to you has the greater sin."

From then on Pilate tried to set Jesus free, but the Jews kept shouting, "If you let this man go, you are not a friend to Caesar. Anyone who claims to be a king opposes Caesar."

Understanding this as a direct threat, and when he saw that he was getting nowhere with the mob that was getting out of control, he took water and washed his hands in front of the people. "I am innocent of this man's blood," he said. "It's your responsibility."

The people shouted, "Let his blood be on us and on our children."[2]

So Pilate released Barabbas to the mob and sent Jesus to be flogged.

Jesus was stripped of his garments and tied to a post by his wrists to be beaten with a cat-o'-nine-tails, a terrible whip with nine woven ropes. At the end of each tail, or rope, there was a knot imbedded with bits of iron, rock, and bone. Manaen had to watch in helpless impotence as the flogging tore the flesh from Jesus's body. Muscles and ligaments were also ripped to shreds and torn from his body. Bone chips and blood splattered Manaen and the crowd.

The men beating Jesus were cursing and laughing like bloodthirsty demons, as if they were enjoying destroying another human being. One stood on each side of him so that the lashes were cutting cross marks in his flesh. They were only allowed to give him thirty-nine lashes, and they seemed intent on doing all of the damage they possibly could with each lash. The blood and flesh from Jesus were splattering all over the courtyard, and his skin was hanging from his body in shreds. The sweat from his agony was collecting in puddles with the blood at his feet.

When they had done all of the damage they could legally do, the governor's soldiers dragged Jesus back into the Praetorium and gathered the whole company of soldiers around him. They put a scarlet robe over his torn flesh and then twisted a crown from limbs with two inch thorns and shoved it down on his head. The blood spurted from the gashes and ran into his battered eyes—eyes that were almost swollen shut until he could hardly see. Then they put a staff in his right hand, knelt mockingly before him and said, "Hail, king of the Jews!" They beat him around the head with the staff, forcing the thorns farther and farther into his head as they spit in his face and ripped his beard out by the handful.

After they had mocked him, they took off the robe and put his clothes back on him. Then they lead him away to be crucified.[3]

CHAPTER 37

Manaen had followed along, helpless as the soldiers led Jesus away. When Jesus began to stumble under the burden of the cross, Manaen had started forward to help, but before he could reach him the crowd and soldiers got in his way. Then the soldiers seized Simon from Cyrene, who was on his way in from the country, put the cross on him, and made him carry it behind Jesus.[1]

There was a large crowd of people following Jesus, pushing and shoving as they tried to get a glimpse of him. Some were throwing things at him or trying to hurt him in some other way; others simply mocked and cursed him. The soldiers were cursing as they used spears and clubs to clear a path through the streets. Jesus was struggling to stay on his feet as the soldiers dragged him along. Part of the crowd included women who mourned and wailed for him.

Jesus turned and said to them, "Daughters of Jerusalem, don't cry for me; cry for yourselves and for your children. The time is coming when they'll say, 'Lucky the women who never conceived! Lucky the wombs that never gave birth! Lucky the breasts that never gave milk!' Then they'll start calling to the mountains, 'Fall down on us!' calling to the hills, 'Cover us up!' If people do these things to a live, green tree, can you imagine what they'll do with deadwood?"[2]

Manaen realized that Jesus was quoting the prophet Ezekiel when God told Ezekiel to prophesy against the southern forest. He understood that a fire had been kindled by the deeds that were taking place here, and destruction was coming. No one would be able to escape what was coming.

When they reached Golgotha, the place of the skull, Manaen stood staring in horror as the scene unfolded before him. He was horrified not only for Jesus, but that Mary and the other women were witnessing the same thing he was. Even Jesus's mother was there with John.[1] He wondered why they hadn't kept her away.

Nothing in his long, violent, jaded past had prepared Manaen for this, not even the slaughter of all the babies just after Jesus was born. Nothing could ever prepare anyone for such barbarism. Jesus didn't even look human. He looked like the bloody, broken carcass of a slaughtered animal.

Two other men, both criminals, had been brought out with Jesus to be crucified. The soldiers threw the three men down on their backs on the crosses, stretched out their hands and feet, and using large iron spikes, nailed them to the crosses. The men screamed and writhed in agony, begging for mercy. Then the crosses were lifted up and Manaen could hear the men's flesh ripping as the crosses were dropped into the holes that had been dug for them. He felt physically sick with anger and anguish from what was happening to his wonderful friend.

The others screamed in agony, but Jesus choked back a scream, gasped, and said, "Father, forgive them. They don't know what they're doing."[3]

Jesus had been stripped of his clothes before they nailed him to the cross in order to further humiliate him. Now Jesus was hanging there, naked, suffering agonies, dying so that the very people who were killing him would have a chance to live. Manaen's mind was numb, but his heart was breaking. He could barely force air into his own lungs as he watched Jesus struggle for every breath he drew.

The soldiers at the foot of the cross recognized the value of his seamless tunic and began to cast lots for his clothes. They laughed and mocked him as they offered him wine vinegar and said, "If you are the king of the Jews, save yourself!" The people stood watching and the rulers even sneered at him. They said, "Let him save himself if he is the Christ of God, the Chosen One."

The high priests, along with the religion scholars and leaders, were right there mixing it up with the rest of them, having a great time poking fun at him: "He saved others— he can't save himself! King of Israel, is he? Then let him get down from that cross. We'll all become believers then! He was so sure of God—well, let him rescue his 'Son' now—if he wants him! He did claim to be God's Son, didn't he?"[4]

Manaen felt like he could have strangled them with his

bare hands to stop their mocking. He realized that he really wanted to do just that and would do it gladly if it would help.

Now the real agony began for the three condemned men as they tried to breathe. Their feet had been nailed to the crosses just above a foot rest that allowed them to push up just enough to get a gasp of air, but this put pressure on the nail holes in their feet and caused more pain. When they bent their knees to take the pressure off of their feet, it put the same pressure on the holes in their hands, causing the flesh to be torn even more. When they were hanging by their hands, their lungs couldn't function enough to draw in air, so the whole agonizing process had to be repeated every few seconds.

The two men who were being crucified along with Jesus were on his left and right. One of the criminals hanging alongside cursed him: "Some Messiah you are! Save yourself! Save us!"

But the other one made him shut up: "Have you no fear of God? You're getting the same as him. We deserve this, but not him—he did nothing to deserve this." Then he said, "Jesus, remember me when you enter your kingdom."

He said, "Don't worry, I will. Today you will join me in paradise."[5]

Manaen had just moved to stand with Jesus's mother, Mary; Mary, the wife of Cleopas; Mary Magdalene; and John, when he heard Jesus say to his mother, "Dear woman, here is your son." And to John he said, "Here is your mother."[6] Manaen was amazed at the love and fortitude of Jesus—that, during the time of his greatest agony, he was making provision for his mother's future well-being.

John had just placed a protective arm around Mary, who was weeping openly.

"John, what will you do?" Manaen asked him.

"I'll take her to live with our family. My family loves her and will welcome her there. Her every need will be met," John replied.

"I don't doubt that for a moment, but if I can ever help in any way, please let me know." Then Manaen looked around and realized that the sky was turning dark. Clouds were piling up, and the wind was starting to gust. Lightning could be seen in the distance.

Just then they heard Jesus cry out, "My God, my God. Why have you abandoned me?"

Some of the people thought he was calling out to Elijah.

Some said, "Let's see if Elijah comes to save him!"

The sun had turned completely dark when Jesus cried out, "Father, I place my life in your hands."

Later, knowing that all things had been accomplished, Jesus said, "I am thirsty." A jar of wine vinegar was there, so they soaked a sponge in it, put the sponge on a long stalk of the hyssop plant, and lifted it to Jesus's lips. When he had received the drink Jesus said, "It is finished!" With this he bowed his head and gave up his spirit.[7] The storm broke loose then with a fury like Manaen had never seen. The only light was from the lightning as it flashed in the strange darkness of the noonday hour. The trees were thrashing about as the wind whipped them into a frenzy. Some broke and crashed into the crowds. The wind sounded as if it were screaming and wailing. The earth began to quake, and the rocks were breaking up and being tossed around. It seemed as if the entire earth was mourning its great loss. People were running in terror of the strange phenomenon. Women and children were horrified, fearing for their lives, and thinking it was the end of the earth.

When the captain of the guard and those with him saw the earthquake and the terrible storm, they were frightened out of their wits. They said, "This has to be the Son of God."[8]

The women realized that he had died and began to shriek and wail. His mother and Mary Magdalene fell to their knees in their grief and would not be comforted. As John lifted Jesus's mother to her feet, Manaen knelt beside Mary Magdalene. Her sobs were tearing at his very soul. He tried to lift her, but she was too distraught to be moved. "Mary, it's over and there's nothing more we can do for him. Please, come back to the house with us now." He had to yell in order to be heard above the fury of the storm.

"No, Manaen," she wailed. "It isn't over! God can still save him! It can't be over! They can't have killed him!"

"Mary, can you make your mind go back to his teaching? Try to remember. He told us he had to die. Please try to understand. No one killed him. He gave up his life willingly. Surely you don't believe that a mere mortal could kill the Son of God? Think now, Mary. Think!"

Reaching out to take the hand that he offered she spoke through her sobs.

"Yes, you're right. He died so that we can truly live. I do remember him saying that." A small smile tugged at the corners of her lips but couldn't quite make it. "He would want us to be brave now, wouldn't he?" She let him put his arm around her and hold her to help her walk against the fury of the wind. It was hopeless. She was too weak with grief. He had to carry her.

"Yes, that is exactly what he would want. Now come. You're getting soaked to the skin, and you'll be sick." He had picked her up just in time to see a soldier with a club breaking the legs of the other men so they couldn't lift themselves up to breathe and would die quickly. He quickly turned her away so that she wouldn't see this final atrocity.

It was the day of preparation for the Sabbath, and, since this Sabbath was the high holy day of the year this year, the Jews didn't want the bodies to stay on the cross during this time. They had petitioned Pilate to have their legs broken so they couldn't breathe. This would speed death, and their bodies could be removed. So the soldiers had come and broken the legs of the first man crucified with Jesus, and then the other. When they got to Jesus, they saw that he was dead, so they didn't break his legs. One of the soldiers stabbed him in the side with his spear. Blood and water gushed out.[9]

Manaen's mind went back to what he had read in the ancient writings, that not one of his bones would be broken. Then he remembered that the prophet Zechariah had foretold that people would gaze in amazement on the one they had pierced.[10] He realized that God was indeed having the final word.

CHAPTER 38

Once the still-grieving women could be convinced to leave, John led them back into Jerusalem, while Manaen stayed to watch the body of Jesus. He promised to protect it and was determined to keep that promise.

As evening approached, Manaen saw Joseph of Arimathea, a prominent member of the council and a fellow believer, leave a group at the foot of the cross and went to talk to him.

"Joseph, old friend, what errand are you rushing to on this dreadful day?"

"Come with me if you want to know."

"I promised to wait here with the body of Jesus."

"My servants are watching him. They'll protect his body."

"Then I'll go with you. I can see from your face that you're intent on something."

"Intent and determined!"

When they reached the governor's palace, they were both so well-known that they didn't have to wait to see Pilate. They were ushered right in and found Pilate sitting, staring out at the parade grounds, wringing his hands.

Without waiting for Pilate to ask what he wanted, Joseph boldly asked for the body of Jesus.

Pilate was astonished.

"Is he already dead?"

"Yes, and I would like to bury his body in my new tomb."

Pilate sent for the centurion who had been at the cross and asked him if Jesus was dead. When he learned from the centurion that it was true, he gave the body to Joseph.

On the way back to Golgotha, they passed through the marketplace where they stopped and purchased some linen cloth. When they got back to the cross, they took the body down, wrapped it in the cloth, and placed it in Joseph's tomb that was cut out of rock. Then he rolled a stone against the entrance of the tomb. Mary Magdalene and Mary, the mother of Jesus, saw where he was laid.

The two men were tired when they finished, because they had refused to let anyone else help them carry the body down from the top of the hill. When they had heaved the heavy stone into place, they sat down on the edge of a wine press there in the garden.

"Have you heard what happened when Jesus died?" Joseph asked.

"The earthquake and storm?" Manaen asked.

"Well, there was that too, but I'm talking about the temple veil."

"No." Manaen was instantly alert. "What happened?"

"At the moment of his death that huge, heavy veil that separated the Most Holy Place from the Holy Place was torn in two from the top to the bottom!"[1]

"How could that happen?" Manaen asked in wonder, as he thought of the weight of the huge curtain. "The fabric in that curtain was seven inches thick."

"No one seems to know, but now the Most Holy Place is totally open to the Holy Place, and the priests are in a furor trying to decide how to repair the damage."

"Has the Holy of Holies ever been exposed before?"

"No. No one is allowed in there with the Ark of the Covenant except the high priest, and that is just one day a year. That's when he sprinkles blood on the altar and intercedes for the people's sins. The priest stands before God as a representative of the people, an intermediary between God and his people, if you will. But you know that.

"It's unthinkable for anyone else to go behind that curtain into the very presence of God! God would strike them dead. Even the high priest has to wear bells on the hem of his skirt and a rope tied around his ankle. Then, if something happens to him while he is in there, the bells will stop ringing and he can be pulled out. Otherwise, he would rot in there because no one could even go into the Most Holy Place to get him."

"I'm surprised that God hasn't struck Caiaphas and Annas dead anyway, considering what they did to his Son." Manaen was frowning.

"Me too," replied Joseph. "But even stranger things have happened. Did you know that tombs opened and many of the holy people who had died were raised to life?"[2]

Manaen was so stunned that he couldn't even answer his friend. He just stared at him, his mouth hanging open.

Joseph continued.

"Yes! It's true! They are appearing to the righteous people in Jerusalem!"

"No!" Manaen shook his head. "You have gone too far now, my friend! Surely you don't expect me to believe that? I'm sorry, Joseph. I don't mean to imply that you would lie. It is just too incredible to believe!"

"All I can tell you is that people saw it happen, and the tombs are empty."

"Joseph, I need to see this for myself! Can you come with me and show me what you're talking about?"

"I don't know if I can show you any of the people, but I can show you the empty tombs."

CHAPTER 39

Later that evening Manaen found many of the disciples gathered in the upper room where they had taken their last meal with Jesus. Everyone sat in stunned silence, except for an occasional sound of weeping. It was almost as if the man, the man they had loved so deeply, had taken their will to live and their voices to the tomb with him. Even the children were still and silent.

Finally, true to their habit, the woman began to move around to prepare for the coming Sabbath. Their movements were slow and awkward, totally lacking their usual confidence and grace. Some of them even staggered and stumbled as they moved around the room, but they wouldn't let the men help them.

Chuza and Joanna joined them there. Joanna's face was swollen, and her voice was still ragged from crying.

"Manaen, what are we going to do now? How can we go on without him?" she asked.

"We still have each other, and he did say that he would never leave us or forsake us. We'll be strong and remember all of the things he taught us. Not only that, but we'll teach everyone we can about Jesus and all of his teachings. I believe that's what he would want us to do. Don't you?" When she didn't answer, he continued, "Don't you think that is what he would want us to do; to carry on and make his life and death count? We have to teach others, everyone we possibly can, about him. That way he will always be alive."

"Yes, you're right. I know that we will continue in his teaching. But, for now, I'll go help the women prepare for the Sabbath. I know that's one thing he would want me to do." She appeared comforted and stronger as she smiled at Chuza and Manaen and went to join the other women.

"I wish I could protect her from all of this," Chuza said to Manaen.

"She's stronger than I had ever realized. But, if you can figure out a way to do that, then perhaps we can apply it to all of the women. They are all in need of protection and comfort. They depended on him as much as he depended on them."

"In what way, Manaen?"

"It amazed me over the time that I traveled with all of you and watched the way the women provided for Jesus and ministered to him. Yes, the wealthy ones provided finances, but all of them, from the wealthiest to the poorest, were always there seeing that he had food and the other necessities that he needed, even cleaning his clothes."

Chuza nodded in agreement as he spoke.

"They were so kind to him, and he was so tender with them. He never ignored them or acted as if they were unimportant. He treated them as equals and valued the women, and all that they did for him, as much as he did the men."

"Yes, it's going to be especially hard on the women. He was so considerate, happy, and cheerful with them. Most men haven't treated them so well. His example will be a lot for the rest of us to try to live up to."

"Yes, and with children too. Were you there when the children were trying to get close to him and the people were pushing them away?"

"I was, and he wasn't happy with the people like me who were trying to keep them away." Manaen's thoughts returned to that day. He remembered how he had watched as Jesus gently and joyfully took as many children as he could on his lap, all the while laughing with them. One boy sat on his shoulders. Then he wrapped his arms around the rest and hugged them close. He reminded Manaen of a mother hen with a brood of chicks. Jesus had laughed with the children, and it was obvious that he genuinely enjoyed their company. He tickled some of them, making them giggle, and some even tickled him back. *What a beautiful, joyful memory. The adults didn't seem to be amused by the scene.* Manaen returned to their conversation.

"Do you really understand what he meant about 'of such is the kingdom of God?'"

Chuza was quiet for a moment before he answered.

"I think that he was saying that when we come to him, we have to believe in him with the simplicity of a child."

"And trust him that way too, Chuza?"

"Yes. I think that is exactly what he meant."

"Children are so simple in their approach to things. They never seem to have to reason things out first." Manaen laughed before continuing. "That would work against them too, just like it does with us."

"Yes, they just seem to trust that everything is going to work out right."

"Trust; there's that word again. It seems to me that Jesus had a way of striking right at the root of men's problems. Trust is one of the hardest issues we men face. I don't know many of us who have been given many reasons to trust people. I know that I certainly haven't. My dealings with Herod, his family, and followers made me believe that you couldn't trust anyone, but I did learn to completely trust Jesus. It took time, but eventually, even I came around. After I learned to trust Jesus, it was easier for me to trust other people. It's still an issue with me at times, though."

Chuza nodded his head.

"I understand completely, but remember, even Jesus said that he trusted no man because our hearts are wicked. And no matter how much we would like to deny it, it's the truth. Just when I think that my heart is trustworthy, I will find my mind going in a direction that I know is wrong. When that happens I know that I'm not trustworthy. It is a struggle at times, but I won't give up. I'm determined to get it right, for his sake as well as my own."

"I'm sure that's all he asked of us. And in time, I know we'll win over our sinful nature if we just keep up the good fight."

"Fight who, Manaen? Is Herod threatening you again?" Joanna looked concerned. She had just rejoined them and heard the last of their conversation.

"I haven't heard anything more from Herod, praise be to God! So it's not who, but what—our flesh, Joanna."

"Our flesh?"

"Yes, our flesh, our sinful nature." Chuza answered. "Doing things like wrong thinking and bad behavior, treating people badly; things that wouldn't bring honor to Jesus."

Joanna looked at them with a quizzical expression.

"Speaking of flesh, the meal is ready."

Manaen wasn't hungry.

"How can anyone think about food at a time like this?" he asked.

Chuza joined in.

"Right now I don't really care if I never eat another meal. I think it would choke me to try to swallow."

"That seems to be the feeling of most of us, but we do need to keep our strength up. Who knows what might happen next?" Joanna struggled to keep her voice calm as she spoke, but her face was full of her unspoken emotions.

"Very well, dear wife," Chuza answered quietly as he stood and put his arm protectively around her shoulders. "We'll join the others now."

The meal was somber and quiet, missing the usual jovial banter between the friends. Everyone was alert to every sound as if they were waiting for the soldiers to come take them away next. And, indeed, the awareness of that possibility was on everyone's minds. Every sound of passing horses or loud voices from outside the house could mean the approach of Roman soldiers who had been incited by another angry mob. Nothing would surprise them.

The following day, just after the morning meal, Nicodemus

arrived from the temple. He came over to Manaen and Chuza after his feet were washed and oil was put on his head.

Manaen was the first to speak.

"Shalom, Nicodemus, I can tell by your expression that you have come with news. I trust that all is well with you and that the news is good."

"Shalom, Manaen and Chuza," Nicodemus glanced around the room before going on. "I'm not sure about the news I bring, but considering the temperament of the Jewish leaders and Pilate it could very easily go either way."

"What is it, Nicodemus?" Chuza asked, impatient to hear any news that might affect the group. "We're anxious to hear. Please…"

"This morning the chief priest and Pharisees came together and went to Pilate, saying that they remembered that that deceiver, referring to Jesus, said while he was still alive that after three days he would rise again. And they commanded that Pilate, yes, I said 'commanded' the governor to do something, if you can imagine that! They commanded that the tomb be sealed until the third day so that his disciples couldn't come at night and steal his body. They said that his followers would then tell the people that he had been raised from the dead. They also said that if it happened this deception would be worse than the first."

"What did Pilate say?" Chuza asked.

"He just told them to take a guard and make things as secure as they knew how."

"Please! And what did they do?" Manaen asked, growing impatient.

"They took a guard and secured the tomb with a seal on the stone that was rolled over the entrance."[1]

"Did they leave a guard there?" Chuza asked.

"Yes. In fact, there are several guards. They're even going to rotate them in shifts to be sure there is always someone guarding the tomb."

Manaen was quiet for a moment before he spoke.

"That's incredible! They really are afraid of a dead man."

CHAPTER 40

ary Magdalene was out of breath and almost hysterical as she talked to the disciples and the others who were still there.

"I'm telling you he's alive!"

Manaen looked at her skeptically.

"Who's alive, Mary?"

"Jesus! Jesus is alive!"

"Calm down, Mary."

"Don't tell me to calm down, Manaen. I have seen him!" she shouted, her face glowing with the joy she felt.

"Where did you see him?" Manaen thought perhaps Mary had had a vision.

"At dawn this morning! After the Sabbath had passed I went with Joanna, Salome, and Mary the mother of James. We took sweet spices and planned to anoint Jesus's body.

But, just as we arrived the ground began to shake violently and an angel of the Lord came down from heaven, rolled back the stone, and sat on it."

"An angel?" Peter asked incredulously. He looked at her like he thought she had lost her mind.

"Yes, an angel! His face was like lightning, and his clothes were gleaming white. The guards were so afraid of him that they shook and fell to the ground like dead men. You should have seen those tough Roman guards. They were as pale as ghosts and shaking all over! Two of them were even crying."

The other women who had gone to the tomb came rushing in. Mary turned to them with tears in her eyes.

"Tell them what we saw. They don't believe me." she said.

"Listen to her, Manaen," Joanna said.

"Go on, Mary," Manaen said. "Tell us more about this angel."

"Well he said, 'There is nothing to fear here. I know you're looking for Jesus, the One they nailed to the cross. He is not here. He was raised, just as he said. Come and look at the place where he was placed.' Then he said, 'Now, get on your way quickly, and tell his disciples and Peter, he is risen from the dead. He is going on ahead of you to Galilee. You will see him there.' That's the message."[1]

Peter looked disgusted and disbelieving.

"What else did this 'angel' tell you, Mary?" he said.

"Nothing, Peter. We just hurried away from the tomb, to tell you what had happened. We were filled with joy, but we were afraid of the guards too, so we ran. But that isn't the best part, Peter!"

"Did you also hear a heavenly choir?" Peter asked sarcastically.

"No, suddenly Jesus met us. I thought he was the gardener and asked him where he had put Jesus. When he said, 'Greetings,' I recognized his voice. We just fell at his feet and worshiped him, but he wouldn't let us touch him. Then he told us not to be afraid, and for us to go tell his brethren and Peter to go to Galilee; there you will see him." [2]

"And I'm supposed to believe this?" Peter was shouting now.

John took Peter by the arm. "Don't yell at her, Peter. Listen, I can understand your doubts. You can stand here all day and argue, but I'm going to the tomb. Won't you come with me? Mary said the angel said specifically to tell you."

As the two men rushed out of the room, Chuza turned to Joanna.

"Are you all right? Were you frightened?"

"Yes, I'm fine. I'm just a little out of breath from rushing back here. But, no, it wasn't really frightening. It was almost as if I could sense his presence even though I didn't know he was there. The guards were terrified, but we weren't. We have no reason to be afraid of angels. Mary was weeping at first because she thought someone had stolen his body. You know how the rumors have been flying since his death."

"Yes, and I also know how quick people have been to believe them."

It hadn't been long when the door burst open, and Peter and John came in shouting.

"It's true. He has risen!"

"Yes! He appeared to Peter! He really is alive! The women really did see him!" John shouted with his joy.

Everyone began talking, shouting, crying, and laughing all at once. Manaen and several people went to the tomb to see for themselves. While they were gone they saw some of the people who had been dead appearing to people in the city. Jerusalem was in pandemonium as people rushed around, some in excitement, some in fear.

Later, after they had rejoined the others, they heard someone knocking, and Chuza came back from the gate with Nicodemus, who was really agitated.

Manaen asked him what was wrong.

"You won't believe what the chief priest and elders have done now!"

"Nothing you could tell me about those vipers would surprise me, friend, especially if it is something dishonorable. I'm sorry, forgive my cynicism. Go on. Tell us what they've done."

"The guard that had been placed at the tomb came rushing back to the temple and told the chief priests a wild tale about earthquakes and angels, and that Jesus's body was missing. When they realized that the guards were telling the truth, the priests met with the elders and devised a plan. They gave the soldiers a large sum of money and said to them, 'You are to say that his disciples came in the night and took him away while you were asleep. If this report gets to the governor we will satisfy him and keep you out of trouble.' The soldiers took the money and that's the tale they are telling.[2] But how is anyone to know what happened to his body? It has just disappeared."

"No, Nicodemus…"

Cleopas and another man came bursting into the room.

"We have seen him! We have seen the Lord!" Cleopas was almost shouting.

Manaen threw his arms around the man and hugged him.

"Cleopas, you've seen the Lord? Tell us what had happened."

"Please forgive me. What a day we've had. We were on our way to Emmaus, just walking along the road, minding our own business, talking about Jesus and the crucifixion, when a stranger came up and joined us. We didn't see where he came from. He was just suddenly with us! While he was walking along with us, he asked what we were talking about and why we were so sad. I asked him if he was a stranger in Jerusalem and didn't know the things that had happened there in the last few days. He said, 'What things?'

"We told him, 'About Jesus of Nazareth; how he was a prophet, powerful in word and deed before God and all the people. And how the chief priests and our rulers handed him over to be sentenced to death, and they crucified him; but we had hoped that he was the one who was going to redeem Israel.' Then we told him about it being the third day since his death and how the women had had a vision and thought he was alive. We told him all we knew. I'm sorry. I know I'm rattling on, but it's important.

"Then he said, 'How foolish you are, and slow to believe all that the prophets have spoken. Did not the Christ have to suffer these things and enter into his glory?' And beginning with Moses and all the prophets, he explained to us what was said in all the Scriptures concerning himself.'

"When we approached Emmaus, the stranger acted as

if he was going farther, but we urged him to stay. When we were eating, he took bread, gave thanks, broke it, and gave it to us. That is when we recognized him as Jesus, but he disappeared from our sight.[3] We did feel foolish then, realizing that we should have known him all along. Then we rushed back here to tell you."

CHAPTER 41

Tension was like lightning in the air. The people were nervous as they worried about their fate at the hands of the temple priest and other Jews who were not believers, excited about all they had seen and heard, and restless because their futures seemed uncertain. When they were about to sit down for their evening meal, Manaen locked the door for fear of the other Jews and what they might do. His main concern was for the women and children. He was careful to keep his sword and knife close at hand.

As they sat eating, they were still talking about all that had happened that day and chastising themselves for their unbelief and hardness of heart. They felt guilty because they had refused to believe the reports they had been given.

"Do you mean you didn't recognize him while he was talking to you?"

"Well, our hearts were burning…"

Suddenly Jesus appeared among them.

"Peace be with you."

Everyone was startled, thinking he was a ghost. One man knocked over a table when he jumped, and a woman dropped a pitcher that shattered on the stone floor.

Then he said to them, "Why are you troubled and why do doubts rise in your minds? Look at my hands and feet. It is I myself! Touch me and see. A ghost doesn't have flesh and bone as you see I have."

When he said this he showed them his hands and feet. And while they still couldn't believe it because of their joy and amazement, he asked, "Do you have anything here to eat?" They gave him a piece of broiled fish, and he took it and ate it in their presence.

He said, "This is what I told you while I was still with you: Everything must be fulfilled that is written about me in the Law of Moses, the Prophets, and the Psalms." Then he opened their minds so they could understand the Scriptures.[1]

Again Jesus said, "Peace be with you. As the Father has sent me, I am sending you." And with that he breathed on them and said, "Receive the Holy Spirit. If you forgive anyone their sins, they are forgiven; if you do not forgive them, they are not forgiven."[2] And instantly, as quickly as he had appeared, he was gone.

There was complete silence in the room for several seconds before anyone could speak. Manaen was stunned from what he had just seen and heard. Then he realized that there was a hand on his arm. Mary was beside him, and when he could finally look down at her, he saw that she was as pale as a ghost.

She was swaying and looked as if she might faint. He caught her just as she began to collapse. He caught Joanna's attention and motioned for her to bring him a pitcher of water.

He was patting Mary's face with a wet cloth when her eyes opened.

"Manaen, dear Manaen, I thought Jesus was a ghost. How could I have been so foolish? I hope that he wasn't too disappointed with me." Tears were mingling with the water on her face.

"We were all startled, Mary. It happened so suddenly. But, no, he wasn't disappointed with any of us. He realizes our humanity." He helped Mary to her feet and realized that only he and Joanna had seen Mary faint. The others were too busy talking about what they had just witnessed and what had happened to them. Joanna had her arm around Mary's waist to support her as she and Mary went to join the other women. Emotions were running high as Manaen listened to the excited conversations going on around him.

"…but John, I've never heard such a thing before. Did Jesus actually say that we can forgive a person's sins?" Peter was saying.

"I believe that he was saying something similar to that."

"How can that be true? Only God can forgive sin! You know that, John."

"Peter, it's all about love. Do you remember when he told us that we have the power of binding and loosening; what we bind on earth is bound in heaven and what we loose on earth is loosed in heaven?" Peter nodded and John went on. "I think he was saying something similar to that. If someone sins against us in any way we should forgive them so that the sin won't be held against them. Peter, he has commanded us to love one another. Love forgives any sin."

"I remember when I asked him if I should forgive a person seven times for the same offense against me, and he said that I should forgive them seventy times seven. That is four hundred and ninety times in one day, and he meant for the same offense! How can a person do that, John?"

"Love. He didn't say that you had to feel like forgiving, just be obedient and forgive them. Feelings come later. But he did say that if we don't forgive others, our Heavenly Father won't forgive us. I think that he was very clear about that. And our love for him should cause us to want to do what he has asked, simply because he asked."

"But, John…"

"Just do what he said, Peter. That's true love."

Peter walked away muttering and shaking his head.

John turned toward Manaen with a smile.

"John, do you think he will ever understand?" Manaen asked him.

"We can only hope so. He's really struggling with the fact that he denied the Lord he loves so much. I hope that he will come to realize that if God requires us to forgive others for anything they do, then that surely must mean that he will forgive us. God would not require us to do something that he's not willing to do himself. And, not only does he forgive, but he forgets! That is something that's totally impossible for us mere mortals."

"Yes! I see what you're saying, and you're right! I've never thought of it that way before. That gives me hope. Let's pray that Peter will come to realize that truth soon. He's so impetuous and unpredictable. Those personality problems get him in trouble, but he'll make it in spite of his shortcomings. He's going to be a great asset to the kingdom of God in the very near future."

"I hope you're right, Manaen."

Manaen nodded, a knowing smile on his face.

"John, what did Jesus mean when he said, 'Receive the Holy Spirit?'" Manaen asked.

"Were you there when he promised us that he was sending us a comforter?"

"No, but I heard some of the disciples talking about it. Didn't he say that after he had gone away he wouldn't leave us comfortless, but would send the Holy Spirit?"

"Yes, and when he said for us to receive the Holy Spirit, that is exactly what I felt—comforted. How about you, Manaen? What did you feel?"

"Like a burden had been lifted. I was at peace. Could that be comfort?"

"Exactly!" John was excited now. "You were comforted."

"Can anything be that simple?"

"Manaen, when will you stop using your brilliant mind and start using your heart? It's a simple matter of trust—trusting Jesus to do and be all that he promised he would do for us and be to us. Surely his resurrection has shown you that, with him, all things really are possible, just like he said they would be."

"I'm trying, John. I'm trying."

John laughed.

"Yes, sometimes you really are, but just love, Manaen. Just love," John said.

"John, you know the story of my life and why I came

to follow Jesus. But, there's something beyond that. There's another reason that I came to believe in him."

"Is it something that you are willing to share with me?"

"Yes. I think I can do that now without feeling like a total hypocrite."

"A hypocrite?"

"Yes. I have had such a judgmental attitude toward the rulers of the temple and Antipas, and that is totally against everything that Jesus taught."

"Manaen, Jesus also said that by their fruits you will know them. And their fruits are surely rotten. Everyone knows that; Jesus especially knew it! Didn't he give them a thorough dressing-down because of it?"

"I understand that, but Jesus still loved them, and I didn't understand that at all. One day, as I sat beside the Sea of Galilee reflecting on the things that had happened, it came to me like a scroll being unrolled. I had heard someone say that the only reason the people followed him was for the miracles he did and the food he gave them. But I don't believe that's true at all." Manaen paused, trying to gather his words.

"Please go on and explain, if you don't mind."

"Well, I see the temple rulers as pious, arrogant, and smugly self-righteous. Their long faces and sour expressions show that they think they are too good to associate with the people. They act like they'll be defiled if they so much as look at a person of a lower social status. It seems as if all they care about is money and their position. I know I sound judgmental and critical again, but do you understand what I am saying? Do you agree?"

John chuckled.

"Yes, I both understand and agree, and there is no other way to say it that I know of. That's just the way they appear to be."

"Jesus wasn't like that at all. He accepted everyone just as they were. He loved the people and obviously enjoyed being with them. He smiled at them and laughed with them. He shared their joy as well as their sorrow. He made people feel alive and good about themselves. I don't mean that he didn't ever correct or chastise, but he did it in a way that wasn't demeaning, harsh, or critical. Well, except for the temple rulers; he did get harsh with them; almost brutal, in fact. I was astonished to hear him call them such vile names. Nothing is filthier to you Jews than anything to do with death, like dead men's bones, tombs, and sepulchers. I will never forget the expressions on the priests' pious faces." Manaen laughed as he remembered their shock and outrage. "Jesus wiped the smug looks right off of their faces. What a sight. I'm so glad that I was there to see them get what was coming to them!"

"But everything he said was true. He painted a very clear picture."

"Oh, yes he did, absolutely, and I'm not criticizing him. I was just surprised at his anger. Of course, I guess I shouldn't have been after the way he cleansed the temple of that bunch of thieves. That must have been a sight to see. But back to what I was saying. He didn't put people down. He just taught them a better way of living and dealing with the pressures of life.

"Yes, you're right. He was trying to teach us his way, our Heavenly Father's way, of treating other people. It would be wonderful if everyone lived by his teachings. It's sad to say, but we fall far short of his teaching far too often. Do you think we will ever really get it?"

"Well it would be heaven on earth if we could, literally. He was amazing. And yet you never felt like he was putting himself on some holy plane that we could never reach. He didn't put himself above other people. It still amazes me that the very God who created everything that has ever been or will ever be, would give up his place in heaven and come to earth. He left a throne to come to a manger. The Creator came to live among the very creatures he had created. Why would he do such an amazing thing? I still don't understand!"

"Love, Manaen, love. He did it because he knew that was the only way to rescue us from our wretched selves and hell."

"It is amazing that God's Son, in fact God himself, loved us so much! And he was always so accessible to the people. He didn't put us off, push us away, or act like he didn't have time for us. He even touched the lepers, the most unclean of the unclean, before he healed them. Didn't the priests just love that! They were furious with him, but he didn't care. All he cared about was the people. His love for us is overwhelming; and he took such pleasure in us.

"No, it wasn't all the miracles and food, John. It was Jesus himself. He was so full of joy that it seemed to ooze from his pores. That's why people were so drawn to him rather than the priests and Pharisees. He was laughing and smiling while they were somber and sour, he was accepting and gracious while they were intolerant and puffed up. He loved the people and enjoyed them, while they seemed to hate the people and wanted to have nothing to do with them."

"I understand what you are saying, and I agree with you."

"Yes, it seems that all the temple rulers care about is their position and the treasury, but Jesus wasn't concerned about either one. His only concern was the people. Everything he did was to show us a better way to live."

"You've summed it up very well indeed."

"I just pray that I can put my palace training behind me and learn to be more like our Master."

"You are doing that more and more every day, my friend. You're nothing like the man I first knew. Jesus has completely turned your life around and your love for him is obvious to all of us who know you."

"Thanks, John, but I have a long way to go."

"We all do, Manaen, but Jesus said there is more to come. He said that he's sending the Holy Spirit to be our comforter after he goes back to the father. He also said that the Holy Spirit would teach us, walk with us, and guide us. I certainly don't understand it all, but I just rest in the fact that he said he would not leave us comfortless."

"But he did have a way of providing physical food too. Do you remember the Sabbath that he and his followers were walking through the field, and he picked grain heads and gave it to us to eat? That certainly caused an uproar!" The two men walked back to the others, laughing as they remembered the outrage of the pious Pharisees over Jesus breaking their Sabbath law.

CHAPTER 42

Later in the day, Thomas came back from the market with some food he had been able to find for them. When he came in they told him that Jesus had appeared to them, but he refused to believe it. He said, "Unless I see the nail marks in his hands and put my finger where the nails were and put my hand into his side, I will not believe it." [1]

"Well, Thomas, I'm glad that the facts are not based on what you believe." Manaen felt sorry for the man, but he couldn't keep the irritation from showing in his voice.

"What do you mean by that remark, Manaen?" Thomas snapped.

"I mean that it doesn't matter what you believe. Jesus has risen from the dead and appeared to us today, and not only to us here, but also to a group of the women, and some of the disciples. He also appeared to Cleopas and his friend when they were on the way to Emmaus."

"I will not believe it unless I see it!"

"Then you may never see him! Where is your faith, Thomas?" Manaen was annoyed that his frustration could be heard in his voice. It seemed that Thomas had a way of bringing out the worst in him, and he hated that.

Without answering, Thomas left the room, his long legs striding purposefully away from Manaen.

"Hum, I guess that didn't go too well."

Joanna laughed behind him.

"I hope that was not one of your prophetic utterances, Manaen. I would hate to think that poor Thomas would never get to see Jesus again. He really loved him, you know."

"I know, Joanna, but his lack of faith gets annoying at times."

"How well I know, but we have to be patient with him. He'll come around, just like we all did."

"Perhaps he will, Joanna. But will faith have any part in his change of mind?"

"You are right there. Probably not, but we still need to be patient with him. I mean, for the Lord's sake and the sake of his teaching, we have to be patient with one another."

Manaen laughed and looked up to see Chuza coming to join them.

Chuza asked them what was so funny.

"Your wife was just reminding me of my faults."

Joanna flushed a deep scarlet.

"Manaen, I was not!" she said.

"Oh, indeed you were, dear lady. You were reminding me of my lack of faith, whether you meant to or not. And I suppose I owe Thomas an apology. I was deriding him for his lack of faith while I have no faith in him. That's no way to treat a friend."

"Please forgive me, Manaen. I meant no harm."

"No harm done, and no forgiveness necessary, but if you want it I will certainly give it to you in large measure."

Joanna nodded and smiled as she left the two men to go back to the women.

"When did you and Thomas become friends, Manaen?" Chuza asked.

"When Jesus said we have to love our neighbors as ourselves. I realized then that I didn't have a choice. I even grew to accept Judas, although I knew that there was something terribly wrong there."

"You knew there was something wrong with Judas?" Chuza looked amazed. "He certainly had the rest of us fooled!"

"I was never comfortable around him. I can't trust anyone who watches a money pouch the way Judas did!"

"What do you mean, Manaen?"

"The man acted as if the money belonged to him and not Jesus. Whenever money was needed for any situation he acted as if it was coming out of his own purse. The man was greedy and covetous. Am I the only one who noticed?"

"I guess that I didn't pay enough attention. My eyes were always on Jesus and what he was doing."

"Perhaps if I had kept my eyes on Jesus I wouldn't have had time to be critical of Judas. Is that what you are saying? If it is, you are right. I would have learned more watching Jesus than I did by watching Judas." When Chuza laughed, Manaen went on. "I'll pay more attention to him now that he's back with us, but I don't think he'll be here very long."

"What do you mean?"

"Just what I said; I don't think Jesus will be here with us long. I believe his earthly ministry is over. Or, that it will be soon."

"Please don't tell Joanna that. She's so happy that he's back, and I don't want to upset her again."

Manaen laughed.

"Most men would be jealous if their wives loved another man the way Joanna loves Jesus."

"Her love is no different than any of our love, even yours, my friend."

"I know. And it still seems so strange to me that I could love this man so much. I didn't think that I would ever love anyone except Joachim. Then there was Lydia, and now there are my grandchildren, but that love is nothing compared to the way I feel about Jesus."

"Is gratitude what you feel?"

"Yes, there is that, but there is something more, Chuza, much more. There is a sense of awe, adoration, and pure joy. There's a peace that I've never experienced before, a knowing that all is well, regardless of what the future holds."

"Do you think that you'll ever go back to Antioch?"

"I don't know. I would like to see my family, and I do have business there that I probably need to take care of, but nothing matters except Jesus, absolutely nothing. And Joachim is perfectly able to take care of all of our holdings there. Still, nothing matters except Jesus. I'm prepared to stay and minister to him or for him in any way he needs."

"What if he needs you to go back to Antioch?"

"Then I would go back to Antioch. I pray that everything

I do from now on will be done to please Jesus, regardless of what he should ask me to do."

"He doesn't ask any more than that of any of us."

CHAPTER 43

Days of fear and frustration passed for the band of believers. They never knew if they were safe from the Romans and the Jewish officials. These were days of speculation as they wondered what their futures held. Manaen knew that Herod could have him arrested and kill him like he had threatened. They stayed together, ate together, prayed together; all the time hoping that Jesus would return. Everyone wanted to see him again. Their lives seemed flat and lifeless without him.

Thomas had rejoined them when Jesus suddenly appeared again. His eyes seemed to glow with love for them all as he said, "Peace be with you. Then he turned to Thomas, extended his hand to him, and said, "Put your finger here; see my hands. Reach out your hand and put it in my side. Stop doubting and believe."

Thomas fell to his knees at Jesus's feet and sobbed, "My Lord and my God."

With great kindness and love Jesus replied to him, "Because you have seen me, you have believed; blessed are those who have not seen me and yet have believed."[1] He reached down and helped Thomas to his feet. Placing his arm around Thomas' shoulders to comfort him, he said, "Remember all I have taught you, Thomas." Then, as quickly as he had appeared Jesus was gone, leaving Thomas sobbing and struggling to regain his composure.

When he was able to speak he turned to Manaen.

"Why, why do I have so little faith? I am too much of a cynic for my own good. Sometimes I think that I will never learn."

"Don't be too hard on yourself, Thomas. I struggled with a lack of faith too."

"That doesn't excuse me. You haven't been a believer as long as I have."

"That's my point. I should have been a believer long before any of you. Remember, I was there when he was born." Thomas only shook his head and moaned.

Manaen went on.

"Thomas, I even heard him teaching the priest in the temple when he was only a boy. They were amazed at his knowledge of the things of God. Amazed and angered too, I'm afraid." Manaen couldn't help but chuckle as he remembered the long, sour faces of the priests that day. "That pompous, sour-faced pack doesn't like for anyone to show them up or try to teach them anything, much less a mere boy."

After a long sigh, Thomas chuckled too.

"I can imagine what they looked like. 'Pompous pack'

is a good description of them. That still doesn't excuse me, though. I vow to stop doubting things that I can't see and touch. That ends today."

Manaen watched as the big man turned and walked away with a new sense of purpose to his step. He was lost in a silent prayer for Thomas when he felt a hand on his arm and looked down into the beautiful eyes of Mary.

Startled, he blurted out, "Hello, beautiful lady."

Then he felt his skin flushing and knew that he was turning as red as Peter's flaming beard.

Looking around as if to see who she was talking to, she spoke softly. "Manaen, I don't know what you said to Thomas, but I think it helped him. You always seem to have the knack to know what to say when someone is hurting."

"I only say what I believe, Mary."

"Then I thank you for your kind remark when I came up. Until Jesus touched my life I considered myself the ugliest of women. Now I know that it was my spirit that was ugly and wretched. My soul was so twisted that it's a wonder Lazarus and Martha didn't despise me. I praise God that they never stopped loving me, even when I was at my most unlovely."

"Family ties are tight bonds that bind us together for life. That's God's plan—to provide love and protection for us within the family unit. Why, I even still love Herod, and he wants to kill me. I don't have any desire to be around him, but I do love him and would love to see him straighten his life out. I'll continue to pray for his salvation."

"I'm always amazed at your grasp of that when I consider the way you were raised."

"Perhaps my lack of a real family tie outside of the palace

is why I do understand it so well. We tend to learn the most from the things we miss the most, don't you think?"

"Yes, that and from the areas of our lives where we've made the most mistakes. I wish I could say that I learned from the mistakes of others, but I'm afraid I didn't. I was too busy feeling sorry for myself and lashing out at everyone around me."

"I can't imagine you lashing out at anyone, Mary."

"Then I thank God that you didn't know me before Jesus healed my pain and set me free to be the person I am today. I am truly a study of his mercy and grace."

"I saw that the night you anointed his feet at Simon's house. I thought then that you were the most beautiful creature I had ever seen. Your love and gratitude were so evident. I didn't understand it then, but I see it clearly now. I even remember how angry I was at Lazarus and Martha for how they had cast you out. Your Jewish laws seem so heartless to me."

"Yes, but Jesus has put the heart into the law, don't you think?"

"He has indeed."

Lazarus walked up to them.

"Mary, Martha needs your help preparing the meal," he said.

Mary's laugh sounded like bells tinkling.

"Here we go again," she said.

Manaen watched her as she walked so gracefully across the room that she seemed to float. He could still smell the aroma of the nard she had used to anoint Jesus.

He was startled when Lazarus spoke.

"What are you thinking, Manaen?"

He turned to Lazarus and met his steady gaze.

"Just that she walks as if her feet don't touch the floor. She is so graceful and has such a delicate beauty."

"Again, I ask what you are thinking."

"Nothing beyond what I said, Lazarus. I was simply admiring part of God's creation. I have no designs on Mary or any other woman right now. I don't know what my future holds. I could even be killed, and there is no way that I would drag anyone into my uncertainty. Besides, I have been alone too long, and I'm too old and set in my ways."

"Any woman would be proud to be your wife. Don't think I haven't heard them talking." With that, he turned and walked away, leaving Manaen puzzled yet amazed.

CHAPTER 44

Time seemed to be flying by as reports reached the disciples about sightings of Jesus and the miracles he was doing. His followers had gone to Capernaum, hoping to see him there. It was one of his favorite towns, and he always seemed to return there.

They also hoped to catch fish while they waited. Peter announced to the others that he was going out to fish and some of the men decided to go help him. They fished all night and didn't catch even one fish. Everyone was tired, hungry, and frustrated.

Early that morning the sun was coming up, turning the water into a carpet of pink, blue, orange, and lavender. Suddenly a man who was standing on shore, smiling as the gentle early morning breeze blew his cloak and tossed his hair around, called out to them.

"Good morning! Did you catch anything for breakfast?"

"No," they answered.

"Throw your net off the right side of the boat and see what happens," he said.

They did what he said. All of a sudden there were so many fish they couldn't even pull them in.

"It's the Lord," John said to Peter.

When Simon Peter realized that it was the Master, he threw on the clothes he had stripped off for work and dove into the sea. The other disciples came in by boat, for they weren't far from land, a hundred yards or so, pulling along the net full of fish. When they got out of the boat, they saw a fire laid, with fish and bread cooking on it.

"Bring some of the fish you've just caught," Jesus said. Simon Peter joined them, and they pulled the net up on the shore—one hundred fifty-three big fish. And even with all those fish, the net didn't rip.

"Breakfast is ready," Jesus said. Not one of the disciples dared ask him who he was. They knew it was the Master.

Jesus took the bread and gave it to them. He did the same with the fish.

After breakfast Jesus said to Simon Peter, "Simon, son of John, do you love me more than these?"

"Yes, Master, you know I love you."

Jesus said, "Feed my lambs."

Then Jesus asked a second time, "Simon, son of John, do you truly love me?"

"Yes, Master, you know that I love you."

Jesus said, "Shepherd my sheep."

Then he said a third time, "Simon, son of John, do you love me?"

Peter was upset that he asked the third time, "Do you love me?" So he answered, "Master, you know everything. You've got to know that I love you."

Jesus replied, "Feed my sheep."[1]

Later when John was talking about all of this with Manaen, they realized that Jesus was probably allowing Peter to declare his love three times just as he had denied the Lord three times.

"John, I think that Jesus was also assuring Peter three times that he had forgiven him and would continue to allow Peter to serve him," Manaen said.

After a few thoughtful moments John replied.

"Then there is hope for all of us, isn't there?"

"Absolutely. That's why he lived and died—to provide hope for everyone. You know that he always taught forgiveness and practiced it in his life and death. Surely you don't think that he would require us to forgive everyone who hurts us if he didn't always do the same thing? His life is our example to follow."

"You're right, but I was thinking of Judas. Do you think he was forgiven for what he did?"

"Yes, if he asked. I've heard that he tried to return the thirty pieces of silver to the temple rulers, but they wouldn't accept it. That tells me that he had some remorse for what he had done, but we won't know the outcome until we get to heaven. Eternity will give us the answers to all of our questions."

John laughed.

"Oh, yes, but the answers won't matter then. We'll be too busy worshiping our Lord and Savior to ask questions and debate their answers. Imagine that! A time when Jews won't ask questions, demand answers, and then debate the answers."

"Isn't that your favorite method of learning?" The friends laughed together as only true friends can.

Later the men were eating supper to the sound of women chatting and dishes clattering. Jesus suddenly appeared to them and said, "Go into all the world. Go everywhere and announce the message of God's good news to one and all. Whoever believes and is baptized is saved. Whoever refuses to believe is damned.

"These are some of the signs that will accompany believers: they will throw out demons in my name, they will speak with new tongues, they will take snakes in their hands, they will drink poison and not be hurt, and they will lay hands on the sick and make them well."[2]

Manaen watched in amazement and wondered about the things Jesus was saying. *Surely I didn't understand what he said. Did he really say all believers? Is he saying that I too will do these things? What an amazing thought! Is it possible?* Manaen shook his head, bewildered to think that it might actually be possible that he would be able to perform these miracles.

Jesus told them to return to Jerusalem and wait for the promise of the Father that he had told them about. He said that John baptized with water; but they would be baptized with the Holy Spirit not many days from then. Jesus said that his followers would receive power after the Holy Spirit came upon them; and they would be witnesses in Jerusalem, and in all Judea, and in all the earth.

"Chuza," Manaen whispered in amazement, afraid to

speak out loud, "What is he saying? Surely he can't mean that mere mortals like us will be able to do these things!"

"That is how it sounds, but like you, I find it hard to believe! What are we saying? Hasn't he tried to teach us that with God all things are possible?"

"Chuza, Manaen, be quiet! Jesus is blessing us," Joanna whispered as she turned back to Jesus. "Chuza, he's leaving!" she shrieked.

To everyone's amazement it seemed that gravity had lost its hold on Jesus, and he was disappearing into the clouds. Then he was lost from sight. Some people were weeping; children were applauding this marvelous feat. But most of the people just stared up into the sky in utter amazement, too stunned to say or do anything.

"Chuza, what just happened?" Joanna asked with tears in her eyes. "Is he gone for good?"

"I don't know. I'm having too much trouble trying to understand what I just saw. I know I saw it, but I still can't believe it! Manaen, who are those two men? They weren't here before, and look at their robes. They are blindingly white," Chuza said in awe.

"I don't know. I've never seen them before. Wait, they're speaking."

"Why are you standing here looking up at the empty sky?" the first man said.

"Jesus will return to you just as unexpectedly and mysteriously as he has left you," the second man said.

Then the two men disappeared just as suddenly as they had appeared. The people were so astonished they couldn't speak. They stood for a while staring up, around, and at each other. They wondered in amazement what had just happened. Who were these men, where had they come from, and where had they gone?

"Angels! We've just seen angels," Joanna finally whispered in awe.

Manaen felt like all of the air had been sucked from around them when Jesus disappeared. He could hardly catch his breath and was, in actuality, afraid to breathe. He wanted to follow Jesus up into that vast expanse of sky, not stay here on this mountaintop feeling so lost and lonely. *Why do I feel so lonely? There must be five hundred people here, including Mary and my other friends. Yet I feel totally alone. It's as if my heart has stopped beating, and I'm dying! I knew this was coming! Why wasn't I prepared for it? How could anyone be prepared to be separated from him for even a moment, and who knows how long it will be before we see him again? Dear God, help me to bear it. Help me to do what he is asking me to do. Help me to be strong and reliable for you and these people.*

As the group made its way back to the upper room in Jerusalem from Mt. Olivet, they still didn't have much to say. Everyone seemed to be deep in thought about these last instructions that Jesus had given them, wondering what it all meant. The children hopped and skipped merrily as if nothing unusual had taken place, singing and chattering like birds. Some did ask a few questions, but when they realized that the adults didn't have the answers, they just went on their merry way, happily accepting everything as only children can.

CHAPTER 45

They did what Jesus had told them to do. They went back to Jerusalem to the upper room where they were staying. For ten days they all joined together, almost constantly in prayer. There were days when they would even forget to eat. It was almost as if Jesus was in the room with them, and they could sense his pleasure in what they were doing.

The days passed quickly as they fellowshipped and began to know and understand each other on a deeper, more intimate level. Manaen began to see James and John as more than just the Sons of Thunder, as some people called them, referring to their boisterous voices. John's ability as a historian began to surface, and Manaen realized why Jesus had spent so much time with him. He seemed to remember details of Jesus's ministry that others of them had overlooked or forgotten. Matthew had some of the same qualities, but saw things from a different perspective than John. It made for some very interesting conversations as they talked about the things Jesus did while he was with them. They grew impatient with waiting, as people tend to do.

Joanna came over to Manaen, and he could tell she was troubled.

"What is it, Joanna? Is something wrong?"

"Not really, but I do have questions. Since Chuza isn't here right now, may I ask you?"

"Certainly, and I'll answer you if I can."

"When Jesus was still with us, he made a promise about sending us a gift, and we've waited and waited here in Jerusalem. It's hard being shut up here with all of these people, away from the rest of our family and friends. There are still about one hundred twenty of us, but many of the original five hundred or so have given up and gone home."

"Yes, that's true. Some of them had responsibilities, but others just lost faith in his words. People are just people, Joanna. Even Jesus said that we would be like that."

"I know, but what could Jesus have really meant when he said that he would baptize us with the Holy Ghost and fire?"

"I'm not sure, Joanna."

"Well, I remember when John baptized me in the Jordan River to wash away my sins. He put me under the water after I had repented. And I did feel forgiven, but the day that Jesus breathed on us and said, 'Receive the Holy Spirit'! Well, it reached a new level. Now I feel totally clean, free, forgiven! But I don't understand. Will we be burned up and consumed in a fire? I have to admit that this is all a little frightening. I just wish that I knew what's going to happen. One whole week has passed; now we're into the second week. I think we've all become a little desperate."

"Yes, we've all grown a little impatient in our waiting and wondering. But stop and think about what has happened. We've started spending more time in prayer, and now we've started to really think alike and in one accord. Please try to be patient, dear lady. Whatever Jesus has planned for us will happen in his time. Just keep praying and believing his promises. Is the food ready for the start of the Feast of Pentecost tomorrow?"

"How like you to change the subject so I won't fret! And it worked!" She was laughing happily as she walked away. Then she turned back to him.

"Yes, everything is prepared. As usual, Martha has everything under control and Mary is singing love songs to Jesus. Have you ever seen two such sisters? The worshiper and the worker! I do love those two opposites. And we need both of them so much."

CHAPTER 46

The next day after the morning sacrifice, the group gathered to celebrate the Feast of Pentecost. Suddenly, just as Jesus had promised, the gift of the Father arrived on the scene. Without warning there was a sound like a strong, gale-force wind. No one could tell where it came from. It filled the whole building until the walls shook. It felt like the huge columns holding the roof up would crash down on them. The noise was horrifying.

Someone shouted that it was a storm, while another one yelled that it was the end of the world that Jesus had predicted.

Someone else screamed that the temple rulers and Romans were coming to arrest them. Dishes were crashing to the floor, wine bottles were breaking, and wine was spilling as people jumped up from the tables.

People were running in every direction, bumping into each

other and falling over the furniture. Children were crying and screaming in fear. Parents were trying to comfort them. Everything was in total confusion and pandemonium.

Then after a few seconds, like a wildfire, the Holy Spirit spread through their ranks, and the people started speaking in strange languages. There appeared to be fire resting on the people's heads. Their fear turned to joy and they started singing songs no one had ever heard before, dancing with complete abandon, spinning, leaping, and laughing with joy. Manaen fell to the floor, speaking in a language he didn't know. He was shaking as if he was drunk, and it seemed like rivers of joy were pouring up from his belly. He realized that he was laughing and crying at the same time. He never wanted this glorious, joyous experience of worship to stop. It was wonderful!

The many devout Jews in Jerusalem from all over the world who had come to Jerusalem to celebrate the feast heard the commotion. They came running to see what was happening. Then when they heard, one after another, their own mother tongues being spoken, they were thunderstruck. They couldn't for the life of them figure out what was going on, and kept saying, "Aren't these all Galileans? How come we're hearing them talk in our various mother tongues? They're speaking our languages, describing God's mighty works!"[1]

One man shouted, "What is going on here?"

Another man was mocking and laughing when he said, "These foolish Galileans are drunk on cheap wine!"

That's when Peter stood up and, backed by the other eleven, spoke out with bold urgency, "Fellow Jews, all of you who are visiting Jerusalem, listen carefully and get this story straight. These people aren't drunk as some of you suspect. They haven't had time to get drunk—it's only nine o'clock in the morning. This is what the prophet Joel announced would happen:

> In the Last Days, God says, I will pour out my Spirit on every kind of people: Your sons will prophesy, also your daughters; Your young men will see visions; your old men dream dreams. When the time comes, I'll pour out my Spirit on those who serve me, men and women both and they will prophesy. I'll set wonders in the sky above and signs on the earth below, Blood and fire and billowing smoke, the sun turning black and the moon blood-red, Before the Day of the Lord arrives, the day tremendous and marvelous; And whoever calls out for help to me, God, will be saved"[2]

Manaen watched Peter in amazement. *Is this the same Peter? What's happened to him?* Then he realized: *This baptism, this total saturation in the Holy Spirit has made this profound change in Peter! Is this is what Jesus meant when he said that we would have power to be witnesses? This baptism is what has changed Peter from fearful chaff blowing in the wind to this fearless, powerful man standing up there before thousands of people talking about Jesus and the things of God. The temple rulers will be furious. They will try to have him killed! First Jesus; now Peter! This could cost him his life, and he doesn't seem to care!*

A man called out, "Brothers, brothers, so now what do we do?"

Peter said, "Change your life. Turn to God and be baptized, each of you, in the name of Jesus Christ, so your sins are forgiven. Receive the gift of the Holy Spirit. The promise is targeted to you and your children, but also to all who are far away—whomever our God invites."

He went on in this vein for a long time, urging them over and over, "Get out while you can: get out of this sick and stupid culture!"

That day about three thousand took him at his word, were baptized and were signed up. They committed themselves to the teaching of the apostles, the life together, the common meal, and the prayers.[3]

Chuza and Joanna looked excited and exhausted later that evening when they met Manaen as they were returning to the upper room.

"Manaen, have you ever seen such a thing?" Joanna laughed joyously before going on. "No, I know you haven't. No one has ever seen such a thing! And it is too wonderful to be a figment of my imagination, so I know it really happened. Still, reassure me, you two; tell me the wonderful events of today really did happen. I want to hear you say it!"

Her excitement and enthusiasm were so contagious that Manaen, tired as he was from helping baptize so many people, couldn't help but join in the laughter.

"Oh, yes, it is all very real! The world was changed forever today, just as we all were. How like our Lord to make a way for so many to come to the truth of the meaning of his life. And how like him to use someone like Peter, the one Satan has tried the hardest to discredit and destroy, as his vessel of honor today to spread the good news."

Chuza looked thoughtful for a moment before he spoke.

"Were you there when the Master talked about putting new wine in cracked bottles?" When Manaen shook his head no, Chuza went on. "Well, he said that you can't put new wine in cracked bottles, and he was right; the effervescence would break the bottles. I think this is what he was talking about—the new wine of the Holy Spirit. Think about it—he had to make us new people in him so he breathed on us and said for us to receive the Holy Spirit. And now he has filled us, his vessels that he made new, with this new wine."

Joanna's laughter spilled out.

"The man this morning wasn't too far off when he said that we were drunk on cheap wine. But it isn't cheap wine; it's new wine, and we can drink our fill without having a hangover. How wonderful!" Joanna spun around laughing and dancing in her joy.

Manaen laughed with her, then grew quiet as he thought about something before he spoke.

"I just realized how perfect Jesus's timing is. We were so impatient for Jesus to fulfill his promise to send the Holy Spirit. We didn't want to wait! We wanted it to happen immediately. Now I understand his plan. There were people from all over the world here for the Feast of Pentecost, and they witnessed these events surrounding the coming of the Holy Spirit. Now they will return to their homes all over the world and share what has happened. It will be like wine pouring from a vat. His message of God's love won't be contained just here in Jerusalem. Instead it will be spilling out all over the world for all people everywhere to hear."

Chuza was laughing now as he realized the truth of Manaen's words.

"How perfect! Our Lord never does anything halfway. His ways never cease to amaze me but, after all, he is the Son of God!"

Chapter 47

The days and weeks passed quickly as the people met together worshiping, teaching, and fellowshipping. Manaen continued to be amazed at the changes in his own life and in others, even as he continued to wonder when Herod would strike again. Peter continued to be a dynamic teacher, unafraid of the repercussions from the Pharisees and Sadducees, but Manaen was only too aware of the ever present danger they faced.

People were being added to the growing group of believers by the thousands. One of those people was a Hellenistic Jew, a native of Cyprus named Barnabas. He owned a great deal of land in Cyprus that he sold and gave the money to the church in Jerusalem. Manaen admired the man and his enthusiasm for the church. He invited him to his home where they shared a meal with Chuza and Joanna. The four soon became fast friends, sharing meals and attending services with the others.

Manaen enjoyed sharing his home with the others in the group. They often had evening meals and services together there.

Manaen, Chuza, and Barnabas were with the others one day when Peter and John were going to prayer meeting in the temple. A lame man who was put there every day to beg alms had asked Peter and John for a handout. Peter told him that they didn't have silver and gold, but he would give him what they had. He told him to walk in the name of Jesus Christ of Nazareth. He grabbed him by the hand and pulled him up. At that moment his feet and ankles were healed and he jumped to his feet and walked. Then he went into the temple with them, walking, dancing, and praising God. The man had thrown his arms around Peter and John, ecstatic with joy, and people had come running from everywhere to see what was happening.

When Peter saw the people gathering, he started talking to them about Jesus and how he had been killed and raised to life. He called on them to change their ways, turn to God, and let him take away their sins. He and John were arrested and thrown into jail.

Peter and John were warned to stop speaking or teaching in the name of Jesus, but they refused, saying that they would obey God, not men.

The outcome was that Peter confidently preached to the rulers, religious leaders, religious scholars, Annas the chief priest, Caiaphas, and everyone else who was there.[1]

Manaen could just imagine how pleased the temple rulers

were with that, but they just threatened them again and then released them because they couldn't make any charges stick against the two men. Peter wasn't worried about their threats anymore. Yes, this certainly was a new Peter! And he was even bolder now than before because there was no fear mixed in with his boldness, no brash bravado. It was also clear to all of them that Peter was following the Lord's leading.

Martha, who had been such a compulsive worker, now joined gladly in the sessions of teaching, and she almost rivaled Mary in her worship. They literally danced around in worship as they cooked and cleaned for the others. Their joyous, contagious laughter spilled over to everyone around them. Mary would sing words that Manaen knew were prophetic.

At the evening meal Lazarus asked Manaen about his future plans. "All I can say is that I am open to the leading of the Holy Spirit. I know that the Lord has something that he wants me to do, but it isn't clear yet just what it is." Manaen answered.

"You clearly have the gift of prophecy. And you are an excellent teacher. Don't you think that he will use you in those areas?"

"Yes, I think that he will, but I want to be sure of where and how he wants me to use those gifts. I do know that wherever I go, I want to be of help to others. God didn't allow my father and then me to amass such wealth for it to be squandered. I want to use it to benefit our people who have needs."

"Like you did that widow that impressed Jesus so much when she gave everything she had into the treasury?"

"Yes, just like that, but how did you find out about that? It was done secretly."

Lazarus threw back his head and laughed.

"Surely you don't expect to be able to keep secrets in this big, happy family! We're too close-knit for that, my friend. And why should you not want people to know that you have a big, generous heart? No one will try to take advantage of it."

"Oh, no, it isn't that, Lazarus! It is just that Jesus told us to do our alms in secret and not to let our right hand know what our left hand was doing. I refuse to be thought of like those hypocritical Pharisees who strut about and blow trumpets when they give so that everyone will see, be impressed, and applaud them. I'm not trying to impress anyone."

"No one thinks that of you. We know your heart, and you have never announced your wealth, which we know is considerable, or been showy in any way. Oh, you were a little unapproachable before you became a believer, but we know you now as you truly are—a humble man with simple taste. But I do understand what you're saying, and I assure you that it hasn't been a matter of general discussion. It is just that your kindness and generosity are known and quietly appreciated. So rest easy, my friend."

"Thank you, Lazarus, for those kind words. And don't forget that you and your sisters aren't paupers either. Speaking of your sisters…"

Later that evening, during the evening meal at the home of Lazarus and his sisters, Manaen realized that he couldn't keep his eyes off of Mary. He admired her grace and beauty, but it was her gentleness that attracted him the most. Then he realized in astonishment, *I love this woman. Amazing! When did this happen? What will I do now? Lord, I'm helpless here. Please show me your will in this. Show me what to do.*

After the evening meal, teaching, and time of fellowship,

Manaen realized that he and Mary were standing alone on the side of the room.

"Mary, will you walk with me and show me your gardens?"

She smiled up at him, and then he heard her gentle laughter.

"You have seen our gardens many times. Why do you want to see them again?"

"Because I've never really seen them. I've only walked through them many times. Now I want to really see your handiwork."

"I would love to show you the gardens. Just let me tell Lazarus where I will be so he can find me if he or Martha need me." In a few moments Mary was back by his side. "I think he approves," she said, smiling up at him.

They walked under the palm fronds that were swaying in the evening breeze as he listened to the soothing sounds of the water from the fountain flowing over the rocks. The moon hanging just above the horizon was deep orange, and it stained the sky and fountain with its beautiful colors of orange, purple, and red.

Mary explained how they had built the gardens out of dry, barren land. She told him about their olive and fig trees, named the flowers for him, and then led him into her favorite place, the rose garden.

"They are so beautiful, perhaps the most beautiful thing on earth. And, oh, the fragrance. Have you ever smelled anything so sweet? I feel so close to God in this place; I feel his love surround me, almost like a lover's arms. It still amazes me that he could love me so very much," she whispered.

"Mary, it's easy to love you." *I feel like a youth again with his first crush.* He realized that Mary had spoken.

"I'm sorry, Mary. Please forgive me, I was lost in thought. What did you say?"

"I asked if you mean agape love or something else? Don't toy with me, because it would be so easy to fall in love with you."

"I mean every kind of love there is. I mean I want to get to really know you. I want to be your best friend, your protector, your …"

"Wait, Manaen, please wait. I'm trying to adjust. I'm trying to take this all in. I feel like we have suddenly changed direction. My head is swimming and my heart is pounding. Please be patient with me. This is too sudden, too …"

"Yes, I realize that I'm going too fast. But, one question: are you willing to pray and seek God's will for us? Is there a possibility that we might have a future together? Do I dare hope for such a treasure?" He laughed. "Okay, three questions then."

"Have you talked to Lazarus about any of this?"

"Not really, but I think he knows my feelings for you. At least he's alluded to it."

"I promise that I will talk to God and my brother about this. I have to know their will before I make any commitment. Meanwhile, rest assured that you are already a dear, dear friend and you would be a most desirable bridegroom." She blushed. "Now who's going too fast?"

Manaen took her arm as they started back to join the others.

"I don't know, but it certainly isn't you. We'll both pray for God's will and seek Lazarus' guidance then. But, Mary, no matter what the outcome is, I want you to always know that I am your friend and greatest admirer. I will always be there for you. My heart and my home will always be open to you."

"Thank you, dear friend. I know that I can trust you. I know that I'm safe with you."

Mary smiled at him, and it was all he could do not to kiss her right there. *Please help me here, Lord. My emotions are almost out of control. I'm too old for this, Lord. What is happening?*

Then they were safely inside with the others and Lazarus had a strange expression on his face. He came over to them and asked Mary to excuse them. She smiled and walked away to join Martha.

"Manaen, what is going on?"

"Can we go somewhere and talk privately?"

"Yes, come with me. We can use the garden."

When the two men were alone, Lazarus asked again what was going on.

"This is premature, and I preferred to talk to you later." The look on Lazarus' face caused Manaen to take a deep breath and go on. "I love your sister and would like to talk to you about seeking her hand in marriage, but only after I fast, pray, and seek God's will. But I would like to know if you would even consider me as a husband for her. Do you consider my age a problem? We won't go against God's will or your will. We would want blessings from both of you."

"Manaen, I need to know what your plans are for the future. I ask you again, will you stay in Jerusalem or return to Antioch?"

"As I told you earlier, I don't know what God's plans are for me yet. I know that he has one, I just don't know yet what it is or how he plans to use me. In fact I don't know if he will use me."

"With your strong teaching and prophetic gifts, God certainly has plans to use the gifts he has given you."

"I understand that, but I don't know yet how or where. Would it matter?" Both men were getting a little annoyed.

"Of course it would matter! Mary is my sister and my delight. Antioch is a long way from Jerusalem. I might never see her again."

"Pray, Lazarus, pray! But, enough of this for now. I have to seek God's will in all of this. I refuse to follow my heart instead of the leading of the Lord. And I'm certain that in his timing, he will reveal his will to us."

"To us?"

"Yes, to the three of us."

"Do you mean that you have declared your intentions to Mary?" Lazarus was obviously annoyed.

"She knows my heart, yes."

"Manaen, you should have discussed this with me first!" Lazarus snapped.

"You're right, but I'm afraid that this old heart of mine overrode my good senses and in our conversation in the garden ... well, you know ... "

"No, I'm sad to say I don't know. No woman has ever completely captured my attention in that way."

"But you will pray with us?"

"Yes, you know that I will."

"Thank you, my friend. Now I need to get on the road. Jerusalem seems a long way off tonight."

"You are welcome to spend the night with us."

"Thank you for your kind offer, but, considering the change

in my relationship with Mary, I need to go. I don't want to do anything that could ever reflect poorly on her reputation."

"I appreciate your consideration." Lazarus was smiling a very knowing smile.

"What is that smirk about?" Manaen felt slightly indignant at this friend's expression.

"You are a lost man, my friend."

"I'm leaving while we're still friends." Laughing, he hugged his friend soundly, thumped him on the back, and left.

"He had better be glad I didn't thump him on his hard head!" Manaen murmured. His heart was light as he made his way back to Jerusalem.

CHAPTER 48

Several days had passed spent in fasting and prayer and wondering and wishing God would answer him about Mary. But there was more to pray about than Mary.

Peter was preaching everywhere, and his shadow was healing people as it passed over them. Multitudes of people were becoming believers, and the temple leaders were angry and jealous. The new believers were being soundly persecuted by the temple priests who were having them arrested. The apostles were arrested and put in jail, but during the night an angel of God opened the jailhouse door and led them out after telling them to go to the temple porch and take their stand.

At daybreak they were back on the temple porch, continuing their teaching. When the temple rulers were told that Peter and John were no longer in jail, they were at a loss. Then someone told them what Peter and John were doing, and they sent for them again, berating them for "filling Jerusalem" with their teaching.

Peter said that they were going to obey God and not man. It made them furious, and they wanted to kill them right then and there. But Gamaliel, a Pharisee and teacher of God's Law, told them to be careful what they did, to keep hands off of Peter and John. He said that if what Peter and John were doing was of man, it would not succeed, but if it was of God, they shouldn't fight against it.

The rulers were convinced, so they just had the apostles thoroughly whipped, ordered them to stop teaching in Jesus's name, and let them go.

The apostles continued teaching at the temple and in people's homes as more and more people were joining them. It became really difficult to minister to the needs of the people and teach them too, so they chose seven men to take care of the needs of the people. One of the men was Stephen, a young man who was full of faith and of the Holy Spirit.

Along with his duties, Stephen was full of God's grace and power and was doing miraculous acts among the people. Manaen admired Stephen, but some men were jealous of him and paid people to lie about him, saying they had heard him cursing Moses and God. Manaen tried to combat the lies, but it seemed that no one except their own people was interested in the truth. The lies were spreading like wildfire and were being fueled by the religious leaders.

The people—especially the religious leaders and scholars—were furious with Stephen. They put forth their bribed witnesses to testify: "This man talks nonstop against this holy place and God's Law. We even heard him say that Jesus of Nazareth would tear this place down and throw out all the customs Moses gave us."[1]

When they asked Stephen what he had to say for himself, he rose up and taught about Abraham, Joseph, Jacob, Moses, and others, right down to Jesus. He told them that they were stiff-necked bullies with calluses on their hearts and flaps on their ears. But when he told them that God had handed his Law to them by angels, and they had squandered it, they went wild.

But Stephen, who was full of the Holy Spirit, hardly noticed—he had eyes only for God, whom he saw in all his glory with Jesus standing at his side.

"Oh! I see heaven wide open and the Son of Man standing at God's side!" he said.

Yelling and screaming, the mob drowned him out, dragged him out of town, and began throwing rocks at him. The ringleaders took off their coats and asked Saul to watch them. Saul was a young man who was a student of Gamaliel, and who had given them the go-ahead with a nod of approval.

While he was being stoned, Stephen prayed.

"Master Jesus, take my life." Then he knelt down, praying loud enough for everyone to hear. "Master, don't blame them for this sin." These were his last words before he died.[2]

Saul congratulated the killers.

That day was the beginning of a horrible persecution against the church in Jerusalem. Many people lost everything they had, including their lives.

After Stephen's funeral, Saul went wild fighting against the new church. He would go into people's homes and drag men and women off to jail.

Manaen realized that it was no longer safe for anyone in Jerusalem and began to be concerned for his friends in the area, especially Mary, Martha, Lazarus, Joanna and Chuza. *Should I go back to Antioch and take them with me?* That thought was never far from his mind. *Please tell me what to do, Lord. I need answers here. So many of our new believers have scattered in fear for their lives. Again, I am asking for your will in this situation. Please give me your wisdom. Lead me and guide me, Lord.*

Manaen had just finished his time of prayer when there was a knock on the door. Nebo answered the door. His hair was white and his joints were stiff, but he would not allow Manaen to retire him.

Manaen could hear joyful greetings and went out to see that one of his servants from Antioch had arrived.

"Greetings in the name of the Lord, Jabez. Is all well? What brings you to Jerusalem?"

Jabez looked confused when he answered.

"Sir, I bring sad news. Dorcas has died and Patrobas is in dire need of you to return to Antioch. Is that possible, sir?"

Manaen felt a terrible surge of grief, but managed to speak.

"Pardon our manners. Please come inside. Nebo, please see that his feet are washed. Jabez, do you need food and water?"

"Oh, no, I'm fine. I just had to bring you this news!" Jabez's face turned red as his sandals were removed, and his feet were washed by a servant.

"This is devastating news." Manaen addressed no one in particular. "They had been together for so long. He'll be lost without her. So will I."

"Yes, he is. In fact, it is making him sick, and there is more, sir—good and bad. Joachim and Lydia have another boy. He is fine and healthy, but Lydia is not doing well. The women are taking care of her, but sir, you really are needed at home. Can you come?"

"Of course we'll come, but I need a few days to prepare. There are things that I need to take care of before we leave. Nebo, will you take care of our guest and begin to prepare for the trip?"

"Your guest, sir? But I'm just your servant." The young man was clearly confused now. His face was a study of emotions. "I can stay in the stable."

Manaen laughed as he put his arm around the youth's shoulders.

"I can hardly wait to tell you about the one who was born in a stable, but, no, you won't sleep outside. We have plenty of room for you here. Nebo will show you to your quarters. Consider this your home while we are here. Relax, Jabez, it's okay. Nebo, will you put him in the apartment next to yours?"

"Gladly, sir. I'll take good care of our guest and weary traveler, and I'll have his mount cared for too." He motioned for Jabez, and they left the room. As they were leaving, Manaen heard Nebo speaking.

"Things are quite different here, Jabez. I know that you were treated well in Antioch, but things will even improve there after we return. You'll see…" Then they were gone, and he couldn't hear anymore.

"Yes, Lord, things will be even better for the people working for me. I promise you that. Now Lord, please help me know what to do next."

There was another knock on the door, and Manaen went to answer.

"Chuza, greetings. Come in. Let me call a servant to attend to you."

"Manaen, there's no time for pleasantries now! I've just come from the palace! I overheard Herod plotting your arrest. He blames you singlehandedly for the things that are happening here. He was saying that you should have warned him. You have to go into hiding now!"

Manaen was so caught off guard that he couldn't even answer his friend.

"Manaen! Did you hear me?"

"Yes, I heard every word, but I don't know how to reply."

"We have to get you out of here right now!"

"Yes, the time has come." He called for Nebo and Jabez. When they came in he told them what was happening. "Have the horses prepared and pack only enough to get us to the coast. We have to leave right away."

Softly, in the depth of his heart, he heard.

"Go see Mary."

"*Is that you, Lord?*"

"Yes, go to Mary."

"*Yes, Lord.*"

"Chuza, thank you for coming, but you need to get back to Joanna now. Don't worry about us. We'll be out of here before they can capture us."

After telling Nebo where he was going and where to meet him, he realized that for the sake of time he had to take his horse, so he headed for the stable, calling for his groom. He arrived in Bethany just as Lazarus was starting prayers with his family before the evening meal. He declined their invitation to join them and asked permission to talk to Mary privately.

Lazarus smiled knowingly as he granted his consent.

"It isn't what you think, although I do want to see Mary. I've had news and have to return to Antioch right away; good and bad news I'm afraid." He went on to share with Lazarus and his sisters what had happened. Then he took Mary to the rose garden.

"Mary, I'm so sorry to have to leave, but I don't have a choice. I love you so much. Do you understand?"

"Yes, I only wish I had more time to get to know you better. But, perhaps it's good that I don't. I would only love you more."

Manaen could only feel despair.

"I don't have any idea when I can come back to Jerusalem, and there is no time for a proper wedding before we leave. I'm so sorry, but this is an emergency."

"Dear Manaen, just knowing that you love me is all my heart needs. God willing, if you ever return, I'll be waiting for you."

Then Manaen knew! He knew beyond all doubt that he would not be returning to Jerusalem. He knew that God was calling him to a life that would not include Mary, and that he had to release her. As he looked into her eyes he knew that she knew too. They clung to each other, and the tears flowed for a few brief moments before they straightened their shoulders and went back to rejoin the others. Manaen wiped the tears first from her face and then his own. He felt like he was memorizing the lines of the face he would never see again. "Manaen, as I said, it is enough just to know that you love me. But it blesses my heart to know that you love God more. To know that I have had the love of someone like you is more than I could have ever dreamed was possible. It is enough. Now go with God, dear friend," Mary said.

It was all Manaen could do to go back and tell Lazarus their final decision.

"I know," was all Lazarus said as he grasped his friend in a final hug, thumping him on the back as men do, knowing that he would never see him again. "Go with God, Manaen, go with God and know that I will always take care of Mary."

"But if you marry…"

"No, she will never be reduced to the place of a servant. If I should ever marry her place is secured, as well as her finances. Each of my sisters is financially secure in their own right; they will always be honored as they should. I would never marry a woman who wouldn't respect their place in our home."

"Thank you, Lazarus. I can go in peace now, but if there is ever a need, please let me know. And if the persecution becomes too great and you need to escape, you can always come to me in Antioch. There will always be a place for all of you there. Please keep me in your prayers." With that final word and hugs all around, Manaen left the home that had become such a place of joy and comfort to him. His heart was breaking, and he knew his life was in peril, but he also had tremendous joy knowing that he was in God's perfect will.

CHAPTER 49

Manaen, Nebo, and Jabez managed to slip quietly out of Jerusalem. They made it safely to the coast, got passage and were in Antioch within weeks and without incident.

Several months had passed, and Manaen was settled in Antioch with his family. Patrobas was slowly recovering from the death of Dorcas. He still had days when he was gloomy with grief and almost unable to function, but they didn't come as often now. Manaen spent more time in prayer for Patrobas on those days when the grief did come.

Lydia had recovered by the time he could get home and the baby was doing fine. He knew that all of this was the result of prayer and was still praising God for healing his loved ones. Now if God would just heal his heart.

He could understand Patrobas' grief. Mary might not be

dead, but she would never be here to share his life. She was the only woman he had ever loved, and he missed her so much that it was almost physically painful. *Oh, yes, I understand Patrobas' grief! My days are full but my heart is empty, broken, and grieving even though I know I did what God wanted me to do. I just don't understand why I had to leave her behind! Please protect her and the others from Saul's persecution. Lord, help me to trust you to take care of them and Chuza and Joanna. You know how hard it was to leave those two. They were my friends when no one else was. And they prayed me into your kingdom. I miss them, Lord. And I miss the long talks with Chuza. Please take care of them.*

Manaen was grateful that his family and friends had been so willing to learn about Jesus and so quick to accept him as their Savior. They had also been baptized and received the gift of the Holy Spirit. The teaching had spread into Antioch, and there was a large band of believers meeting in his home now for worship and teaching.

"What? I'm sorry, Joachim. I didn't hear you come in. What did you ask me?"

"That's okay. I'm sorry to interrupt. I know you were deep in thought."

Manaen chuckled.

"I'm glad you interrupted. I was being self-pitying, missing Mary and the others. I wish you could have known her, Joanna, and Chuza too. Enough of that!" He chuckled and went on. "What did you need?"

Joachim laughed.

"I don't know which to do first—comfort you about Mary, tell you that I too wish I could have known her and your friends, or ask you how many people to expect for tonight's teaching. You choose."

"The usual number, I expect. But have the women prepare for a few extra in case some of the regulars invite friends. What are we having?"

"In deference to your fine palate, we will have roasted flamingo tongues."

"Stop joking; that's too reminiscent of Antipas! How he does love his delicacies and the richer, more exotic, and expensive the better."

Laughing again, but struggling to look solemn, Joachim answered.

"Okay, I'll behave. We're having the usual: olives, dates, pomegranate wine, and that wonderful thing Lydia bakes with the thin, thin layers of dough, dates, nuts and honey—lots and lots of sweet, wonderful honey! Do you want anything else?"

Manaen laughed.

"Oh, yes, I want a whole tray of the last thing you said…just me!"

"You're too old to risk getting that fat!"

He ducked and rushed out when Manaen laughed, threw his sandal at him and shouted.

"You impudent young upstart! I can get the best of you on my worst day!" *Being with my family makes it all worthwhile. I'm so thankful for the way God has blessed the teaching we're doing here. So many have come to understand who you are, Lord, and what your life and death meant. I've lost count of how many have accepted you as Savior. Help me to teach them what you want them to know. I can't do it without you. And to think—the people here have started calling us Christians. What an honor.*

When the people were arriving, Manaen was there to greet them. There were Jews and Greeks along with men from Cyprus and Cyrene, who had come to Antioch to teach the people about Jesus. All at once Manaen was being hugged from behind and lifted from the floor. Then he recognized the laugh!

"Barnabas, put me down and tell me what you are doing here!" As soon as his feet hit the floor, Manaen spun around and returned the bear hug. He was laughing with the joy of seeing his friend again. "What are you doing here?" Then he looked around to see who else might be with him.

"No. I'm sorry to say that I'm alone." He hugged Manaen again when he saw his disappointment. "We heard in Jerusalem that some men from Cyprus and Cyrene had come here to share the good news about Jesus, and they sent me to check on things."

"How long have you been here? Where are you staying?"

"I just got here today, and I'm staying with some of the believers in town. I didn't realize that your estate was so close to Antioch."

"Would you consider moving out here with us? We have plenty of room and you're more than welcome."

"I would like that very much, if you're sure it isn't too much trouble."

"No trouble at all. I'll have an apartment prepared for you. And why did you say that you're sorry to say you're alone?"

Barnabas' face was a study of emotions as he replied.

"I meant that Mary isn't with me. Everyone knows that you love her, Manaen; and she loves you. But we also know that obedience is better than sacrifice."

"Barnabas, this obedience is a huge sacrifice."

"God knows that, and he will honor your sacrifice. It's just that we all understand and admire you, but wish it could be different for you."

"I wish that too, but God's ways are perfect, and he has his reasons. Otherwise she would be right here with me, along with Martha and Lazarus. How are things in Jerusalem? Are the believers there still being persecuted? I have been so concerned about them, but trusting God at the same time. Does that make sense?"

"Absolutely, that's faith in action. Doing something when you are afraid to do it takes a lot of faith! I've seen that faith at work in you on more than one occasion. You were a strong pillar in the church at Jerusalem, but I can see why God needed you here. The people here are strong in their faith. You have taught them well."

"My constant prayer is that I'll always teach them the one simple truth: how much God loves them. He told the prophet Jeremiah that he has our lives planned out; he has great plans for us—plans to take care of us, not abandon us, plans to give us the future we hoped for."

"That tells me that he loves us more than we realize."

Manaen grew still before he spoke again.

"You know, Barnabas, that he also told Jeremiah that when we call on him he will answer; that when we seek him with all of our hearts we'll find him.[1] That doesn't sound like some far-off, impersonal God to me. It sounds like God loves us and wants a personal, up-close relationship with us. That's what I want our people to know more than anything else: that God loves them and actually wants to be their friend."

"There's nothing better to learn. For too long we thought he was just our judge, keeping score of our sins so he could punish us. And now we know that nothing is further from the truth. I heard John say that God *is* love. If he *is* love then he can't do anything other than love us."

"It really is too simple to believe, but it's true. Praise God, it's true. Otherwise he would have struck me dead long, long ago!"

"Praise God indeed. Don't let me hold you up any longer. The people are waiting for you."

"Come, let me introduce you to all of our people and we'll get on with the meeting for tonight." Arm in arm, the two old friends joined the group to worship God and learn all they could about the teachings of Jesus.

CHAPTER 50

The meeting was over and everyone except Patrobas had left. Even his houseguest had gone to bed for the night. Patrobas was still struggling to understand what Manaen had taught that evening about love and forgiveness.

"No, Patrobas, it isn't just that my sins were forgiven. Or that I forgave my father for his bitterness toward me. His rejection and abandonment of me were devastating blows, but it goes much deeper than that. I changed my thinking from what had been done to me and began to think of what had been done to my father. What caused him to feel the way he did? What had happened to him, perhaps in his own childhood?

"But, Manaen, he stripped you of everything a child needs!"

"Not everything. I still had food and clothing, I received the best education available, and I also had you and Dorcas in the beginning—a fact for which I will be ever-grateful. Your loving care was a balm for a young boy's heart, and it did help reinforce my sense of self-worth. But, yes, he had taken away the love and companionship I needed. Yes, he denied me the training and guidance any son needs from his father. Yes, I had been deeply wounded by his actions. But perhaps he too had been deeply wounded at some point in his life. I do know that the loss of my mother devastated him, but most of us overcome those losses."

"He couldn't. Or he wouldn't! He was too angry and self-absorbed!"

"I know, but why? That became my all-consuming question for a while. Then I realized that I could never really know why. It was all conjecture on my part, and he was dead, so I couldn't ask him."

"What did you do? How did you manage to go on with your life and become the man you are today: a prophet and teacher here in Antioch and our strongest leader?"

"One day when I was deep into trying to figure it all out on my own, I remembered hearing what Jesus said at the synagogue in Nazareth, when the crowd wanted to kill him for saying it. He said, 'The spirit of the Sovereign Lord is on me, because the Lord has anointed me to preach good news to the poor.' Then he said what I finally began to understand and what became my personal salvation, 'He has sent me to bind up the brokenhearted, to proclaim freedom for the captives and release for the prisoners.'"

"I don't think I understand. You haven't been in prison!"

"Oh, but I have—a prison of my own making! When I refused to grant forgiveness to my father and was consumed by bitterness and anger toward him, I was in the worst prison possible. There may not have been bars, but there were chains. Granted, they were not visible, but actual, physical chains don't bind us as completely as the chains of sin that bind us."

"Go on, Manaen; I know this isn't all you have to say. And you have my complete attention now. This is all so new to me."

"Jesus's teachings were new to all of us who were privileged to hear them. I certainly didn't understand at the time, but it's clear to me now that I have opened my heart to them. He was talking about setting the inner man free. He wants to set the heart of men free to be all that he has created us to be. King David wrote about us being fearfully and wonderfully made, formed in our mother's belly by him! Think about that! We were created by God—in his very image and likeness—each one of us."

Patrobas nodded in agreement.

"I think I understand that."

"God does everything for a purpose, so he did have a plan and a purpose for each one of us. A good one, I might add, but the enemy of our soul has been at work trying to twist and pervert that plan since the day Adam was created. And, I'm sure you'll agree, he has certainly done a good job of it! He does it by inflicting wounds so deep that we spend our lives trying to hide them."

"Why, Manaen? What makes us do that?"

"Shame. We are ashamed of being found out! I spent my life trying to keep anyone from knowing that I was so wounded. It seemed like a weakness to me, like something to be ashamed of. I felt like it was my fault that my father didn't love me and want me. I thought something was wrong with me and that he would love me if I wasn't lacking in something. I didn't know what the something was, but I knew that whatever it was, I lacked it. And if I lacked that elusive 'thing,' I wasn't the man I should be. So, I hid behind a mask, like a thief or leper, always afraid of being exposed!"

Patrobas' big, white head shook in bewilderment. He looked as if he couldn't take it all in. Manaen waited patiently for his friend, knowing that he was trying to sort out all of the things he had told him and not wanting to rush him to any conclusion. He knew Patrobas had to come to his own understanding, just as he himself had. Finally Patrobas spoke.

"I thought that you said that all we had to do was have our sins forgiven."

"Well, yes, that is the first step. But imagine that your son was out running a foot race with another boy, fell, and broke his ankle. They brought him to you and you said something like, 'Okay, I forgive you for falling, now go win that race.' No, you would take him home, nurse him to health, and then send him back out to run again after the bone was completely healed and his strength had returned. And he would probably win."

"Go on."

"That's what Jesus was saying in Nazareth. We hear the good news and accept him as our Savior, then, if we are willing, he heals our broken hearts, breaks the chains of the past that are holding us captive, and sets us free to serve him with our whole heart. We can never really be the men he intended, or live the lives he has created us for, until we allow him to take our broken hearts and make them whole. Then we can be the people he has created us to be."

"Manaen, is it really that simple?"

"Yes, but only if we are willing to trust him, yield to him, and let him do the work. Otherwise, it's impossible. Do you remember when I told you his parable about the vine and the branches?"

"How Jesus is the vine and we are the branches that have to stay connected to him?"

"Yes, Patrobas, but why do we have to stay connected to him? Come on, you have been in charge of the orchards and gardens here for years and years!"

"In order to produce fruit?"

"Yes, but there is something else. The life of the vine comes from the root. If the branches don't stay connected to the vine, which is fed through the root system, we will be all weathered, shriveled up, and unable to produce good fruit. In other words, our Heavenly Father is the root that feeds Jesus, the vine, and we, the branches, produce fruit. Without struggling and striving we just produce good fruit—if we stay connected."

"But men have to work and make things happen. This sounds like a lazy man's way out to me; just too good to be true."

"It does sound too good to be true, but it isn't. Jesus was the strongest man who ever lived, but he always said that he only did what the Father did and said what the Father said. If Jesus needed to stay connected, then how much more do we need to do that?"

"I'm beginning to glimpse the truth of what you're saying. But, how do I make this happen for me?"

Manaen threw back his head in laughter and then struggled to stop rather than offend his old friend.

"I'm sorry, but listen to you. 'How do *I* make this happen?' The only thing *you* can do is submit yourself to his perfect will for you and *ask him* to make it happen for you. In other words, pray.

"I admitted that my wounds were a source of concern for me rather than continuing to pretend that they didn't hurt. Then I asked him to heal them and do what the prophet Isaiah said he would do, 'give me the oil of joy for mourning.'

"All I can say is that you see before you a man who is free from the pain of the past. I have forgiven and released everyone who ever hurt me. I hold nothing against anyone, so I'm the free man Jesus talked about—free from hurt, bitterness, anger, unforgiveness and any other chains that would keep me bound. I'm healed and free to be the man God created me to be and I'm so thankful to him for doing it for me."

Patrobas sat quietly for a moment.

"Pray with me, Manaen. Please pray with me," he said. After a time of prayer, Patrobas lifted his head and looked at Manaen.

"It is well with my soul now, Manaen. It is well with my soul!"

"Have you forgiven my father?"

"Yes, and everyone else too!"

Manaen felt like he had been given one of life's greatest gifts: the gift of helping someone he loved break the chains of bondage.

EPILOGUE

Manaen's time was filled with his family, teaching, running his estate, and meeting the needs of the people. His wealth was a blessing to many people, as he shared all that he had with the people of God. His gardens flourished, and he fed the people; his knowledge grew, and he taught the people; his wealth increased, and he clothed and sheltered the people. All were labors of love.

The man, Saul, who had persecuted the followers of Christ, had his own conversion experience and became Paul, a dynamic man of God. Paul and Barnabas had been sent out from Antioch as missionaries. The church was thriving and the followers of Christ in Antioch were now being called Christians.

Manaen had grieved deeply at the death of his friends and servants: Nebo, Patrobas, and Dorcas. He had rejoiced greatly at the birth of more grandchildren and even a great-grandchild.

Manaen had grieved even more deeply when he learned of the death of Herod the Tetrarch after he had been stripped of his kingdom and banished to Gaul. Manaen would never see him again. *Why did Antipas have to refuse to believe the truth when it was right there before him? Why did he have to be so proud and arrogant?*

He even grieved over Antipas's old enemy Agrippa, King Herod of Judea. When the people of Tyre and Sidon had requested an audience with him, hoping to continue in peace and to receive food supplies from Judea, he became pompous and gave a long-winded speech.

"The voice of God! The voice of God!" the foolish men shouted. That was the last straw. God had had enough of Herod's arrogance and sent an angel to strike him down. Herod had given God no credit for anything. Down he went. Rotten to the core, a maggoty old man if there ever was one, he died.[1] As his emotions swung back and forth from anger to grief, Manaen wept bitter tears to think that his cousins and Antipas, his child-hood friend would not spend eternity with him in heaven.

Occasionally word would come from Jerusalem, and he knew that Mary, Martha, and Lazarus were still safe—a fact for which he praised God. He was an old man now with white hair and weary bones, but he still missed his Mary. His only comfort came from knowing that they had been faithful in obedience to what he knew God wanted them to do. He also knew that his life was winding down, and eventually he would be reunited with Mary forever.

Manaen felt closest to Mary when he walked in his rose garden; he remembered the times they had walked and talked in her gardens. He spent a lot of time there praying for his loved ones who were still in Jerusalem; praying for their continued growth in the Lord and their continued safety as the persecution of the followers of Jesus grew more intense.

Joachim was sitting, talking with him in the rose garden one day. They had just finished reading a letter from Paul that was being circulated among the churches. They were discussing the letter's contents when Manaen looked at him.

"Son, always remember that nothing, absolutely nothing matters but Jesus. Make sure that everyone knows that simple truth." With that, he took a deep breath, smiled toward heaven, and went to be with the Savior and Lord that he had loved and served for so long.

BIBLIOGRAPHY

All references from The Message unless otherwise noted. Some scriptures may be slightly reworded to reflect dialogue, but no content is changed.

Some references are included, not as quotes, but so that content can be verified for authenticity.

Chapter 1

1. Jer. 31:15

Chapter 8

1. Luke 1:47, 51–53

Chapter 16

1.   Luke 2:49

Chapter 18

1.   Matt. 3:2–12
2.   Luke 3:7–17
3.   John 1:6–18
4.   John 1:29–31
5.   Matt 3:13–14
6.   Matt. 3:17

Chapter 19

1.   John 2:4–10
2.   John 3:31–36

Chapter 20

1.   John 4:50–51

Chapter 22

1.   Luke 5:1–11
2.   Luke 4:33–35

Chapter 23

1.   Luke 4:16–30 NIV
2.   Matt. 5:1–7
3.   Luke 7:36–50 NIV

Chapter 24

1.   Luke 8:2
2.   Luke 8:40–48
3.   Luke 8:52–56

Chapter 26

1.   Matt. 14:3–12 NIV

Chapter 27

1.   Luke 9:1–5 NIV
2.   Mark 6:14–15 NIV
3.   Luke 9:12–17 Message and NIV

Chapter 28

1.   Matt 14:22–36
2.   Matt. 15:21–28 NIV
3.   Mark 9:17–27
4.   John 9:1–41, 10:19–21 Message & NIV
5.   Luke 10:38–42
6.   Mark 8:30–33

Chapter 29

1.   Luke 10:38–41
2.   John 3:1–18

Chapter 30

1. John 11:19–37
2. John 11:38–44

Chapter 31

1. Luke 17:30–36
2. Luke 18:15–17
3. Mark 10:46–52
4. John 12:1–11

Chapter 32

1. Mark 11:1–3
2. John 12:12–13, 17–19
3. Luke 19:41–46
4. Matt. 21:14–16
5. Mark 11:20–25

Chapter 33

1. Matt. 22:15–40
2. Matt. 22:41–45
3. Matt. 23:1–12
4. Matt. 23:23–26
5. Matt. 23:37–39
6. Luke 21:1–4
7. 2 Samuel 24:21–24

Chapter 34

1. John 2:19
2. Matt. 24:1–51

Chapter 35

1. Luke 14:12–15
2. John 13: 6–17
3. Luke 22:17–23
4. Luke 22:48
5. John 13:27
6. Luke 22: 33–34
7. Luke 22: 58–62
8. Matt. 27:3–7 NIV
9. Luke 23:1–7

Chapter 36

1. Luke 23:8–1
2. John 19:8–12
3. Matt. 27:27–31

Chapter 37

1. Luke 23:26
2. Luke23:28–31
3. Luke 23:34
4. Matt. 27:41–43
5. John 19:19–22
6. Luke 23:39–43

7. John 19:25–26
8. Matt. 27: 50
9. Matt. 27:54

Chapter 38

1. Matt. 27:51
2. Matt. 27:52
3. Chapter 39
4. Matt. 27:62–66

Chapter 40

1. Matt. 28:5–7
2. Matt. 28:11–15
3. Luke 24:13–33

Chapter 41

1. Luke 24:36–45
2. Matt. 18:21–22

Chapter 42

1. John 20:24–25

Chapter 43

1. John 20:26–29

Chapter 44

1. John 21:1–19
2. Mark 16:14–18

Chapter 46

1. Acts 2:1–11
2. Acts 2:14–21
3. Acts 2: 37–41

Chapter 47

1. Acts 5

Chapter 48

1. Acts 6:12–13
2. Acts 7:55–60

Chapter 49

1. Jeremiah 29:11–13

Epilogue

1. Acts 12:20–22

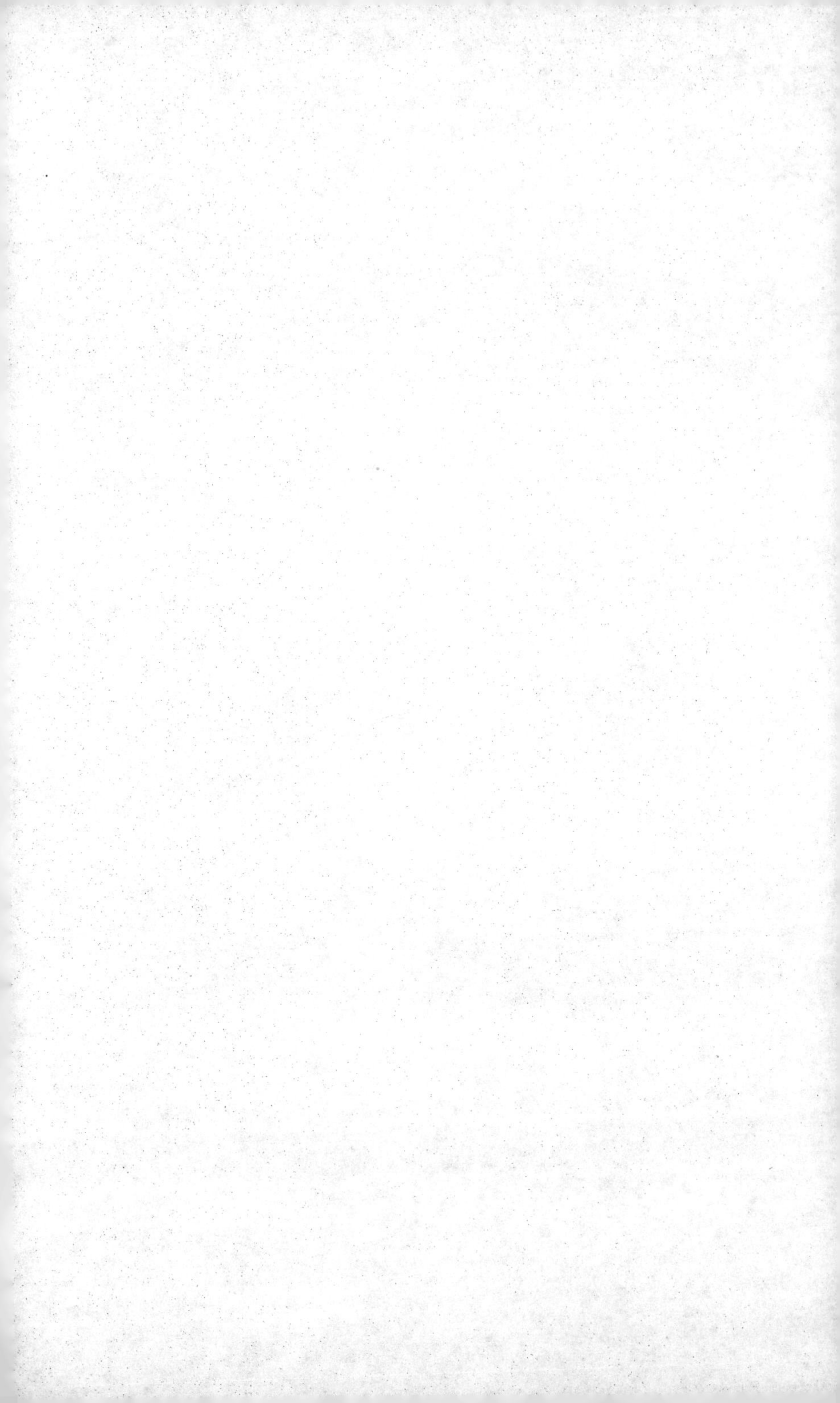